the peacock cloak

Chris Beckett

NEWCON
PRESS

NewCon Press
England

First edition, published in the UK March 2013
by NewCon Press

NCP53 (hardback)
NCP54 (paperback)

10 9 8 7 6 5 4 3 2 1

ISBN: 978-1-907069-48-2 (hardback)
978-1-907069-49-9 (paperback)

Cover art by Eugene Kapustyanskiy
Cover design by Andy Bigwood

Minimal editorial interference by Ian Whates
Text layout by Storm Constantine

Printed in the UK by Lightning Source, Milton Keynes

con.ten.ts

in.troduction.

My previous short story collection, *The Turing Test,* included stories written over some sixteen years, but excluded quite a number of stories written during that time on the basis that much of the material in them had already appeared, or would soon be appearing, in one or other of my novels. *The Peacock Cloak* is a more concentrated sort of collection, since it includes my entire output of short stories over a much shorter period, the four years since *The Turing Test* was published in 2008.

I do not know what other differences readers will notice between the two collections. I noticed myself, when compiling this book, that there are fewer stories written in the first person, and that, for whatever reason, there are fewer female main protagonists. In fact there is only one main female protagonist (Cassie in 'The Caramel Forest'), while several stories have two male characters at their core. This has been a time for confronting and setting aside some aspects of myself, I think.

There are continuities with the earlier collection too, of course, and even some characters who have found their way from the previous book into this one, but I will leave readers to spot these for themselves.

Once again I would like to thank the editors who first published these stories: Sheila Williams at Asimov's, Andy Cox and his colleagues at Interzone, and Pete Crowther and Nick Gevers at Postscripts. These people create a habitat in which life-forms such as myself can flourish, or, if not flourish, at least crawl around in the undergrowth, and yap and bark a bit. If it wasn't for them, we'd have to keep all this stuff in our heads. An awful thought.

Many thanks too to Ian Whates at Newcon Press.

And, as ever, my love and thanks to my dear wife Maggie.

Chris Beckett
August 2012

atomic truth

Jenny Philips emerged from the revolving doors of Rigby, Rigby & Stile into the dirty drizzle and the glistening lights of a London November night. It was a Friday and she'd been working late, clearing her desk in preparation for a week's leave. This time tomorrow she and Ben would be in Jamaica, dining under palm trees and stars.

She badly wanted to call him now, to make some kind of contact. But she knew he was busy wrapping things up at *his* work and he'd specifically told her he didn't want to be disturbed until he was done. Ben could get quite cross about things like that. He'd promised to call her as soon as he was through and she'd have to be content with that.

Jenny looked up and down the busy street, judging the severity of the rain, turning up her collar, opening her pink umbrella and then, of course, putting on a pair of large hemispherical goggles. She was pretty, smartly dressed, twenty-eight years old, the p.a. to the senior partner in a City law firm. The goggles made her look like a fruit fly but this didn't worry her because everyone on the street looked the same. Ocular implants were on their way, but there were still unresolved safety issues – a small but unacceptable percentage of laboratory animals were still going blind – and for the moment everyone wore bug eyes.

Or almost everyone. In the burger bar next to Jenny's office, Richard Pegg slid off his stool, pushed a dog-eared notebook into his pocket, zipped up a very large anorak which stretched down almost to his knees and pulled his woolly hat even lower down over his head. He was one of the few people in London under seventy who didn't even own a set of bugs. Even the people who slept in shop doorways had bugs, even the beggars. But Richard still went out into the rainy street with a bare face and naked eyes. The truth was he didn't need bugs to provide him with phantoms and visions and voices. He had to take pills, in fact, to keep that stuff at bay.

Richard was twenty-eight, like Jenny, but he'd never had a job. He'd come up to town from his little one-bedroom flat in Surrey for one of his trips round the museums with his notebook and pencils.

'Doing research' was what he called it to himself, looking for the hidden meaning of the world among the fossils and the hieroglyphs, the crystals and the cuneiform tablets. He'd filled up another notebook with his dense scrawlings in three different colours about clues and mysteries and conspiracies, full of capitals and underlinings and exclamation marks.

Emerging from the burger bar, Richard too confronted the drizzle and the electric lights: orange, white, green, red, blue. But while Jenny had taken the everyday scene for granted, for him, as ever, it posed an endless regress of troubling questions. What was rain? What were cars? What was electricity? What was this strange thing called space that existed in between one object and the next? What was air? What did those lights mean, what did they *really* mean as they shifted from green to amber to red and back again, over and over again?

And unlike Jenny he also saw Electric Man. Four metres tall and outlined in white fire, Electric Man towered over the passing people and cars and stared straight at Richard with its lightbulb eyes, because it knew that he could see it, even if no one else could. Pursing his lips and hunching down into his anorak, Richard avoided its gaze as he headed off towards the station.

"Atomic truth," he muttered to himself, drawing together the fruits of his day's work. "Atomic truth. Hidden by the world's leaders. Hidden *from* the world's leaders because none of them has atomic eyes. They can't see it, not truth in its atomic form. Or not as far as I know."

He laughed loudly, opening his gap-toothed mouth. People turned to look at him. He ignored their bug-eyed stares.

"Hi, Sue, it's Jenny!" The slender woman waiting in front of him for the pedestrian crossing sign to change from red to green had taken the opportunity to put through a bug call to one of her friends, an older woman who she used to work with in a previous job. "Ben is too busy to talk and I *had* to phone someone. I'm so excited! But nervous too. Our first holiday together. Do you think it's all going to be all right?

Thanks to her bug eyes, Jenny could see and hear her friend right in front of her. Richard couldn't see or hear the friend at all, of course, but he gathered up whatever fragments of the conversation that he could and stored them in his mind with the same reverence with which he copied down hieroglyphs in the British Museum. The way people talked to each other, were at ease with one another, the way they shared things and held one another's attention, these were as much a mystery to him as the inscriptions on the mummy-cases of pharaohs: a mystery, but, like the hieroglyphs, pregnant with mysterious meaning.

"Hi, Sue, it's Jenny!" he muttered.

He laughed. It struck him as funny. And then he tried just repeating the name, "Jenny, Jenny, Jenny."

It had such a sweet sound, that name, such a sweet, sweet sound.

Jenny had her bug eyes set at low opacity. She could still see the world that Richard saw – the traffic lights, the taxis, the cars throwing up their fans of brown water, the shops like glowing caves of yellow light – but for her, soothingly, all this was enclosed in a kind of frame. Wearing bug eyes was cosy, like being inside a car. It reduced the city streets to a movie on a screen, a view seen through a window.

Near the bottom of her field of vision – and seemingly in front of her in space – was a toolbar with a row of icons which allowed her to navigate the bug eye system. Near the top of the field there was an 'accessories bar' with a clock and a variety of pieces of information of the kind that people find comforting, like the many blades of a Swiss penknife, even if they never use them: things like the air temperature, the Dow-Jones Index, a five-year calendar, the TV highlights of the evening ahead, the local time in Sydney and Hong Kong…

Above the accessories bar, advertisements rolled by:

"*Even Detectives Cry*, the powerful new novel from Elgar Winterton, now in bug-book format at Finlay and Barnes for just £2.99… *Froozli*, the great new snack idea from Nezco. Because being healthy needn't mean doing without…"

Of course Jenny wasn't paying any attention to the ads.

"Ben's spent so much money on this," she said to Sue. "You wouldn't believe it! Jet-skiing, and diving, and rafting, and… Well, loads of things he's booked up for us. I keep worrying that he's done *too* much and that it's going to be hard to… I mean, I keep saying he doesn't have to…"

A young couple passed by in the other direction, arm in arm. Although physically together, thanks to their bugs they were at that moment in entirely different worlds. He was blink-surfing the net. She was chatting animatedly into the air.

Sue regarded her friend Jenny. Bug eyes did not transmit a visual image requiring a camera, but a virtual image in which movement and expression were reconstructed from facial muscle movements. Now Sue's virtual face regarded her gentle friend Jenny with narrowed, worried eyes

"Just try and enjoy it, Jenny!" she said. "Grab it while you can and enjoy it!"

She hesitated, wanting to say more but unable to find quite the right words. She was nine years older than Jenny, and rather tougher.

"Enjoy it, Jenny dear," she ended up repeating. "It's not every day you get a trip to Jamaica with everything paid for by someone else."

Communicating through bug eyes, paradoxically, allowed you to see other people bug eye free. But since he never used bugs himself and since he never entered other people's actual homes, where folk removed their bugs to watch TV, Richard saw people with bug eyes on most of the time. He inhabited a world of human fruit flies. They saw his naked face and looked away.

"Jenny," he whispered, "Jenny."

And he laughed, not mockingly but with delight.

Jenny finished her call with Sue. She crossed a busy road, then glanced at the mail icon on her toolbar and blinked twice. Her e-mail window opened and she skipped through the unread messages. One came from a bug-book club she subscribed to and needed a quick answer or she'd have to pay for a book she didn't want.

She blinked her message on its way. A relay station half a mile away picked it up, extracted its cargo of digital code and translated this into tiny flashes of light which travelled underground, at 300,000 kilometres per second, along filaments of glass, to a satellite station down on the Cornish coast which turned the light flashes back into a radio signal, a single phrase in a never-ending stream, and beamed it into space. Five hundred kilometres out, a satellite received Jenny's signal, along with hundreds of thousands of others, amplified it and sent it back down again to Earth.

"1010111010010100101000101110101110101001010100010101000 ..." called down the satellite, high up there on its lonely vigil at the edge of the void. "...10001010100011101..." it called down to the busy surface of the Earth:

"No thank you," it was saying on Jenny's behalf. "Please do *not* rush me my discounted bug-book edition of *Even Detectives Cry*."

A satellite dish in Cape Cod picked up the signal, and sent it on its way.

Richard looked down a little side alley and saw two foxes. They'd knocked down a pile of wooden pallets at the back of a restaurant, and were now rummaging for scraps of meat and fish. In the electric light of the city, they were pale and colourless and not at all like those foxes in story books with their merry faces and their cunning eyes. No one but Richard had noticed they were here.

"Hey, look! Foxes!" he said out loud, stopping, and hoping that Jenny might turn and look.

He'd picked up that she was worried and he thought the foxes might cheer her up. Women liked animals didn't they? He was pretty sure they liked things like that.

"Look at that!" called Richard again, "Two foxes! Right in the middle of a city!"

Behind and above the foxes he also saw Jackal Head, the presiding spirit of dogs and foxes and other doggy creatures. Jackal Head regarded him with its shining eyes, but Richard looked away and said nothing. He knew from long experience that no one else could see the likes of Jackal Head, bug eyes on or not, so he concentrated on the foxes.

"Two foxes!" he called out again.

A man in a brown raincoat glanced at Richard quizzically but didn't bother to look where he was pointing. You didn't have to look at Richard for very long to realise there was something odd about him. His anorak was several sizes too big. His hair was lank. He had two days growth of stubble on his chin. He had no bug eyes.

"Two foxes!"

No one else took any notice. A sense of weariness and desolation swept over Richard. They were all so busy with their bugs, that was the problem, talking to people far away about things that he couldn't understand, no matter how hard he tried.

Then he noticed that Jenny was some way ahead of him – he could see her umbrella bobbing along above the crowds: pink with white polka dots – and he ran to catch up. He liked the feeling of being near her. She made him feel warm.

"Jenny," he said to himself, "Jenny, Jenny, Jenny."

And once again he laughed with pleasure, showing his gap teeth.

"Jenny, Penny, Henny," he said out loud.

"Zero, the only yoghurt with less than one tenth of a calorie per serving…"

Jenny walked quickly, checking through in her mind the things she still needed to do before tomorrow. Ben would get cross with her if she ended up having to run around looking for things at the last minute. He hated disorder. He hated inefficiency of any kind. She herself was a very successful p.a. and spent all of her working days doing pretty much nothing but imposing order. But for some reason Ben made her feel bumbling and incompetent.

"Fateful Summer, the heartrending story of doomed love in the shadow of a global war…"

Jenny's bug eye provider knew she was twenty-eight, single and a member of the 'aspirant middle-upper clerico-professional' class – and it knew from her purchasing record that she liked low fat yoghurt and middlebrow novels – so it told her many times each day about interesting new diet products and exciting new books, as well as about all the other things that aspirant middle-upper clerico-professionals were known to like or be concerned about.

"Is one pound a day so *very* much to pay for life-long security…?"

"Single, childless and fancy-free? The *best* time to think about school fees! Talk to *School Plan*. Because life's too short…"

But if Jenny was 'aspirant middle-upper clerico-professional', what was Richard? He wasn't even a typical member of the 'chronically unemployed/unemployable welfare claimant' class – a low-income class which nevertheless, in aggregate, constituted a distinct and lucrative market – for he'd been adopted at the age of one and had grown up in a well-to-do professional family, and had never associated with other claimants. (The 'chronically unemployed/unemployable welfare claimant class' lived, on the whole, apart from the population at large in social housing projects). In fact, since he had no bug eyes, no computer, no phone and no credit card, there was hardly enough of a trace of him out in the public domain on which to base a valid class evaluation.

Richard was an isolate, a one-off. He had been a strange introverted child who his adoptive parents had never quite learnt to love. He left them at 17 and now had very little contact with them, though they had bought his little flat in Guildford for him, and his mother still sent him money and food parcels.

Three young men in suits came by, walking briskly and overtaking first Richard and then Jenny. They worked in the City as commodity traders. They'd all got bugs on, and they were using the setting called LCV – or Local Consensual View – which allowed bug eye wearers to retransmit the signals they were receiving on an open channel, so that others in their immediate vicinity could pick them up. This enabled all three of the young men to banter with a fourth young commodity trader called Freddy who wasn't physically present.

"Freddy, you stupid fuck. Is it true you lost 90k in one hour yesterday?"

"*Freddy you stupid fuck,*" muttered Richard under his breath, storing away for later examination this strange and utterly bewildering amalgamation of affection and abuse.

"Freddy you stupid fuck," he said out loud.

He laughed. One of the young men turned round and glared at him.

Richard couldn't see Freddy, of course, or hear his reply. But Jenny, out of momentary curiosity, blinked on LCV in her bugs to get a look at him. (This was the principle behind the bug eye boom: the one who *isn't* there was always more interesting than the one who is.)

"Yeah, I lost 90k," Freddy was saying. "But last week I netted 50 mill. Being a decent trader's about taking risks, my children. Watch Uncle Freddy and learn."

So he was just a boastful little boy in a suit like his friends, Jenny concluded, glancing at the clock on her tool bar, then blinking up the internet to check the train times. Options were offered down the left hand side of her field of vision. She blinked first the 'travel information' folder, and then 'rail'. A window appeared, inviting her to name the start and end points of her proposed journey. She mumbled the names of the stations, blinked, and was given details of the next two trains. It seemed she was cutting it a bit fine, so she paid for a ticket as she walked – it only took four blinks – and walked a little faster.

Suddenly a famous TV show host called Johnny Lamb was right in front of her. His famous catchphrase was 'Come on in'. Now he invited her to 'come on in' to a chain store behind him that specialised in fashion accessories. Jenny smiled. Shops had only recently taken to using LCV to advertise to passers-by and it was still a novelty to see these virtual beings appearing in front of you in the street. She walked straight through Johnny Lamb, blinking LCV off again as she did so.

Richard, of course, had no means of knowing that Johnny Lamb was there at all, but he noticed Jenny's increase in speed and hurried to match it. They were almost at the station. He felt in his pocket for his ticket – his cardboard off-peak return ticket paid for with cash – and entered the station concourse.

Two police officers called Kenneth and Chastity were waiting below the departures board. They wore heavy-duty bug eyes with specially hardened surfaces, night vision and access to encrypted personal security data, and they were watching for illegals in the crowd.

ID cards contained tiny transmitters which could be located by sensors mounted in streets and public places. Ken's and Chas' bugs showed little green haloes over the heads of people who had valid ID and giant red arrows above people who didn't – illegal immigrants, for instance, or escaped prisoners. It was rather entertaining to watch illegals trying to slip unnoticed through the crowd, with one of those red arrows bouncing up and down over their heads.

Jenny (of course) had a halo. Richard had an amber question mark. It indicated that he was carrying a valid ID card but that he'd either got a criminal record or a record of ID problems of some sort, and therefore should be questioned if he was behaving suspiciously in any way.

Well he *was* behaving suspiciously, thought Constable Kenneth Wright, nudging his partner. The man didn't even have a set of bugs!

"What kind of Neanderthal goes around with a bare face these days?" he said.

It was almost obscene.

Chas nodded grimly and pulled up Richard's file by looking

straight at the amber question mark above his head and double-blinking

"Mental health issues. Diagnosed schizophrenic. Detained in hospital three times. Cautioned two years ago for failing to carry an ID card," she read from the file.

Not the crime of the century as even she would reluctantly have to admit.

"Probably left his card at home on principle," Ken said with a sigh. "Probably some stupid nutty principle. Probably the same reason why he doesn't wear bugs. No need to pull him up, Chas. He's got his card on him today."

Chastity found Ken's attitude very lax. This was not a perfect world, of course – one had to accept that there were liberals in it, and human rights lawyers – but why let potential trouble-makers walk on by when you were perfectly entitled to haul them up, ask them questions and, at the very least, let them know you were watching them?

"Excuse me Mr Pegg," she said, stepping forward. (She loved the way this new technology let you have people's names before you'd even spoken to them: it put them on the back foot straight away.) "Would you mind telling me why you aren't wearing bug eyes?"

Richard blinked at her, glancing anxiously round at the receding figure of Jenny, who he might never see again.

Why didn't he wear bugs? It was hard to explain. He only knew that if he wore bugs he would drown in them.

"There isn't a law that people have to wear them is there?" he muttered, glancing again at Jenny with her pink polka dot umbrella, who, cruelly, was getting onto the very same train that Richard would normally travel on.

Chastity didn't like his tone one bit.

"Maybe not yet," she said, "but there soon will be, like carrying an ID. And while we're on that subject, I'd like to see your..."

But here her colleague nudged her. Away across the concourse, a big red arrow was jiggling into view, pointing down at a young man from Malawi called Gladstone Muluzi, whose visa had expired the previous week.

"Bingo!" breathed Chas.

"Gotcha!" hissed Ken.

"Can I go then?" interrupted Richard, glancing longingly across at the sacred train that now contained the sweet and gentle Jenny.

"Yeah, go on," said Chas.

She didn't even look round at him. Her eyes were fixed on her prey.

Richard ran for the train and climbed on just before the sliding doors locked shut. Then he barged through three carriages looking for Jenny, stepping over suitcases and pushing past people stowing their possessions on the luggage rack. He upset several of them, because it didn't occur to him to say "Excuse me" or "Sorry".

But who cared? Not Richard. He didn't notice the reaction he was getting. There was Jenny, that was the important thing, there was Jenny sitting all on her own in a set of facing seats. Richard approached her and, with beating heart, spoke to her for the very first time.

"Are these seats free?"

"Yes. They are," said Jenny.

Her voice was like music. He laughed. Jenny gave a small clipped smile and looked away, reading him as odd but harmless, wondering why he wasn't wearing bugs, and noticing with distaste the faint sour smell on him of slept-in clothes. Her older brother was autistic so she was used to oddness, and her feelings towards Richard were not unfriendly ones, as many people's might have been. But all the same she didn't want the bother of thinking about him just now. And she could have done without the whiff.

Then the train began to move and she glanced at the opacity icon on her toolbar and blinked it up to 80%. Out on the street she'd kept opacity low to let her negotiate traffic safely and avoid walking into other people. But, now that it was the train driver's job to watch the way ahead, Jenny no longer needed reality and could reduce accordingly its net contribution to the nervous signals reaching her visual cortex. Objects and people in the physical world became thin and ghostlike. It was the bug world that was solid and real.

Shame you can't shut out smell as well as vision, she thought, screwing up her nose.

Richard, incongruously, laughed, and Jenny glanced at him, or at the dim ghost of him she could see with 20% of her vision, and wondered what it was that had amused him. He wasn't looking at her. It was something he'd seen outside the window. This struck her as endearing somehow, and she smiled.

To varying degrees – 75%, 90% – almost everyone in the carriage had made a similar adjustment to the opacity of their bug eyes after settling in their seats. And now a soft tide of voices rose up from passengers up and down the aisle, as they called up family members and friends to tell them they were on their way.

But Jenny looked at the clock on her status bar.

Ben will be calling soon, she thought. *Best not to call anyone else until then, or he won't able to get through.*

Ben had a bit of a short fuse when it came to things like not being able to get through.

So she blinked up mail instead and sent a quick message to her boss.

"Remember to talk to Mr Jackson in Data Services before the staff meeting!" she reminded him.

It was already in his diary, but he'd grown so used to being reminded about everything that he often forgot to look. Imposing order, she did it all day. But when it came to Ben she felt like a chaotic fool.

Around the carriage the tide of voices receded as, one by one, calls came to a conclusion and passengers settled down into their own bug eye worlds. Some watched bug TV. Some read bug newspapers and bug books. A Canadian student picked up on a game of bug chess she was playing with a bug friend across the Atlantic. A young boy from Woking played a bug shoot-'em-up game. A woman lawyer with red hair had a look at the balance on her bug bank account. An insurance broker surfed bug porn, having first double checked that his LCV was properly switched off. (For he'd had an embarrassing experience last week with a group of leering schoolboys.)

Outside the window a building site passed by, lit by icy halogen spotlights. Diggers and cranes were still at work and would be through the night,

"*UCF London*," read giant banners all round the site. *Building the Dream.* It was a new kind of bug transmitter station, one of a ring around the city, which would create the new Urban Consensual Field. When it was done, every bug-wearer in London could inhabit a kind of virtual city – or one of several virtual cities – superimposed upon the city of brick and stone.

There would be ghosts in the Tower of London; there would be writing in the sky; there would be virtual Bobbies on every corner... The past would be made visible; the future would rise like a phoenix from the concrete and tarmac of now; and people would even be able, if they wanted, to stay at home in the warm, and send out digital avatars to walk the city streets.

The door at the end of the carriage slid open. A ticket inspector entered. His rail company bug eyes showed giant tickets hovering above every passenger in the carriage except one and he could see at a glance that every one of these tickets was in order. Only Richard had an empty space above his head. The inspector came to look at his piece of cardboard.

"Forget your bugs today, sir?" he inquired pleasantly, feeling in his pocket for his little-used clippers.

Jenny jumped slightly, startled by the inspector's voice. She had been vaguely aware of him entering the carriage, but he had been a barely visible presence, remote, out there, like a parent outside the bedroom of a half-asleep child. So she had quite forgotten him and gone back into her bug dream by the time he had spoken.

Not just for Jenny, but for almost everyone there, the carriage, with its white lights and blue seats and aluminium luggage racks, was now no more than a hazy dream. As to the used car lots and crumbling factory units that were flitting by in the dark outside, they were too insubstantial to make out at all with bugs set anything above 70%

Richard was alone in the atomic world, the world of matter and space.

"One day they won't see it at all," Richard thought. "It'll just be me that keeps it going."

He laughed.

"One day aliens will invade the earth, and only I will be able to see them. Like I see the foxes and those mice that run around under the trains. Like I saw that deer."

That was a powerful memory. One night he'd woken at 2 a.m feeling a need to go to the window of his little bedroom and look outside. The street had been empty, the traffic lights changing from red to amber to green and back again, secretly, privately, as if signalling to themselves.

But a white deer had come trotting down the middle of the road: a pure white stag, with great branching antlers, trotting past the convenience store with its ads for bug card top-ups, past the silent pub, past the shop that sold discounted greeting cards and remaindered books, past the darkened laundrette. It had trotted past them and on, round the corner and out of his sight again.

A solitary car had come by after that, way too fast, screeching its brakes round the corner, shooting across a red light and roaring off in the opposite direction to the deer. And then silence had returned again, and nothing had moved but the traffic lights, shifting every few minutes between green and amber and red.

"It had a rider on its back," Richard said out loud in the railway carriage, suddenly remembering this fact. "It had a...."

Then he stopped, for Jenny had looked at him and smiled.

It was a lovely smile, even when partially obscured by bug eyes. A smile of tenderness and delight.

Richard laughed his gap-toothed laugh.

"Hello sweetheart!" whispered Jenny to the 3D image of her boyfriend Ben, suspended in the space where Richard was sitting. "Have you had a good day darling? I am *so* looking forward to spending this time with you!"

Of course Richard couldn't see Ben frown back at her, and tell her he hoped she wasn't going to be silly and girly and go over the top about everything.

After she'd hung up, Jenny turned opacity right up to 95 and watched the new fly-on-the-wall documentary called *Janey* about the daily life of a young secretary like herself.

"Just remember I'm on national TV," Janey was saying to her boyfriend Ray. "All over the country people are watching me on their bugs. So now tell me the truth. Are you really going to *commit?*"

According to a recent poll, nine million out of eleven million bug viewers agreed that Ray wasn't good enough for her, but tragically, heroically, crazily, she stayed with him anyway.

21

Jenny thought about Ben and his sharp tongue. It really hurt her, it made her feel small and foolish and insignificant. Were they going to be all right in Jamaica? Was that even a possibility? Was there really any chance of it at all?

Richard meanwhile was looking out of the window at abandoned industrial estates.

"No one sees this. No one except for me."

He looked at ruined factories and warehouses and engine sheds.

"I know who'll show up now," he thought with an inward sigh.

And sure enough there was Steel Man, with its iron hands, suspended by magnetic forces in the orange city sky. And of course it spotted Richard at once, regarding him intently with its burning eyes.

Richard turned away uncomfortably, like a child avoiding the gaze of an adult who had once told him off. He hunched down in his seat, with a wince and a tightening of his lips, and turned his attention determinedly to the smoke-blackened walls of Victorian tenement buildings, with buddleia sprouting from the chimney stacks, and to old billboards with their fading and peeling ads for obsolete products. (No one would ever again be bothered to paste up those wrinkly paper images. Any day now advertisers would be able to use the Urban Consensual Field to put pictures in the sky.)

"If it wasn't for me," muttered Richard Pegg out loud, glancing at the opaque goggles that covered Jenny's eyes and avoiding the gaze of Steel Man. "This would all just…"

He broke off.

A tear had rolled out from under Jenny's bug eyes, a mascara-stained tear. Richard watched, fascinated and profoundly moved, as it rolled down her right cheek.

Jenny flipped down the opacity of her bugs and began to fumble in her bag.

But Richard beat her to it, retrieving a squashed packet of tissues from under the notebook in his right anorak pocket, and leaning forward to offer it to her.

Jenny lifted her bugs right off her eyes, smiled at him, accepted the packet.

"Thank you," she said, pulling out a tissue and dabbing at her eyes, "thank you so much. That's very kind of you."

Richard laughed.

"It was an invisible man," he offered.

"Sorry?"

"Riding on the back of that deer. An invisible man with horns."

He didn't normally speak of such things, but Jenny he knew he could trust.

"Wow," Jenny exclaimed. "That sounds like quite something."

Richard laughed.

"It was," he said. "That's why the Need woke me. It was an atomic truth."

Jenny smiled, handed him back his tissues. Then more tears came, and Richard handed the tissues back again and watched her, fascinated, uncomprehending, but full of tenderness, while she once more dried her eyes.

"I'll tell you something," Jenny sniffled. "I'm *going* to have a good time in Jamaica, whatever old misery guts decides to do. I'm going to have a good time no matter what."

She smiled.

"Is that an atomic truth do you reckon?"

Richard laughed loudly.

At the far end of the carriage someone else laughed too, but it was nothing to do with Richard or Jenny, nothing to do with anything present.

"Thank you," Jenny said again. "You really are very kind."

She had done with crying. She passed Richard his packet of tissues, smiled at him one more time, and pulled her goggles back down over her eyes.

Richard settled into his seat, trying to avoid looking at Night Man, who he couldn't help noticing was out there hovering over the dark fields like a giant owl, and staring gloomily in at him with its enormous fiery eyes. Gloomy old Night Man he could do without, but he felt he'd had a good day all the same.

two thieves

Two thieves stood glumly at the railings of a ship, watching their destination slowly transform itself from a blemish on the horizon to a toy island with a single green papier-mâché hill and then, finally, to an actual place that was no longer 'there' but 'here'. Dockhands waiting for the ropes, seagulls squabbling on the quay, weeds poking up between the flagstones: it would all be 'here' for a very long time to come, if this place's reputation was anything to go by.

"Oh crap," muttered Pennyworth

He was short, bald, fat and prone to sweat. His friend was slight and wiry, with a pockmarked face and shock of almost vertical ash blond hair that made him look a little like a toilet brush. Their full names were Penitence Worthiness Gestas II and Surefaith Solicitude Dismas III, but Pennyworth and Shoe were what they always called themselves.

Shoe looked out at the settlement's score or so of stone buildings, the vegetable gardens, the lighthouse. He looked down at the faces peering up from the quay, strangers, but soon to become all too familiar. He ran his hands through his spiky white hair and gave out a groan of despair.

"Dear God, I swear I will die of boredom."

The police had ambushed their gang in a jeweller's shop, acting on a tip-off from an informer. Three gang members were shot dead in the firefight. Another was wounded and died two streets away from loss of blood. But Shoe and Pennyworth were old hands and knew, or thought they did, when to play the game and when to throw in their hands. They'd surrendered themselves at once, expecting perhaps eight years in jail, with time off for not resisting arrest.

But this time they'd got the calculation wrong, for when the panel of judges was reminded of their long records of extortion, pimpery, house-breaking, drug dealing and deceit, it decided the time had come for Last Resort.

"*What?*" the two thieves bellowed in dismay.

Up to that point they had been off-hand and nonchalant, acting as if the trial was a matter of indifference to them and they were keen to get on with more important business. Now they both leapt howling to their feet.

"We never wanted to rob that shop in the first place!" protested Shoe. "We were set up!"

"It's not fair!" cried short, fat Pennyworth, "You let other people have another chance!"

But the judges bowed to the court, and gathered up their robes, and filed out to their chambers.

"Gentlemen," said the voice of the ship's captain over the pa system. "Please pick up your things and disembark."

A couple of dozen prisoners trudged down the gangplank onto the quay, some surly, some silent and alert, some trying to make light of their situation with jokes.

"It doesn't look such a bad place," observed a tiny timid-looking little man, glancing anxiously at Shoe.

And he was right. With its pleasant stone buildings, its blue sky and sea, its wheeling gulls, Last Resort looked more like a fishing village or holiday retreat than a penal settlement. Even the warders checking off their names on clipboards were informally dressed and could almost have been tour guides or couriers. For this wasn't so much a place of punishment as a place of quarantine, a place where inveterate offenders could be sent indefinitely when they showed no sign of changing their ways, not for purposes of vengeance but to prevent them causing further distress.

"Not such a bad place if you like doing sweet nothing," grunted Shoe, his wiry frame taut with dislike, as he turned to one side to spit.

"Greetings everyone," called out a tall white-haired man. "My name is Humility – Humility Joyousness Fortunas – and I'm the governor of Last Resort. It may sound an odd thing for a prison governor to say, but I sincerely hope that your time here will be interesting, pleasurable and rewarding."

No one had ever escaped from Last Resort, for it was on an island surrounded by hundreds of kilometres of open ocean, one of the remotest places on the planet. But (as the governor now made clear) the regime here was far from harsh. They'd find their accommodation plain but comfortable, he explained, they were free to roam, and they'd have plentiful opportunities work at trades, or to study, or to engage in sport and the creative arts. There was even a unique opportunity to take part in the excavation of an archaeological site.

Not all the prisoners were grateful or impressed.

"Who wants to make pots?" growled Pennyworth. "Who wants to dig up bloody old stones?"

He and Shoe had lived their whole lives in the seamy underbelly of a city where you could walk for a whole day and still not come to its edge. All their notions of what was exciting and fun were formed from that experience. They'd lived for the whiff of violence, the heady joy of getting one over on some foolish sap, the sound of gunfire, the thrill of the chase. But here the cry of seagulls was the loudest sound, and you could see the island's only hill at the end of its single empty street.

"I'll die of boredom," Shoe gloomily repeated.

"I wouldn't have bothered to lay down my gun if I'd know this was coming," said Pennyworth. "I'd have kept on shooting till they put a bullet through my head."

A few days later, the two thieves were riding in a bus along a bumpy coastal track, carefully avoiding looking out at the great blue ocean glinting with sunlight, for fear they might find themselves enjoying it.

"So what is this dump we're going to, anyway?" Pennyworth asked one of the other prisoners, a large toothless black man who was sitting across the aisle from them.

The black man shrugged.

"A settlement from the Old Empire or some shit like that."

"What, and we have to dig it up?"

"Yeah, but the guy in charge is really soft. You don't have to do much."

Pennyworth snorted.

"Why do they want to dig it up anyway?"

"Find out what it was for," the black man said. "Or some shit. No one knows apparently."

"Or gives a crap," said Pennyworth.

The black man laughed.

"Yeah," Shoe said, "but you never know what we might find, do you? It's amazing what people pay for that old crap."

He'd once been involved in a scam involving some fake Old Empire artefacts, and he had some idea of their worth. It was why he'd suggested to Pennyworth that they chose this work, as opposed to, say, potting, or working on the colony's single farm.

They came to a picturesque ruin on a slope above a rocky shore, some three kilometres from the main colony, with diminutive trees clinging picturesquely to its crumbled stonework.

As they alighted from the bus, the young officer in charge came rushing to greet them with his hand outstretched.

"Gestas? Dismas? Welcome to the Place of Wells! Wonderful to have you aboard, my friends! My name is Gravitas but most people just call me Officer Graves. Well, I *am* always down a hole in the ground!"

The two thieves declined to smile.

"I think you'll really enjoy this work," Graves continued undaunted. "I know the site doesn't look much at first but I promise you that it's one of those places you really fall in love with, once you get a feel for it."

Officer Graves beamed at them, full of benevolent hope.

"What once stood here looks to have been a square building with a flat roof," he told them. "A large building in terms of length and breadth but only a single storey high. You see the walls here? And here? The top of the roof was paved to make a flat terrace – you can see a few bits of it left round the edges – and the terrace was completely enclosed with a colonnade. There's just that one single complete arch still left over there, look. Almost the whole roof has collapsed into the rooms below, as you can see, and what we're doing now is removing the remains of it to see what lies beneath. It's all very exciting because we really have no idea."

Not much excitement was evident, however, in the faces of Prisoner Gestas and Prisoner Dismas. Officer Graves gave a small sigh.

"One note of caution," he went on. "We really don't know what function this place used to serve, but we do know they had some mighty advanced technology back in those days, and played with materials and forces that we no longer understand. Wear these radiation counters at all times, and if they ever start to bleep, or if you come across something that seems in any way odd, do please report back to me before going on. It's for your own safety. I really don't want anyone to come to any harm here."

Shoe and Pennyworth shrugged and spat and grudgingly shoved the proffered counters onto their belts, and Graves led them to a part of the site where a shaft of some kind had been filled up with rubble. Some four metres of this debris had already been lifted away. Now Graves led them down into the shady hollow and, under his direction, the two thieves reluctantly began removing more loose stones and putting them in large bins for removal later by crane.

"People say that this dig really isn't very important compared with the big ones on the mainland where they are finding all those wonderful artefacts," Graves enthused as they made a nominal pretence of working. "But we don't know what it will throw up, do we? And we won't know until the whole dig is done. I think you'll find it a fascinating place. All digs are, like books of secrets waiting to be read."

"Wow," said lean-faced Shoe in a flat, bored, sarcastic voice.

Graves blinked and looked momentarily hurt – the thieves' surliness was starting to wear him down – but he was a man with a determinedly positive outlook on life.

"We look up the stars today," he said, "and we know their names and we know what they're made of, but for all practical purposes they might as well be lights projected onto a screen. It was different for our ancestors at the time of the Old Empire. When *they* looked out at the stars, they were looking into a vast cave of delights going back and back and back, a cave through which, in some way we no longer understand, they were able to move freely – just imagine it! – bringing back strange beasts and fabulous wealth and wonders that we can only dream about."

He glanced hopefully at Shoe and Pennyworth. Both were gazing into the distance with the determinedly vacant expressions that people and animals wear when they are keeping their minds entirely blank.

"And yet," Graves doggedly continued, "technological prowess is only part of what we lost when the Great Calamity brought down the Empire, and I would say not the greatest part. What strikes me most at these sites is the architectural grace, the calmness and at the same time the playfulness of that wonderful civilisation. Again and again we find details, flourishes, ornaments, whimsical little touches, that seem to serve no purpose other than to give delight, or raise a smile, or serve as food for thought."

He glanced again at the two thieves and finally resigned himself to the fact that he might as well be talking to the stones.

"Anyway, it gives you a good appetite, that's for sure," he said a little sadly, "all this digging and shifting rocks in the open air, with a nice sea breeze to keep you cool."

Pennyworth turned to the side and spat.

"So are there any questions, lads?" asked Graves, making one last effort to force cheerfulness into his voice.

A seagull screeched. The ocean sighed.

"I'll leave you to it then," Graves concluded. "Have fun. Lunch will arrive back at the sorting area at twelve. Just come over and find us when you're ready."

Shoe and Pennyworth grunted, watched him go, and then slumped on a slab of rock and lit up cigarettes.

"A *fascinating* place," Pennyworth mimicked. "A wonderful book waiting to be read."

He put two fingers into the back of his mouth as if to make himself gag.

"What a *dump*," he concluded.

"Yeah," agreed Shoe, "what in God's name made us pick this job?"

After half an hour of this sort of talk, boredom finally drove them to interact at least a little with their surroundings, and they chucked a few stones at each other. Then they set up a bit of ancient marble paving slab and lobbed more stones at it until it split in two. Finally, when they couldn't think of any other games, they began picking up rubble and dumping it into Graves' bin, settling in spite of themselves into a slow rhythm that was certainly more pleasant than doing nothing at all, though both of them would have strenuously denied it.

Then Pennyworth's counter began to bleep.

"What the. . .?"

Before Pennyworth could finish the sentence, Shoe's counter went off as well. Both men laughed raucously.

"So are we going to go and tell that Graves guy?" asked Pennyworth at length.

"Are we shit!" said Shoe. "This might be something interesting."

Pennyworth nodded and tried to turn off his counter. Unable to find the switch immediately, he lost patience with the thing and silenced it by banging it repeatedly on a rock.

"Piece of shit," he growled.

"You dick, Pennyworth," said Shoe, turning off his own device. "The switch is right here on top. Where it says ON/OFF."

"Yeah, well," grumbled Pennyworth.

He poked the switch, found it no longer worked, and tossed the counter aside.

"Come on then," said Shoe. "Let's find out what this is."

Working at a speed that would have delighted Graves' heart, they shifted more stones and finally reached something that looked like a circular lid, about a metre across, made of shining and untarnished metal.

"It'll be locked, or rusted up underneath," Pennyworth said glumly. "Then we'll bloody well *have* to go and get help."

"You never know," said Shoe, tossing aside a cigarette and kneeling in front of the lid with his fingers under the edge.

Pennyworth joined him with a sigh.

"One – two – three," Shoe called out, and they both lifted.

The lid came away quite easily, and they found underneath it a well. This explained the name of the place, of course, but that was not what was on their minds just then. The thing that struck them was what they saw inside it. There was no water in that well, nor was there the dark echoing space you expect in a well that has dried up. There was – nothingness.

Of course the human eye doesn't see the essence of things, but can only detect light or its absence, and you might argue that what was visible there must therefore have been amenable to description in such terms. But it didn't seem like that to them. There was neither light nor darkness down there. There was no surface, solid or liquid, rough or smooth. There was just nothing.

"Holy crap!" intoned Pennyworth.

Shoe turned his radiation counter back on. It was bleeping away so fast that it was pretty much giving out a continuous screech. He listened to it for a moment, then laughed.

"Sweet!" he exclaimed.

Others might have worried that the radiation would do them harm, but to these men danger and uncertainty felt like home.

Shoe and Pennyworth hadn't known it, but their counters were connected to a monitor back at the sorting area which Graves checked at regular intervals. He had picked up that they had detected radiation and, running and scrambling across the ruins, he quickly reached the broken wall at the top of the shaft and looked down at the two of them standing there on the edge of the well, with Shoe's counter still giving out a continuous plaintive screech.

"Hey guys," he called to them softly in what he hoped was a calm, kind voice, "you're going to need to back off from there."

He squatted down so that only his head was above the wall, in order to minimise his own exposure to whatever force of nature was pouring out of the well.

"Take a couple of steps back," he called, "mind you don't trip on the stones, and then come up here and get behind this wall with me."

Shoe and Pennyworth looked up at him peeking fearfully down at them. Then they glanced back at each other, and laughed.

"What *is* this thing, then?" Shoe asked.

Graves made a further effort to control his voice.

"Not sure guys, but it looks as if you may have come across some sort of spatial gateway. We've never come across a live one before. But never mind that for the moment, eh? Really, guys, I'm not kidding. It's a lot of radiation we're all soaking up right now. I need you to step away from the edge and then we really ought to get away from here."

Gateway? They had no real idea what Graves was talking about, but 'gateway' sounded like a way out. Shoe looked at Pennyworth. Pennyworth nodded, and, with a defiant yell, both of them jumped into the well. The last thing they heard was Graves yelling "No! Don't!"

After the first quarter-second or so, they didn't experience themselves as falling. In fact they found they were already standing on smooth, solid ground. There had been no jolt or impact at all, but they were aware of a sharp change of temperature and light intensity, and a feeling that they had become slightly heavier. Wherever they were, it was much cooler than the dig at the Place of Wells, and it seemed to be night time, although, once their eyes had adapted, it was certainly not pitch dark.

"Bloody hell!" said Pennyworth.

They stood under a starry sky on a wide platform perhaps a hundred metres square, paved in chequerboard style in black and white marble. A colonnade ran round the edge, with an urn containing an olive tree in front of every third arch. Beyond, there was a sandy desert.

The air was completely still, and the silence was absolute.

They stood there for a few seconds, looking around themselves with open mouths. Then Shoe gave a low whistle and pointed at the sky.

Shoe and Pennyworth weren't big on moons, for the moon back in the city had been at best a pale smudge above the brash electric lights, and there were always brighter and more vivid things clamouring for attention all around. But one thing they did know about moons, and that was that there was only supposed to be one.

And here… Well it was regrettable, but it couldn't be avoided. Here there were three of the things shining down.

Standing there side by side, their mouths gaping foolishly open, they both felt an icy shiver of almost superstitious terror. It was a deep and primitive fear, the animal dread of the inexplicable and the unknown. One moment on Earth, in an island in the middle of the ocean. The next moment: this.

"Oh crap," murmured Pennyworth.

"Yeah, I know," said Shoe.

"We're on another planet, aren't we?" Pennyworth whispered.

Since Shoe didn't reply, Pennyworth answered his own question, addressing himself to the three cold moons themselves.

"We must be. Another bloody planet. What are we going to do?"

The moons, of course, had nothing to say on this point. Their sole contribution to the story of the two thieves was to illuminate the scene and to provide incontrovertible evidence that this was not the planet Earth.

And Shoe also said nothing. He sniffed, and spat, and then began to walk across the wide platform to the colonnade.

"What are you doing Shoe?" moaned Pennyworth.

Again Shoe declined to answer.

"Talk about out of the frying pan," Pennyworth complained as he hurried after his silent companion.

He caught up with Shoe as he reached one of the archways. They looked out over the planet surface, turned and looked back at the artefact on which they stood, then looked out at the planet again. The chequered platform, strewn here and there with blown sand, was raised some three metres above the surrounding desert. A flight of marble stairs led down onto the surface, its lower steps buried in sand.

And this was a *proper* desert. There are half-hearted deserts that have cacti growing in them, or shrubs, or tufts of yellow grass, or even small trees. But there were no features at all in this one but rocks and stones, each with an overlapping set of faint moon shadows.

"We can't cross that," said Pennyworth

"No," said Shoe, finally breaking his silence. "And anyway, the whole place might be like that for all we know. You can't cross something if it hasn't got another side."

"We've had it, haven't we?" groaned Pennyworth.

Shoe shrugged and began to walk round the edge of the colonnade, noticing, now that they were close, that all the olive trees in their urns were dead. The twigs were grey and had long since lost their bark.

Reaching the corner of the colonnade, they turned and continued along a second side of the platform, passing another flight of stairs that led down into the sand.

"Maybe we should have listened to that guy," said Pennyworth. "What's his name? Graves."

"What?" said Shoe. "That drip? Nah. Never. Start doing what men like that tell you and you might as well be dead anyway."

They turned along the third side.

"Hmm," said Shoe.

Like the other sides, this side had stairs going down from it, but they didn't lead directly onto the ground but onto to a subsidiary stone floor, also paved in black and white marble, a little below the current ground level of the desert. A wall protected it from being overwhelmed with sand, though blown sand was still building up on the flagstones, and especially in what had once been an ornamental pond in the middle, partially burying the dried bones of several carp. Two huge urns, one on each side of the pond, held the brittle white skeletons of substantial trees.

Pennyworth and Shoe ran down the steps. They found that the stone floor opened into a hall underneath the raised platform they'd been walking on. The hall was a hundred metres long and twenty wide, its floor paved once again in black and white, its walls and ceiling very smooth with a faint decorative design carved into them of swirling organic shapes. Two thick columns like tree trunks stood in the middle of the long space, holding up the platform above.

"I don't like this place one bit," Pennyworth muttered, and, even though he spoke quietly, his voice seemed to echo right up and down the hall. "It's like a museum or something."

Away from the light of the three moons, the cavernous room was illuminated only by cube-shaped objects set at intervals into the walls that gave off a low pinkish light. Some of the light cubes were dimmer than others, and some were at their last ebb, not really illuminating anything at all, just glowing and flickering like old embers. A few had died completely.

"Yeah," said Shoe, "but if there's going to be a way out, it'll be somewhere down here, I reckon. Think about it, Pennyworth. That well back at Last Resort was way down below that old ruin."

The odd thing about the hall was that there was nothing in it, and no doors either, other than the one through which they'd entered. But right in the middle of it, between those two fat columns, was the balustrade of a descending spiral staircase.

Shoe and Pennyworth leaned over the balustrade and looked down.

"*Yes!*" Pennyworth shouted, and his triumphant cry echoed from the stone all around them and up and down the stairwell.

Shoe gave an exultant hoot and kissed his fellow-criminal wetly on the cheek.

"Piss off, you pervert," protested Pennyworth, laughing and pushing him away.

The staircase wound straight down into the ground, dimly lit by more of glowing cubes, to a depth equivalent to four or five storeys. There was single landing half way down. But none of these details were of any interest to the two thieves, for down at the bottom of the stairs they'd seen just what they'd been hoping for: another well, like the one they'd uncovered at the archaeological dig at Last Resort. Even from five storeys up they could see the same mysterious absence within it, neither a surface nor a gap: neither light nor dark, neither rough nor smooth.

Shoe smiled broadly.

"Lead on my friend," he said.

"We did it!" shouted Pennyworth gleefully, setting off down the stairs at a run. "We are the best, you know that, Shoe? We found a way out of Last Resort, and now we've found a way out of this dump too. We are the best."

"Where do you think it'll take us this time?" asked Shoe.

"Who gives a shit? As long as it's somewhere that's not here."

"Yeah," said Shoe, "or back in Boringsville on Last Resort."

But on the landing halfway down, deep below the surface of wherever this empty planet was, he stopped and grabbed Pennyworth by the arm.

"What?" demanded Pennyworth impatiently, wincing at the sound of his own voice echoing up and down the stairwell.

They had been surrounded by silence ever since they arrived on that chequered platform, had heard literally nothing at all in their whole time here except for the sounds they made themselves. But down here, where every breath and footstep echoed and re-echoed from the silent stone, the stillness seemed even more intense. You really had to *make* yourself speak, for it felt dangerous to break that stillness with the rough echoey self-conscious sound of a human voice.

"Look," said Shoe, "a door."

"*What?*"

Pennyworth glanced, without curiosity, at an archway that led off the landing into a corridor. It had writing over it in the old, cursive script, quite different from the spiky letters that shouted from billboards and illuminated signs in the city where they grew up.

"You ran straight past it," Shoe said.

Pennyworth looked at him incredulously.

"Of course I bloody ran straight past it, Shoe! There's one of those well things at the bottom, remember? Who gives a shit about anything else?"

"May as well check this out while we're here, surely?"

"Why? What's the point?"

"There might be something here we want. We'd be nuts not to have a look."

"I guess," Pennyworth reluctantly acknowledged, rubbing his bald head. "I don't like this place though. It's like… Well, it's like people were here a long time ago and…"

Shoe laughed mockingly.

"Afraid of ghosts, Pennyworth my old mate?"

"Nah, of course not. It's just that..."

"Well okay then," Shoe interrupted and he passed through the arch. The corridor was cut into the rock rather more roughly than the hall or the stairwell so it had something of the quality of a mine tunnel, and it was lit at intervals with the same glowing pinkish cubes as the stairs. The time was clearly approaching when all these underground structures would sink back into total darkness. Every fifth or sixth cube here was already guttering or entirely extinguished, and one of them gave a final flicker and expired just as they were walking past it.

After ten metres or so, a large chamber opened up on the right. Its whole floor space was stacked with plastic boxes, piled untidily on top of each other, perhaps put there by someone in a hurry, or perhaps disordered by previous intruders rummaging through them.

Short, plump Pennyworth immediately ran forward to check them out.

"Holy shit!" he breathed "Look at this!"

Shoe looked, and his hard lean face broke into a smile.

Diamonds! Every box they looked in was full of diamonds. Diamonds in their thousands, diamonds in their tens of thousands, were all around them.

Pennyworth shouted with incredulous laughter.

"Bloody hell, Shoe! We'll be *rich!*"

Shoe glanced wryly at his companion, running his hands through jewels all the while.

"Worth pausing on the stairs then was it, mate?"

"Too bloody right, my old buddy. Good job I've got you to knock some sense into me."

They stuffed their pockets to bursting point. Then Pennyworth took off his shirt and tore two holes in the shoulders. He tied up the ends of the arms, stuffing them both with more diamonds until they bulged, then put the shirt back on with his own arms sticking out through the torn holes, so that the shirt-arms dangled in front of him like bloated extra limbs.

"You dick, Pennyworth," said Shoe. "You look like you're wearing some dumb octopus suit or something."

For some reason, Shoe's initial elation had faded slightly, but

Pennyworth was still far too excited to notice or care.

"Who cares what I look like?" he retorted. "This is my future I've got here. This is my bloody future."

He rubbed his shiny head.

"Now let me see. How am I going to carry more?"

He had an idea, hesitated, and made a decision.

"Damn it," he said, "I'll do it. We've all done it when we've had to hide stuff in prison, haven't we? I can shove six big diamonds up my arse, and swallow half-a-dozen little ones too."

"Whatever turns you on," said Shoe with a slightly distant laugh, and he went back into the corridor.

Pennyworth wasn't joking. He whipped down his breeches at once and winced and grunted as he shoved stones up himself, his eyes bulging and streaming. Then he picked out a handful of little diamonds, gathered what saliva he could in his dry mouth as lubrication, and swallowed them one by one, gagging as each one went down. Finally, he heaped diamonds into a box and picked it up to carry with him.

"At least take a box Shoe!" he exclaimed, waddling uncomfortably out into the corridor, with the heavy box in his arms and the bulging octopus arms dangling down his front. He was in obvious pain. His eyes were watering, and he walked gingerly. Diamonds, after all, are hard and angular things.

"Yeah I will," said Shoe. "But later. I'll pick up a box on my way back past here."

Pennyworth stared at him, dismayed.

"Way back? Aren't we going straight to the well now?"

"Hurts to walk, huh?" said Shoe laughing. "That's your problem, buddy. I want to see where this leads."

"Come on, Shoe my old friend," Pennyworth pleaded, looking up with dismay into the face of his tall learn friend. "Don't fool around, eh? Let's just get down to that well."

But Shoe shook his head and insisted on continuing along the corridor.

"I'm not fooling around. Remember what you said when I wanted to come along here? If we'd done what you wanted then, you'd never have found all this, would you?"

"Yeah, okay, but..."

Reluctantly, Pennyworth conceded, picking his way painfully

along behind Shoe, still for some reason clutching his box of jewels and still wearing his diamond-packed shirt, though he could have put both of them down and come back to them later.

At the end of the corridor there was another archway, this a very narrow one, leading to some descending spiral steps, very steep and narrow, and quite crudely cut into the raw rock.

Shoe examined the writing engraved above the arch, and noticed it was the same as the inscription over the entrance to the corridor.

"Your heart's desire," he read out.

"Crap," said Pennyworth laughing. "You don't know what it says. That's not in our language. It's not even in our letters."

He shook his head.

"Sorry, buddy, nice try but I'm not going a step further. You go down there if you want to. I've *got* my heart's desire, mate, I'm holding it now. I'll wait for you up here."

Shoe shrugged and climbed down the narrow stairs. At their foot, the equivalent of two storeys down, he reached a small but pleasantly proportioned room, its walls and ceilings decorated with a fine tracery of stone in an abstract pattern vaguely suggestive of vines and seashells. In the middle of the room, and filling up a good proportion of its floor area, was a circular pool of clear still water. On the far side of the pool was a stone seat like a throne. Cubes in three of the four corners of the room gave out gentle pinkish light. The fourth cube had died.

Suddenly aware of how weary he was, of how long a journey his life so far had been, and how long it might still be, Shoe felt an overwhelming desire to go and sit in that stone seat and rest. Never mind Pennyworth waiting up there with diamonds shoved up his rectum and diamonds like a yoke round his neck.

"More fool him," muttered Shoe. "He can wait."

"Shoe! *Shoe!*"

The voice came at first from far away and he didn't take much notice of it, just noted it, and frowned slightly, and let his thoughts return, like fish released back into a stream, to the silent and peaceful chambers where they had been so happily engrossed.

"*Shoe! Shoe!*"

This time, annoyingly, the voice was close by, coming not from some remote place but from just across the small space where he was sitting.

"Hey Shoe! What in God's name do you think you're doing?"

With a start, Shoe looked up and remembered where he was. He saw fat Pennyworth standing in the doorway of the room, still laden with his heaped box of stones and his ridiculous octopus arms. Sweat was running down the bald man's face, which was a caricature of outrage and incredulity.

"*What are you bloody doing?*" shouted Pennyworth, too angry to remember his unease about disturbing the echoey silence. "I've been up there all this time, trying so hard not to crap these diamonds out again that I've got a cramp up my butt, and you've not found anything at all. You're not even *looking* for anything."

"Oh, yeah, sorry," said Shoe, indifferently. "I didn't notice the time passing."

"You didn't notice the... I don't believe I'm hearing this! We're stuck in the middle of a desert on some godforsaken planet, in case you'd forgotten, and here you are sitting around like... like some old guy in a movie relaxing on his veranda in the sun. I could hit you, Shoe, do you know that? We want to get *away* from here remember? We're on an alien planet!"

Shoe reluctantly stood up.

"You should try sitting here," he said, "It..."

"I haven't got time for a sit down," interrupted Pennyworth (for whom, it must be admitted, sitting down had every reason to be a particularly unappealing idea).

He eyed the water. "Might just wash my hands though. They're a bit shitty."

"Don't you *dare* touch that water," snapped Shoe.

Pennyworth frowned.

"Why shouldn't...?" He shrugged. "Oh suit yourself. If you want to act all weird, be my guest. But let's get going to that well."

"So what were you looking at anyway?" asked Pennyworth, after he had completed the painful ascent from the room with the pool and they were making their way back along the corridor towards the landing.

"I sat in the chair and I looked at the water, and... It was just peaceful. It was like I..."

They were approaching the room full of treasure and Pennyworth interrupted him.

"You going to pick up a box?"

"I guess."

Shoe went into the room and absently tossed a few extra diamonds into one of the boxes to top it up.

"I was like I remembered something," he mused, "like I remembered something really obvious which I keep forgetting. I remembered... Well, it's hard to explain but I remembered that everything is..."

"Tell you what," said Pennyworth, "we should carry a few boxes to the well down there, stack them up and come up for more. Then we could chuck the extra boxes into the well before we go through ourselves."

"Uh. Yeah, okay. What I'm trying to say is that I remembered that everything is fine, you know? There's no need to..."

"Are we going to move or what?"

Shoe picked up his box. As they made their way back to the stairs, he opened his mouth to try one more time to explain again what he had seen down there, but then changed his mind. It was obvious that Pennyworth wasn't listening or interested or capable of hearing. But, more than that, he sensed that the simple act of trying to put it into words would dissipate the experience. With every word you spoke about a thing like that, the less you knew what it was you were trying to say.

"Now all we need," said Pennyworth, panting and gasping, as they set down the boxes beside the well and headed back up the stairs for more, "is to get to a place that isn't Last Resort and isn't a desert. Anywhere with people in it will do. Anywhere with people in it, my friend, and you and I are going to be rich."

Pennyworth was so excited about this prospect that he seemed to have temporarily forgotten his discomfort, though Shoe couldn't help noticing, as he followed his companion up the stairs, that Pennyworth's breeches were now soaked with blood. The dark stain had spread right across the seat and halfway down one thigh.

"I'm going to get a bloody great swimming pool," Pennyworth said as they reached the room full of treasure. He was so short of breath that his words came out in short bursts. "A bloody great swimming pool with... with underwater lights and a bar and... and all of that... And twenty bedrooms... And a high wall... And one of those big metal gates with my own guards minding it... And I'm going to have a wine cellar, and drink wine that costs... that costs more than its weight in gold, if I feel like it..."

They picked two more boxes, headed back towards the well.

"Maybe I'll buy my own.... my own football team or something, to have a bit of a hobby..." Pennyworth went on as they headed down the stairs again, though he could hardly find the breath.

"Yeah," he wheezed as they reached the well again, "and I'm going to get myself so... so many women.... so many pretty woman. Actresses. Models. A different one every day... And every night of course."

"Right you are," Shoe said distractedly. "Now let's jump into this thing and get it over with."

Pennyworth looked at him in horror.

"No way!" he panted out, wincing as he carefully lowered his second box to the ground. "We need more boxes! We need two more at least."

Shoe shook his head.

"We need to go," he said.

"No, Shoe! Not yet!"

Pennyworth's plump face was pale with blood-loss and slimy with sweat. His hands were shaking.

"Man," said Shoe, "you should really see yourself."

He dropped the box he'd been holding into the well. The nothingness sparkled and hissed as the treasure fell through it.

Pennyworth looked longingly up towards the landing and then back at the well, his glistening face knotted up with strain. He ran his tongue round his lips as he struggled with the conflicting pressures of greed and pain. But he didn't have the energy to argue any more. Wincing, he bent down, picked up a box and tossed it into whatever lay beyond that surface that wasn't really a surface at all.

Shoe picked up his other box. He too glanced up the stairwell, and remembered the room with the pool that he'd never see again. He shrugged the thought away.

"Are you ready?" he asked Pennyworth, who was now standing in a small puddle of blood.

With a grunt of pain, Pennyworth picked up his remaining box.

Again he ran his tongue round his lips and he looked sadly up the stairs one final time. Then he turned to Shoe and nodded, and they both jumped.

The harsh white sunlight hurt their eyes and at first they could see nothing but its overwhelming glare. But they could feel the heat of a tropical sun on their skins immediately, and smell the city smells of sewage and sweat and rotten vegetables. And they could hear the shouting and screaming of a hysterically excited crowd.

They were standing in a market square strewn with diamonds and bits of plastic box, and all around them men, women and children were jostling, shoving and screaming abuse at one another as they scrabbled on the worn paving slabs for the precious stones.

"Holy crap," breathed Pennyworth, whose glistening face was now grey as a corpse's.

Nearby, a tall woman with a baby on her back stood up, triumphantly clutching a single diamond in her fist, and glanced in their direction. The baby was screaming and screaming, but she was oblivious to it. Her hard, bloodshot eyes darkened as she saw the new arrivals with their piled boxes of jewels. There were four bloody scratches on her right cheek.

"*Get them!*" she shrieked.

The actual words were unfamiliar to the two thieves, who knew no languages other than their own, but the meaning was very plain. Immediately the woman started to run towards them. A few other people reluctantly lifted their heads, saw the two thieves, and took in the implications. And then there were more shrieks and more people looked up. In a matter of seconds half the crowd was heading straight for them.

"Throw it down, Pennyworth," yelled Shoe. "Throw down the whole boxful and run!"

He hurled the contents of his box out into the crowd, followed by the box itself. Pennyworth gaped at him for a moment, then looked back at the faces rushing towards him, crazed and murderous with longing. He swallowed once, then flung out his own box just as the tall woman with the scratched face was almost upon him. Once more there were diamonds everywhere. The crowd screeched as it took in this second helping of instant wealth. (The first lot had appeared out of nowhere only a few seconds previously.) Everyone dived to the ground, snatching and snarling and clawing. The boxes were torn to shreds in moments.

Dodging pedestrians and rickshaws, the two thieves ran. But they'd only covered the length of one block when Pennyworth fell to his knees with a sob and threw up copiously, immediately scrabbling in the vomit for stones.

"I've got to crap," he whimpered to Shoe, "I can't hold on any longer."

His foolish octopus limbs dangled into his stinking sick. Passers-by turned to stare at them. Rickshaw drivers beeped horns to try and make them look round.

"Well crap yourself then, Pennyworth. We need to move."

Shoe looked back the way they had come. Any moment now, he knew, the diamonds on the market square would be exhausted and the first hungry outriders of the crowd would start to come after them.

He pulled his sick companion to his feet, and put an arm round his shoulders to hold him up, trying not to breathe in too much of Pennyworth's spreading stench, but gagging all the same. He looked down the streets to the left, the right and straight ahead, weighing up his options with a speed and detachment that came from long experience.

But even as he did so, other thoughts came unbidden into his mind.

"There's probably another well buried under that market square", he found himself thinking. And he remembered what Officer Graves had said about the Old Empire and its playful mysteries strewn out across the stars, and it seemed, in that moment, to make sense to him. And with a sudden pang of loss, so sharp as to bring tears up into his eyes, he recalled the room with the pool.

"Hey! There they are!"

"Over there!"

The harsh shrieks of recognition were coming from the direction of the square.

"We'll go to the left," Shoe decided, "the road's busier and it'll be easier to hide."

Then he tightened his grip round his foolish friend and gave himself back to the moment.

johnny's new job

Monday it was all round the factory where Johnny worked that a little girl called Jenny Sue had been killed by her wicked stepfather. He had dropped her down a dry well and left her there to starve.

Wednesday, the case was officially declared by the government to be an instance of Welfare Knew And Did Nothing (within the meaning of the Summary Judgement Act) so of course everyone kept their ears open and sure enough pretty soon the thrilling voice of the Public Accuser came booming out of the factory Screens, demanding on behalf of everyone there that culprits be identified for him to Name.

"Ordinary decent folk have had enough!" the Public Accuser told the city government, while every single soul in the factory stood raptly listening. "Those responsible must pay the Price."

Everyone cheered.

"Too right! You go, Accuser!"

Accuser's dark unsmiling face stared down at them from the giant Screen.

And then on came Factory Manager Number One and suggested they all do two hours of extra work for nothing, in memory of the little girl.

"Let's all do our bit extra," Factory Manager said, "It's what Jenny Sue would have wanted."

And everyone cheered once more and returned to their looms, working with such gusto that their output for the next two hours was the same as it would normally be in half a day. And some of them had tears running down their faces as they worked and worked for that poor dear dead little child.

They knew they'd need time off, you see, when Welfare's Name was announced.

Friday afternoon at 3, Screen gave out that the Announcement of Welfare's Name would be in an hour's time at City Hall, to be done by the Public Accuser himself.

"Work hard as you can to half three," said Factory Manager, "and then knock off early and go with my blessing on full pay. I know you all want to do your bit. And I will do mine."

And once again everyone cheered, and told each other he really wasn't so bad at all as bosses go, and they set to and worked at the looms as hard as they could until half-past three. Then it was down tools and on with coats and down through the grey streets to City Hall where a big crowd was already gathering, with a brass band playing solemn music in memory of the little girl and a big flag hanging from the balcony.

Announcement was never on time. The last time it had happened was when Welfare took a little boy away from his loving mum and dad, and they both begged her not to, but the Welfare Officer didn't care, that heartless cow, even though the mum was pretty and the dad had once served in the wars in Araby. The wait had been over seventy minutes that time and the crowd was going crazy with impatience by the time the Announcement was made. But in a way that was all part of it. Announcement on time would spoil things really. It wouldn't give folk a chance to wind themselves up for what had to be done.

Anyway, at ten past four the Mayor came out onto the balcony.

"Fellow citizens, it is my sad duty to announce that a dear little girl from our city has died *due to the criminal negligence of Welfare.*"

There must have been two, three thousand there. Everyone cheered and pretty soon the old familiar chant went up.

"The names! The names! The names!"

And the Mayor gave a little wave as if to say, I do know and I'd like to tell you but I'm afraid it's not my job. And on the big Screen above, where his face was shown as high as a double-decker bus, you could see his little smile as if he were sharing with everybody the impatience he felt as a human being, whether or not he was Mayor. And everyone said to themselves, well, he's not so bad, he's just like us really.

Then the Mayor went back inside – "The names! The names! The names!" – and presently out he came again with that same shy little smile and held up his hands for quiet. It was nearly half-past four by then.

"Citizens! Citizens! Thank you as ever for your commitment and concern. You make me proud to lead this great city. It is my great pleasure and honour now to give to you that mighty defender all that is good and decent in our community, that fierce guardian of everything that is right. I give you… The Public Accuser."

And out came Accuser in his black robe, and you could see on the screen that he never even nodded to Mayor, never even smiled.

"The names!" yelled out Johnny, just as everyone else was settling down, so you could hear his individual voice right across the square.

And Accuser looked at him, looked over the top of his half-moon glasses right across the square at poor little Johnny down there in the crowd.

Johnny went bright red.

"Well I was only saying…" he muttered.

"My fellow citizens," boomed out Accuser, "a terrible crime has again been committed by Welfare in whom we generously placed our trust. We did not ask much of them. We did not ask of them that they make our city rich. We did not ask of them that they heal the sick. All we asked of them – the one little thing we asked – was that they protect our children, our precious little ones, and to ensure that none of them came to harm. And yet they failed; again they failed, again they betrayed the little ones. And it is has been looked into, as ever, by the proper people, and we are now at that point we always reach on these occasions when I tell you the name, or names, of the officers concerned."

He slowly unfolded a piece of paper, placed it on the dais in front of him and smoothed it out.

"I have so far identified just one Welfare Officer who must take the blame, though more names may likely follow later."

Accuser paused, looked out over his half-moon glasses to make sure the people were ready for the full seriousness of what he was about to say.

"That negligent and heartless Officer is…" again he paused. "That blundering and incompetent fool… That disgrace both to manhood and to our city… is…"

And here he looked down at his paper.

"…is Officer David Simpson of 15 Lavender Grove, Uptown."

The crowd booed and hissed. Accuser took off his glasses and scanned the faces below, as if to make sure that everyone present had fully understood.

But he need not have worried. The people were already surging out of the square, bellowing with grief and rage.

And off Johnny went with them, striding and sometimes even running through the streets, adding his own impatience to the general haste to get to 15 Lavender Grove and get the job done, and enjoying being part of a big crowd who were all feeling the same thing.

"Welfare Officer David Simpson," announced Screens along the way, "had been receiving a salary of seventy thousand gold crowns a year…"

There were cries of incredulity and rage.

"…owns a real car," the next Screen was saying.

You heard bits as you passed the Screens every fifty metres or so, and then in between you couldn't hear.

"…and this year he went for a holiday in sunny Tartary with his wife Jennifer and his two children, Horace and Portia, both at Younger's Infant School. That's on Upton High Street, by the way, and here are the pictures of the kids…"

The crowd looked up at the children and hissed.

"How would he have liked it if it had been one of them?"

"Tartary, eh?" the announcer was musing aloud on the next Screen. "Tartary. Not bad. Not bad at all for a man who was paid to care for little children *and instead stood back and did nothing while an innocent little girl was killed.*"

"The bastard, get him!" yelled Johnny, who wouldn't have minded a holiday in Tartary himself.

"Yes, get him," agreed the folk all around him, hurrying earnestly through the streets, determined that what happened to Jenny Sue must *never ever happen again.*

"We're doing this for you, Jenny sweetheart!" shouted out a woman nearby, in a voice that started strong and ended with a sob.

"For you, Jenny Sue!" the crowd yelled with her, and many joined her in angry tears.

"Someone ought to chuck *his* little girl down a well and see how he likes it," a man said to Johnny: a tiny little man with a huge moustache. "See how he feels about that."

Well that sounded fair enough to Johnny so he yelled it out.

"Let's get his little girl Portia," he yelled. "Let's chuck *her* down a well!"

"Yeah, let's get her," a few people around him called out.

But it was a bit half-hearted and quickly petered out, as if the crowd sensed that there was a contradiction here somewhere, even if it was hard to put your finger on it.

Poor Johnny felt a bit crushed that his contribution had gone unappreciated but a kindly woman beside him put her hand gently on his shoulder.

"We might hate her," the woman said, "and we might well hope that she dies too, a horrible cruel death, so he can see what it's like, and be truly sorry. But she is only a child after all, whatever we might think of her. We've got to remember that."

When they reached the sign that said "Welcome to Upton" everybody cheered, and for a little while the crowd milled about in the middle of a cross roads, wondering where to go next, growing and spreading out into the surrounding streets as more people poured in from behind. Traffic lights went red, orange, green, orange, red to no avail while cars and vans waited respectfully for these good but justifiably angry people to move on in their own good time.

"Where's Lavender Grove, mate?" the crowd called out collectively to the people of Upton.

"Up that way, turn right and then left, you can't miss it, mate," the people of Upton called back in strong stern voices, only too glad to be of help. And some of them came along.

Pretty soon the crowd reached Lavender Grove, and, shouting and yelling all the while, began squeezing itself in as best it could.

It was street of little detached houses with tidy front gardens. Outside every house on the street there were law officers in blue to make sure that no one got carried away.

"Frustrating, isn't it?" said a tall man near Johnny. "You want to do over the whole damn street of them, don't you?"

"Course you do," Johnny said.

But the man's friend opined that it didn't *really* help to take it out on the neighbours. A neighbour's proper role in this situation was more to come out and tell stories to Screen about the one being Named.

"...about how they never would have thought it, and all that," the man said.

"Well, I suppose," the first man reluctantly agreed.

There were law officers in front of number 15 too. But they were there for a different reason. Their job was to ensure that the people inside did not slip away before it was time. They had a couple of cars ready with their engines running and red lights going round and round on top. Pretty soon the sergeant in charge decided there were enough people crammed into the street. He nodded to the officer by the door, and the officer gave a sharp rap and soon out came the wife Jennifer and the two children Horace and Portia, their faces white with the knowledge of their sin. For, as everyone knows, to be in the presence of sin *is* sin. It's something you catch like a disease.

And the crowd booed and hissed and yelled and a couple of hotheads rushed forward to lay into them, dear good passionate young fellows that they were, and had to be gently pushed back by the law.

Cold and stern, the law put the mother and the two children in one of their cars and off it went down the street with the other car following after. You could see the law didn't like it any more than anyone else, letting Welfare's family get off lightly like that, but they had their job to do, and all credit to them.

"Chuck *them* down a well and see how he likes it," yelled a fat woman, and a great roar of approval went up.

Johnny looked at her enviously and wondered what she'd got that he hadn't. But he noticed that the crowd seemed to sense somehow that these were only words, not an actual proposal. It let the car go by and out of Lavender Grove and off to wherever they were going.

So now came the *real* business. All these good honest people who'd come up here from City Hall were standing looking at the front door of 15 Lavender Grove and everyone knew there was no more wife and kids or anyone else in there, just Named Welfare himself on his own. And it was a strange feeling, a strange exciting feeling that you felt going right through you, in your body as well as in your mind, a bit like sex, knowing he was inside there, scared witless, and knowing that somehow or other they would soon get him out.

And then there was a rustle of excitement from the back of the crowd, and calls of "Gangway! Gangway!" and people moved back to make a path for Accuser himself, arriving not in a car but on foot, there in the actual flesh, moving among them. He passed so close that Johnny could reach out and touch his black robe as he went by.

Straight up to the house went Accuser and rapped hard on the door.

"David Simpson!" bellowed the Public Accuser. "Come out and face the people of this city."

Nothing. No sound from inside at all. So Accuser, grim-faced, picked three strong men from the crowd and they all went into the house and pretty soon, after a little bit of muffled shouting, came out again with the despicable man who had let little Jenny die. The crowd, the poor wounded grieving crowd, went crazy with rage, screaming and yelling at him that he was scum and vermin.

Accuser held up his hands for quiet, and then he turned to the snivelling Welfare and demanded of him loudly and firmly and with great dignity that he own up to what he had done.

"Do you deny that it was your fault that that dear little girl was thrown down the well?" boomed Accuser in his great and dreadful voice.

The Welfare Officer said something that no one but Accuser could hear.

"He says *he did his best*," Accuser repeated, as if he was handling something dirty with tongs. "He says it's not always easy to know what is going to happen in advance. He says he had a lot on. "

Accuser looked out at the crowd, letting that contemptible drivel sink in. Then he roared out the rage that they all felt.

"*What* could he have had on that was more important than saving a little girl? What is more important than that? Holidays in Tartary, perhaps?"

He held his hands out wide in a gesture of helplessness. Even Accuser, it seemed, with all his wisdom and experience, was still dumbfounded by the flimsiness of these people's excuses. Even Accuser shared the bewilderment of ordinary decent folk.

"Do we need to hear more?" he asked

"No! No! No!" hollered the crowd, for it was anxious to get on.

And it trusted Accuser, knew it could rely on everything he said. He was so good at exposing these wretched Welfare Officers, and laying bare their craven willingness to be led and misled by others. Why should anyone else even bother to try?

As he walked away from the lynching with the rest of the crowd, Johnny felt a little… strange. Not that he didn't felt cleansed, not that he didn't feel uplifted. But yet all the same he did feel just a little bit uneasy.

And actually people in general were rather quiet as they trailed out through the grey old streets. A few enthusiasts were chanting and shouting – "Well! Well! Well! Welfare! Well! Well! Well! Farewell!" – but on the whole most people were quiet.

"It was for Jenny," Johnny reminded himself. "It was for little Jenny Sue, and to make sure it never happens again."

And even as he thought this to himself he heard a woman nearby saying the very same thing to her friend.

"We had to do it didn't we? For Jenny Sue."

Everyone talked about that little girl as if they knew her.

"It's not like we *want* to do stuff like that," the woman told her friend.

"Of course not," her friend agreed. "It's the last thing we'd want to do if there was any choice in the matter."

Soon afterwards Johnny ran into some people he knew from the factory, Ralph, Angela, Mike and a few more, who were going to get a drink. Johnny had always been a bit of a loner, a bit on the edge of things, and people like that wouldn't normally have thought of asking him to come along, but at a time like this you stuck together.

"You coming for a jar Johnny, my old mate?" said Mike. "I think we deserve one after all that, don't you?"

They found a big bar in the city centre and began to drink quickly, their thirst not easily quenched. And while they drank, Screen gave out more news. There would definitely be more Names, it seemed. More would be announced next week.

"Well," grunted Ralph, who'd been near the front when the Price was paid. "I just hope they get it right when they name these Names."

Mike looked sharply up at him.

"What do you mean?" he demanded.

"Well, if they Named the *wrong* people, it would…"

Ralph's voice tailed off. Everyone looked at him, dismayed.

"What exactly are you saying, Ralph?" asked Mike coldly.

His voice had a warning edge and he looked round significantly at everyone there to confirm that he was speaking for all of them and that he counted on all of them for support.

"You want to be careful, Ralph mate," Mike said. "If I didn't know you better I'd think you didn't care about Jenny Sue."

"Yeah that's right!" said Johnny, seeing a chance to establish himself. "You want to watch what you're saying, Ralph. If we don't go after the bastards that let her die, that poor little girl will have died for nothing."

Ralph looked a bit scared.

"Of course I care about Jenny Sue," he said indignantly. "I'd lay down my own life if it would bring her back."

"Oh that's a lovely thing to say," exclaimed Angela, who liked to make the peace.

"And anyone who let her die," Ralph went on, "deserves everything they get."

Mike was mollified. He reached out and warmly grasped his friend's hand.

"That's better, Ralph my old mate. That's the good old Ralph we know."

But here's the funny bit of the story. When Johnny was staggering home with seven pints inside him, he ran into six big blokes with shaven heads, stripy tops and cudgels in their hands. They came straight at him and he tried to run but he just couldn't manage it with all that beer in him.

"Steady! Steady!" they told him, laughing as he wriggled and squirmed in the grip of two of them.

There was a law man over the other side of the street and he was laughing too. And even Johnny gave a rueful smile, because of course he knew these blokes were government men and were only doing their job.

"You don't need me to tell you who we are do you, son?" asked the chief of them, a great neckless barrel of a man.

"No you don't, mate," Johnny said. "I know who you are. You're the press gang and it looks like you've got me fair and square."

"That's right, mate," said their leader. "We're the press gang all right, and my name's Bobby Grab."

He put on his special electric glasses and reached out his fat hand so that Johnny could give him his government card.

"Johnny," Bobby Grab read out, "Johnny Jones. Works in the blanket factory for two hundred crowns a week. Well this is your lucky day, Johnny Jones, because in this job we've got lined up for you, they'll pay you twice that."

"Oh," said Johnny, very surprised, "so what service is that?"

"The Welfare, mate. They've had a bit of a recruitment problem lately for some reason, so they've had to get us on the job. Which means you're pressed mate. Five years national service in Welfare. Could be the making of you."

Johnny's face was white.

"The Welfare? You've got to be kidding me. I don't want to be in Welfare!"

"Why not mate? Why on Earth not? The money's good and you'd be doing important work. Protecting children, protecting innocent little ones. What could be better work than that?"

"But… But look what happened to that Welfare today… I was there… They… We…"

At this Bobby Grab's face grew dark.

"What are you saying Johnny boy? Are you saying that David Simpson didn't deserve what he got? I find that hard to believe, I must say, after what happened to that poor little Jenny Sue."

"No, mate, of course not."

"Would that little girl have had to suffer if he'd done his job?"

"No, mate."

"You sure?"

"Of course I'm sure."

"I should hope you are. Otherwise what were you doing there, as I could see on your card, helping out at Lavender Grove this afternoon? What were you doing there if that was a man who didn't deserve it?"

"I'm not saying that."

"Well I'm relieved to hear it, mate."

"But… I might not be any good at the job. That's what I mean. I might not know what to do,"

The gangman laughed indulgently.

"You're forgetting something, mate. You're forgetting what always happens when a little child dies like Jenny Sue. First the Public

Accuser does the Naming and sees that the Price is paid. But what comes next, eh? What comes next?"

"Um... I... er..."

"Then comes the Healer, doesn't he?" the gangman reminded him, as if he was talking to a child. "The Healer comes in, dressed in white, just as Accuser comes dressed in black. And Healer looks into it all doesn't he? And he listens to those who know about these things, and he makes new rules to ensure that it will never ever happen again. You must know that, mate! He does it every time!"

Johnny nodded yes, he supposed so. Truth be told, you didn't pay so much attention to these things after the Naming and the Price were done. And it wasn't on Screen much either.

"Trust me, my lad, that's how it works," said Bobby Grab, indulgently pinching Johnny's cheek between a fat finger and a fat thumb, as if he was a kind old uncle and Johnny was a little boy.

Bobby turned his neckless head to look at his men.

"I'm right boys, aren't I?" he asked.

"Spot on, boss, spot on."

"So what I'm saying," the gangman went on, "what I'm saying is that by the time you start work as a Welfare Officer, Healer will have come, and he'll tell you just what to do, and then all you'll have to do is do what he says and you'll be fine. Beats working in a blanket factory every time if you ask my opinion. And it's not as if you've got the build for our sort of work."

He beamed round at the big men around him. All the gangmen laughed.

"Just listen to the Healer, Johnny, and you'll be fine," advised Bobby Grab, and he nodded to his men to let Johnny go.

"Take the week off," he said. "That's the law. A week on full pay. And then you'll get a letter telling you what to do. All right? You won't play silly buggers will you? You know that we'd only come and find you? 'Course you do. And anyway when you think about what I've said, you'll realise that this could be just the chance you need. After all a fair-minded young fellow like you wouldn't have gone to the lynching if you didn't know perfectly well that any half-decent human being could do a better job than Officer Simpson. It wouldn't really have been right."

He gave Johnny a hearty slap on the back to send him on his way, and then the gang headed off into town looking for more young men and women. And Johnny headed home.

But all the way he kept noticing the Screens with their promises of new Names next week. And he dreamt that night that he was alone at the bottom of a well, like poor little Jenny Sue.

the caramel forest

In the caramel forest the leaves, trunks and branches were all made of the same smooth flesh, like the flesh of mushrooms. It was yellow, grey or pink. A kind of moss covered the ground, pink in colour, and also fleshy and mushroom-like. And there were ponds, every hundred yards or so, picked out by the pale sunlight that elsewhere in the forest was largely filtered out by trees. The ponds were surrounded by clumps of spongy vegetation, pink or white or yellow.

But the children, pressing their faces to the car windows, were trying to spot something more interesting than trees and ponds. Cassie told Peter he would win five points if he spotted an animal of some kind, and one hundred points for a castle. They'd only ever seen one of those and that had been in ruins, its delicate, butterscotch, shell-like architecture smashed and kicked to pieces by settlers.

But the forest, with its spotlit ponds, remained an empty stage. There were no castles, and no animals either, only the occasional solitary floater drifting through the space between canopy and forest floor, trailing its delicate tendrils, and bumping from time to time against the trees. Cassie didn't consider floaters either sufficiently animal-like, or sufficiently interesting to deserve a point.

"We see those all the time," she told her little brother, who persisted in pointing them out.

"Those aren't really ponds, you know," she presently informed him. "Under the ground they're all joined up. It's like a sea covered over by a roof of roots and earth."

"Quite right, Cassie," said her father, David, from the front passenger seat.

"I wish we'd see some goblins," said Cassie, glancing defiantly at the back of her mother's head. "I'll give you twenty points, Peter, if you spot us one, and I'll let you have turn with my microscope as well."

"We don't call them goblins, do we?" David reminded her. "We call them indigenes. They're just living creatures like us, going about their lives."

"Everyone at school calls them goblins," said Cassie.

"Well, most kids in your school are the children of settlers," said her father, "and they don't know any better. But we're Agency people. We're supposed to set a good example."

Another floater (which Peter, annoyingly, still pointed out), more ponds, more silent empty space beneath the mushroom-like trees.

"Most of the kids say that goblins are only good for shooting and nailing up," Cassie said off-handedly. "They say the Agency is soft."

"Well that's just silly, Cassie. There's no reason to persecute the indigenes. They harm no one, and they were here for millions of years before the first settlers came."

"They give you funny ideas though."

"Well, maybe. But that's probably just their way of protecting themselves."

"Protecting themselves?" Cassie weighed this idea for a moment, tipping her head to one side, then dismissed it with a shrug. "Well whatever it's for, I…"

"*Must* you talk about those horrid things *all* the time?" interrupted Cassie's mother, Paula.

She turned a corner, leaving it rather too late, and the car only narrowly avoided a particularly large pond, a small lake almost, with the road running along the edge of it. David winced, but did not comment.

Peter pointed out two more floaters drifting by above the water.

"You'd better play in the garden when we get back," Paula said, half-turning her beautiful but bitter face as they left the pond and headed back into the trees. "I need you out of the way so I can get ready for the visitors. We've hardly got enough time as it is, let alone with you two getting under my feet."

"Honestly Paula," David whined. "I can't win. You keep saying how bored and lonely you are. I thought you'd appreciate the company."

"Yes, David, but it was just stupid to invite people to come to dinner at six o'clock, when you knew that we ourselves would still be two hours' drive away at three."

Cassie tensed. She dreaded her parents' quarrels.

"And anyway," Paula went on, "my idea of company is people who might be interested in talking about things that I like talking about. Not two of your workmates who will just talk shop."

She sighed.

"And one of whom you obviously fancy, incidentally," she added, "judging by how often you mention her name."

"For god's sake, Paula. What was I supposed to do? They called me. They said they'd be passing our way. They asked if we'd be around."

"You could have said we were doing something else. You don't seem to find that hard to say that to me."

"Let's sing some songs," Cassie said firmly to her brother.

The bungalow sat in the middle of a wide bare lawn, surrounded by a two-metre chain link fence to keep indigenes and animals at bay, with floodlights on poles at regular intervals. The lawn, rather startlingly, was green, a colour entirely absent from the surrounding forest.

Juan, the caretaker, sat outside his hut cleaning a gun. He laid it down and limped to the gate to open it for them, nodding, but not smiling, as they passed through.

"Bo da, senar senara," he greeted them with small stiff bow. He could speak English well enough but usually confined himself to Luto.

Cassie organised a game outside in which Peter was a dog called Max, and she was the dog's owner. Peter was five. She was ten.

"Woof! Woof!" said the dog.

All around them was the silent forest. It had a strong sweet smell, like caramel, but with a faint whiff of decay.

"Woof! Woof! Woof!"

"Quiet now, Max, I can't hear myself think."

It was odd. The one thing Cassie did not want to hear was the sound of shouts or sobs from within the house, and if she *had* heard them, she'd had covered them up at once with noisy play. Yet she couldn't help herself from listening out for them: listening, listening, listening, all the while glancing down the road back into the forest on the far side of the chain link fence, willing their visitors to arrive.

But the forest, that silent, waiting, spotlit stage, was still. Nothing made a sound. Nothing moved except for yet another floater drifting through the trees.

"We're on an alien planet," Cassie informed her dog Max, who was too young to remember anything else. "This is Lutania. We come from Earth, where the trees are green like this grass, and there are no goblins or unicorns, and none of the creatures can talk to you inside your head. One day we'll go back there, across all that huge huge empty space. Imagine that."

Was that a sound from the house? She held up her hand to tell her brother to be quiet. But no. It was just something banging in a gust of breeze in the garden of the other house behind hers, the empty house, which, apart from Juan's hut, was the only other building in the vicinity. They were on their own out here. It was five miles to the next human settlement, and that was a Luto village, the one where Juan's family lived, with no Agency inhabitants at all. School was another ten miles beyond that.

"Come here now Max and eat this bone. If you're good I'll stroke your head."

"Woof!" said Max, crawling obediently across to her.

"Oh, wait a minute," she said. "Here are the visitors. You'd better be Peter again."

Every single night, through the thin wall of her room, Cassie heard her mother crying.

"I *hate* this place..." she'd hear Paula sob, "I *hate* this stinking forest..."

"Ssssssh!" her father would hiss.

Or, after half an hour of muffled sobs and murmuring, she'd suddenly cry out:

"Of course the kids don't bug you when you're away all the time."

"Shut up," Cassie would mutter, on her own in the dark. "Shut up, shut up, shut up!"

She'd try and distract herself by thinking about the immense tracts of space between Lutania and Earth. If she could only understand how big that was, she felt, this little house, and this little local difficulty of her mother being miserable and her parents not getting on, would become so small that they'd be of no consequence at all. It was a bleak sort of comfort.

Peter, meanwhile, would sleep peacefully in the room on the other side of hers.

Right now, though, there were the visitors to attend to. Ernesto and Sheema

"Sorry about the short notice, but it seemed a shame not to call by when we were in these parts."

"Hope we haven't put you out. Good lord, look at this spread! You shouldn't have gone to all this trouble!"

"Nonsense, nonsense," cried Paula. "No trouble at all. Lovely to see you. We'd have been most offended if you'd passed this way and not come to see us."

Standing in the corner of the room, hand in hand with Peter, Cassie watched her mother with narrowed eyes. Paula really did seem pleased to see these people, that was the strange thing. She really did seem to mean what she said. She was smiling. She had laughter in her eyes. But that was how she was. You never knew. You could be laughing and joking with her one minute, thinking you were having a lovely time, and then the next look round and see her collapsed and broken, crying hopeless tears.

"My," said Sheema, "what *beautiful* children!"

Cassie turned her attention to Sheema, accepting the compliment with a severe half-smile and a gracious inclination of her head. Sheema was *quite* pretty, she supposed.

"Such wonderful red hair too!" Sheema said, quailing in the intensity of the little girl's gaze, and turning back hastily to the grown-ups.

"Okay, okay," Cassie's father conceded over the empty dinner plates. "They have an electromagnetic sense. They communicate with microwaves in some way. The trees act as antennae. I grant you all that, and I grant you that it may allow them to detect human brain activity. But it doesn't explain how they *interpret* it..."

"They *don't* interpret it, Dave," Sheema said. "They pick it up and beam it back to us."

"Sure, but you're not getting my point. They don't just beam back random signals, do they? They're able to home in on certain things..."

"Or perhaps just stimulate certain parts of..." Ernesto began.

David ignored the interruption.

"And anyway, Sheema," he said, "the 'beam it back to us' theory doesn't explain how we manage to *receive* the signal."

"You're both complicating this unnecessarily," Ernesto persisted. "Like I say, they don't receive or send a *signal*; they just stimulate certain parts of our brains. They disorientate potential predators by stirring up uncomfortable feelings. They don't have to know what it is they're dealing with or what effect they're having, any more than a skunk has to understand the chemistry of his stink, or what it smells like to you."

Peter was already in bed. Cassie knew she would soon be sent to bed as well. She glanced between the adults with sharp appraising eyes. Dad and the two visitors were talking louder and louder as the evening went on, and crossly interrupting one another more and more, and yet they were smiling too. They seemed, for some reason, to be having fun. Mum was a bit quiet – she wasn't a scientist like the other three – but even she was smiling. She did seem very thirsty, though. She was drinking glass after glass of wine.

For a moment, David glanced uneasily at his wife, noticing warning signs. But he returned to the argument all the same.

"What you're stubbornly missing, Ernesto," he said, laughing angrily and banging his hand on the table. "What you're refusing to consider is this. How can a creature whose nervous system is absolutely nothing like ours at all, home in on our 'uncomfortable feelings' and stir them up? One can just about envisage how they or their trees might do this with other Lutanian creatures with similar nervous systems. But with humans? How? How are they able to locate those feelings in our quite different brains?"

"A good point," Sheema acknowledged with a laugh. "But what alternative are you suggesting?"

"I suspect we may eventually need an entirely new theory of the mind. Think about it. We have completely different brains from goblins." (For some reason, he was using the word freely, though he always corrected his family when they used it.) "They don't even have neurons, as we understand them – they don't even have an *analogue* of neurons – and yet indigenes are able to reach right through the species-specific particularities of the human brain, to find and stimulate the places where we keep our troubles. How can this happen unless pain and distress has some kind of universal form that transcends the particular nervous system which expresses it? And that being so, perhaps we need to radically rethink the place that mind has in the scheme of things. Perhaps we need to stop speaking about space-time, and starting talking about space-time-mind."

"But that's mystical nonsense, David," laughed Ernesto, angry and friendly all at once. "With great respect, it's just lazy mystical nonsense.

Just because we've failed so far to find an explanation in terms of the parameters of physical science, it doesn't mean we have to give up and rewrite the entire rulebook."

"Why not, Ernesto? Why not at least consider that possibility? Space, time and mind."

David's eyes were bright. He was in a playground where he felt at home, and he was full of energy, with the cowering, haunted look, so often there, quite absent from his face. But he was careful to avoid looking back at his wife, whose eyes were shining in quite another way.

"Because it's *twaddle* David," Ernesto laughed. "It's mystical twaddle!"

Paula rose to collect the plates.

"Are we ready for dessert?" she asked in a loud bright voice that Cassie recognised at once as dangerous.

David glanced at her. There was a brief flash of fear in his eyes, but he still turned back stubbornly to his friends.

"One other point, Ernesto. One other point that people sometimes forget. We've been assuming this evolved as a defence against predators, but what predators exactly do we have in mind? It's not as if..."

"That was delicious, Paula," cut in Sheema, glancing with sudden anxiety at her hostess. "I'll come and help you."

"What was it you were saying about goblins?" Cassie asked the two men as the women left the room. "What were you saying about their minds?"

"*Indigenes*, darling," said her father, barely concealing his irritation at being distracted. "Yes, we were just talking about how they somehow make people have uncomfortable thoughts when they get up close."

"They don't make *me* have uncomfortable thoughts," Cassie said.

"Ah, well maybe you haven't been near enough to one," suggested Ernesto, with a friendly wink.

"I have so, loads of times. Here and at school. One came right up to the school fence a couple of weeks ago. I *liked* the thoughts it gave me."

"Did you indeed, sweetheart?"

Her father glanced at Ernesto, smiling and raising one eyebrow in a superior and theatrical way that Cassie knew was only made possible by the presence of visitors.

She shrugged.

"It happened, Dad," she said coldly. "Whether you choose to believe it or not. I liked being near it. But the other kids threw stones at it."

David laughed uneasily, glancing again at his friend.

"Nearly time for bed," he announced.

"I haven't had my pudding yet."

There was a loud wail from the kitchen.

"They're out there *again!*"

David rushed to his wife. Cassie hurried after him.

They could see the goblins through the kitchen window: two of them, one squatting, one standing.

"Make them go!" sobbed Paula. "For God's sake make the horrible things go away!"

They were thin grey creatures, about the same height as Cassie, picked out by the bluish electric lights around the fence. Neither one of them was looking at the house. Both seemed engrossed in some object that the squatting one was holding up for the other's inspection: a shell, perhaps, or a piece of stone.

"Get a grip now, Paula," muttered David. "You know quite well they're completely harmless."

Sheema put her arm round Paula's shoulders.

"Easy now, love," she said in a warm and gentle voice.

But the look she gave her husband wasn't warm at all, and seemed to Cassie to refer to some prior exchange between the two of them. Sheema hadn't wanted to come here, was Cassie's guess: Sheema had warned Ernesto that Paula would be difficult and make some sort of scene.

David and Ernesto went out through the kitchen door and starting running across the unnatural green of the grass towards the fence, shouting and waving their arms, each one of them with his own set of multiple shadows thrown out by the floodlights.

"There there," Sheema murmured soothingly to Paula. "There there. Remember it's just a silly trick they play. Just a silly trick they play on our minds."

Cassie stepped just outside the kitchen door, so she could watch everything: the women indoors, the goblins and men outside. The caramel smell wafted from the forest, carrying its faint hint of decay. The moss under the trees glowed softly. The many ponds shone with phosphorescence. And creatures were moving out there, whichever way you looked. The stage was no longer empty.

"Go *away*!"

David ran up to the fence, kicking it and banging on it with the flats of his hands. After a few seconds, the squatting indigene rose very slowly to its feet, and then both it and its companion turned their narrow faces towards David and regarded him with their black button eyes. Their V-shaped mouths resembled the smiles in a child's drawing.

"Go on, be off with you!" David shouted again, quite pointlessly, for the creatures had no ears.

Both goblins tipped their heads on one side – sometimes indigenes could look thoughtful and cunning; at other times they seemed as devoid of intelligent thought as a tree or a toadstool – but neither of them moved away. Behind them, far off in the softly glowing forest, a column of white unicorns was making its way through the trees.

Cassie started to walk down towards the fence.

"Cassie darling," called Sheema without much conviction. "Don't you think you ought to...?"

She tailed off – she had no confidence with children – and in that same moment Cassie heard in her head the voice that always spoke in the presence of goblins: her own voice, speaking her own language, but not under her control.

"Fear," it said, "but no love."

Again David banged impotently on the fence. This had no effect on the goblins, but it brought Juan out of his hut, swearing in Luto, with a heavy pulse gun in his hands. He limped to the fence and pointed the gun at the goblins at point blank range, barely acknowledging his employer or his employer's guests.

"Be careful Juan," began David, "no need to..."

Ignoring him, Juan pulled the trigger. The gun only made a faint thudding sound, like a beanbag dumped on a table, but the goblins staggered and clasped their heads.

"I think that was excessive Juan," David said, as the creatures loped off into the forest.

"You want them to go or not, senar?"

65

Juan shrugged and turned back to his hut. Cassie knew his children – they went to the same school as her and Peter – and she knew that, if Juan had been given the choice, he'd have killed the goblins without compunction, or maybe caught them and nailed them to a tree. It was what Juan and his friends did for fun when they went hunting out in the forest, with no Agency do-gooders there to pry or to spoil things.

David and Ernesto walked back to the house. Cassie, unnoticed, followed behind them. She could see how David deliberately turned slightly away from his friend, so Ernesto couldn't see the strain in his face.

"So?" asked Ernesto. "What did *you* hear in your head, David? What wisdom came to you through the channel of pure mystical being?"

"I didn't pay much attention," David said shortly. "You know what, though. I really wish Juan would listen to me a bit more, and do what I ask him to do, instead whatever he happens to think best. The Agency pays his salary after all."

He still hadn't noticed his daughter following quietly behind them.

"I heard the voice telling me that I was second rate," sighed Ernesto, "and that no matter how hard I tried, I would never be as good a scientist as you."

In the kitchen, Paula was sobbing on Sheema's shoulder. No one asked her what *she'd* heard in her head.

David noticed Cassie and told her to go to bed.

Some nights were sobbing nights. Some were sniffing and snivelling ones. But that night, after Sheema and Ernesto had gone, was the worst kind. Tonight was a *wailing* night.

"I can't *stand* those things, David. I can't stand them. Can't you see that? I just can't bear another whole year of them. Why can't you get that? Why doesn't it *matter* to you? I know you don't love me, but don't you care about me one little bit? Don't you care at least about the children?"

"The children are fine with goblins, you know that. And please keep your voice down, or Cassie will hear us."

"They're not fine with goblins. You really don't understand *anything* do you? Cassie *pretends* she's fine with them as way of coping and trying to keep the peace."

"No I don't," hissed Cassie in the darkness. "Stop lying about me. Stop *lying.*"

She banged angrily on the wall. Her parents' voices subsided immediately to a murmur, but she knew the wailing would soon start up again.

"Run away, why don't you?" asked a voice inside her head. "Why hold on to this dream?"

She went to the window. Sure enough, the goblins had come back. They were squatting side by side with their backs against the fence.

Cassie sighed. It was only a matter of time before Paula also sensed their presence, and then there would be no peace at all.

"My dad said you had goblins round yours last night," said Carmelo next day in the school playground.

Cassie was in her usual refuge, a place close to the fence where she could squat down behind a spongy clump of pink vegetation and be shielded from the general view. Juan's son had come over specially to seek her out. He was dark and wiry, with clever mocking eyes.

Cassie shrugged. "Yeah, we did. I didn't mind though. I quite like them."

Beyond the fence lay the silent, empty forest.

"You quite *like* them?"

The boy took a cigarette from his pocket and lit it. He was only eleven but he drew the thick soupy smoke into his lungs like a smoker of many years, releasing it slowly with a contented sigh.

He squatted down beside her.

"Dad said your mum yelled and yelled when those goblins came back again in the night."

"Yes, she did. We had to get your dad out of bed again to chase them away. Mum hates goblins."

"Well, that makes one person in your family who's got a bit of sense."

"Why? What's the harm in goblins?"

"They slowly take over your head, Agency girl. Slowly, slowly. Funny thoughts and dreams: that's just the beginning. Next thing you know, you've forgotten who you are or where you came from, and then you belong to them. That's why we shoot them and string them up.

We'd be goblins ourselves if we didn't."

He drew in more smoke and regarded her with narrowed eyes as he let it back out through his mouth and nose. The two of them were still only children, but there was a certain electric charge between them all the same. Carmelo constantly mocked Cassie for her stuck-up Agency ways, and she scolded him for his ignorant settler beliefs, and yet he often came on his own like this and sought out her company, when he could have stayed with the other settler children, or brought them over to tease her.

"But you're not allowed to harm goblins," she told him primly. "It's against the law. You're supposed to treat them like people."

Carmelo made a scornful noise.

"Like people! We've been dealing with goblins here since long before your Agency came here with its stupid laws. My dad says, when he was a kid, every single village had dried goblins nailed up on gibbets at the gates to warn the others away."

He drew deeply on the cigarette, regarding her carefully.

"Goblins were here long before you were," Cassie pointed out.

Carmelo laughed as he released the smoke.

"And we were here long before you, Agency girl. And Yava *gave* us this world."

Yava was the settlers' god, and Cassie knew from experience that there was no point in even discussing him.

"You shouldn't smoke, you know," she said. "It'll mess up your lungs."

"Don't do this, don't do that!" the settler boy mocked her, and took another deep drag. "You agency people are all the same."

"Well it *is* bad for you. That's just the fact of it."

Carmelo exhaled.

"Those goblins didn't come back again after their second visit, did they?"

"No. Not after your dad chased them away again."

The boy snorted.

"Chased them away!"

"What? What's funny about that?"

"He chased them out of your sight, more like, and then did for the two of them with an axe. That way he got to sleep the rest of the night, without your mum and dad yelling for him every hour or so."

Cassie stared at him.

"He *killed* them?"

"Of course he did."

"But we didn't want that!"

"Oh come on, Cassie, they're only animals."

"How could they take over our minds if they were only animals?"

But Carmelo had spotted a floater drifting in over the fence. Taking one quick final drag from his cigarette, he took careful aim and flipped the glowing butt end upwards. There was a hiss of gas as the burning tip made contact, and then the floater sank, slowly deflating, onto the ground.

Carmelo walked over to it, and squeezed out the remaining gas with his foot.

One night, a month or two later, Cassie was woken in the early hours of morning by her parents quarrelling yet again on the far side of the bedroom wall.

"Why don't you *listen*, David? *I – don't – want – to – stay*! Which part of that don't you understand?"

She got up and went to the window. The lawn outside shone its unnatural green in the bluish glow of the electric lights. Far off in the forest, tall shadowy giraffe-necked creatures were solemnly processing round a shining pond.

"*Why* is it impossible, David, why?" came her mother's voice. "Why can't you just go to the Agency and say 'sorry, we made a mistake, we need to go home before my wife loses her mind, and my kids become even more weird and goblin-like than they already are'? Why is that impossible?"

Cassie considered knocking on the wall as usual. Her parents had already had one row that night. Surely they could see it wasn't fair to wake her up again?

But she didn't do it. Something in her mind had clicked into a new position, though she couldn't have said why, just now, after months and years of this nightly torment. Giving a little firm nod of assent to her own impulse, she pulled on some clothes, and tiptoed quietly to the door. As she touched the handle, her mother's voice rose yet again in the next room.

"I *know* David, but what you've got to understand is…"

She closed the door carefully behind her.

Her brother woke with a start.

"Peter. Wake up. We're leaving."

"What?"

He always obeyed his sister unquestioningly, but he'd been deeply asleep.

"Where are we going?" he wanted to know, while Cassie passed him clothes.

"Away from here. Mum's shouting at Dad *again.*"

Cassie took the key to the compound from the shelf beside the kitchen door, then crept out across the grass with her brother, bleary-eyes, behind her. She slid back the bolt on the gate, very slowly and carefully so as not to disturb Juan, then led Peter briskly through. She headed quickly away from the brightly lit fence and then immediately off the road and into the forest.

"Dad says you could walk five hundred miles this way," she said, "and still not reach another road."

All around them were ponds, and phosphorescent moss, and creatures moving under the dim mushroomy trees.

"Where are we going?" Peter asked again as he trotted behind her.

"I don't know yet," Cassie said. "But don't keep asking me, eh?"

From a pond straight ahead of them, unicorns emerged, scrambling one by one out of the bright water to snuffle and flare their nostrils in the caramel air, before heading off in single file through the trees.

Peter began to count them.

"One, two, three, four..."

"Seventeen," Cassie told him shortly.

About twenty ponds later, they came to one where a single, very small, goblin sat at the bottom, lit by the pink phosphorescence of the pond's floor. The creature was not much bigger than a large cat, and was quite motionless, staring straight ahead, apparently at nothing in particular.

Peter pulled at his sister's hand, troubled by the presence of the goblin and wanting to move away. But Cassie resisted, making him wait until the little goblin glanced up, its black button eyes taking in the two of them looking down from the air above.

"Mummy is going mad," said a calm cold voice inside Cassie's head. "Daddy is a scaredy-cat, who hides away at work."

"Yes, sirree," she muttered with a grim chuckle. "You got that right, my friend"

Peter began to cry, and Cassie turned to him with a frown.

"Go on then," she said, "Spit it out. What did it say to you?"

Her little brother just sobbed.

"Well, whatever it said," she told him firmly, "you may and well face up to it, because it's true. They don't tell lies."

Peter nodded humbly.

"So go on then," Cassie persisted. "Tell me what it said."

"It said…" snuffled Peter, "it said that Mum wishes I'd never been born."

"Oh *that*," Cassie snorted. "Is that *all*? I could have told you that. I've heard it often enough through my bedroom wall. She wishes she hadn't had either of us. Spoiled her career apparently, and anyway she doesn't like kids. Come here, you silly boy. Come to big sis. *I* love you don't I?"

She pulled Peter close to her, putting her arm round his shoulder in a rough masculine way. Three baby water dragons appeared in the pond, supple as eels and slender as human fingers, and began to chase one another round and round the little goblin, which was once more staring straight ahead.

"There you are, Peter," Cassie said, hugging her brother against her, and absent-mindedly patting him. "There there. That's better isn't it? You've got *me* to look after you, haven't you? You've got your big sis. So you don't need them, do you? You don't need anyone else at all."

Peter sniffed and nodded.

"There's all the food anyone could want out here, after all," Cassie told him, giving him a little encouraging shake. "We'll be *quite* happy having fun out here all by ourselves. No Mum blubbing. No Dad whining."

She thought for a moment, a little sadly, about Carmelo.

"And no horrid school with settler kids," she added firmly, "who think killing things is fun."

At the bottom of the pond, the goblin suddenly swum off, disappearing, in a single, frog-like stroke, into one of the water-filled tunnels under the trees.

"Come on then, trouble," Cassie said to her brother. "Let's get moving again, before someone notices we've gone."

All that night, with pauses for food and rest, they wandered through the caramel forest, Cassie telling Peter stories to keep his spirits up, or providing him with improving pieces of information, or making up games for them to play together. Who could find the biggest tree pod? Who would spot the next dragon?

"Why don't you be Max the dog again, Peter," she suggested when he seemed to be flagging, "and then you can snuffle things out for us."

Snuffling things out wasn't exactly hard to do, with the show in full swing all around them.

"Woof! Woof!" said Max almost at once, spotting a gryphon fanning a pair of incandescent wings that crackled with electric charge.

"Woof! Woof!" he said again, as a white hart darted away from them, and plunged into the underground sea.

"Woof! Woof!" he shouted out, as an agency helicopter came thump-thump-thumping over the mushroom trees, probing down into the forest with long cold fingers of light.

"Good boy Maxie," Cassie told her brother. "*Good* boy. Now quickly come and hide."

Not long after the helicopter had passed over, dawn began to break. The phosphorescent glow faded from the moss and the ponds, the stage emptied, and the two children found themselves walking alone through ordinary sunlight that filtered down through the trees, as in pictures of Earth, that faraway world across the void, that place where leaves were green.

They lay down to sleep in deep soft moss.

When Cassie woke the sun was already setting. Beside her Peter still slept peacefully, sucking the edge of one finger, and for a while she just lay there watching the shadows of dreams rippling across his face and his eyes darting about under his closed lids.

During the quiet still hours of daylight, Cassie realised, creatures had come to watch her dreaming, just as she was watching Peter now.

She'd had strange thoughts running through her sleeping mind, and a familiar voice in her head had been telling her that there was no faraway home, no great void of space, no 'Earth' or 'Lutania', only a single whispering, seething world, strange and familiar all at once.

From a nearby pond climbed a small winged quadruped, shaking its sparkling wings.

"Come on Peter," Cassie called out gaily. "Wakey, wakey! It's another lovely night."

They were deeper into the forest that night, further away from Agency stations and settler villages alike, and they came across many goblins.

The creatures were sometimes on their own, often in twos and threes. They watched the children with their black button eyes and smiled their V-shaped smiles. One of them held out a white stone, another a piece of twig. One even showed them a small brown button from a settler's jacket.

"There is no space," said the voices in Cassie's head, as the goblin's eyes watched her. "There are no people. There is no such thing as far away."

It seemed strange to her that she'd ever been persuaded to believe in an immensity of empty space beyond the caramel forest and its sky, for it seemed obvious now that everything that existed was as close as could be to everything else: close enough to whisper and rustle and murmur, close enough to touch...

She looked at the button. She nodded. She turned away.

Peter clutched her hand so tightly that it hurt.

Several more times they heard the thud-thud-thud of a helicopter passing overhead, and saw the Agency searchlights sweeping officiously through the mushroom-like trees, leaching the colour from leaves and trunks.

The children just hid until they passed, surrounded by the whispering and rustling and murmuring of the caramel forest.

Cassie had no desire to be plucked up into the empty sky.

In the early dawn they came to a castle beside a pool. It was very small, only about Peter's height in fact, and in the dim grey light it looked like a little smooth stalagmite that had grown there for some reason beside the water. But one side of it was open, and they could see the intricate little chambers inside it, with their amber whirls and coils that enclosed even smaller chambers, and yet-tinier whorls...

When they tired of looking at it, the children gathered the spongy vegetation that grew around the castle and made themselves a secret nest nearby, well hidden from the sky. Then they found some savoury chicken fruit to have for their supper and a couple of toffee apples for afters.

"Now wash your face and clean your teeth in the water, Peter," Cassie said when they'd finished. "And then let's get you settled down."

She stroked his head and told him a story, while the sun rose in the sky, turning as it climbed from a syrupy rosehip red to pale lemon.

"I'll look after you, my little bruv," she whispered to Peter's already sleeping face. "I'll always look after you."

Three goblins arrived. One by one they caressed the little amber castle, and bent down to stare into its interior. Then they settled on their haunches on the bank of the pond, without even a glance at the two children.

"Won't find your way back now," said the voices in Cassie's head.

"Not if I can help it," muttered Cassie contentedly, stretching out in her improvised bed.

Crack!

There was a gunshot, followed by human voices and barking dogs.

Peter lurched into wakefulness with a whimper.

Crack!

One of the goblins dived into the pool.

Crack! A man ran to the bank and fired into the water.

"Is all right now, darlings. We take you back to your Ma!" growled another man's voice, right next to the children in a thick Luto accent. "Goblins won't scare you no more."

Sitting up, Cassie and Peter clung together. The whispering and murmuring of the caramel forest was suddenly far away.

"And maybe this time Agency go listen eh?" grumbled a third man, helping Cassie and Peter to their feet. "Maybe this time they go understand why goblins is bad."

The air was full of smoke. These weren't pulse weapons that these men were carrying. They were proper old-fashioned guns, blasting out deadly balls of hot, hard matter.

Dogs came sniffling and snuffling, first round the children, and then, rather more interestedly, round some smooth greyish stuff that was strewn over the ground nearby.

Cassie gazed at it, uncomprehendingly.

"Don't worry about nothing," said the leader of the search party. (It was one of dozens spread out across the forest, linked by radio to the Agency helicopters overhead). "Is only crazy ideas these goblins put in your head. That's all. Only crazy ideas. They'll went away soon enough."

He ruffled Peter's hair kindly, and gave Cassie a friendly wink. She stared at him. The other men were breaking up the castle with their gun butts.

One of the dogs took an experimental mouthful of the grey stuff, then sneezed and spat it out. It was goblin flesh, smooth all the way through, like the flesh of mushrooms.

greenland

I was afraid once, Dr Brennan, thank you for asking, muchas gracias, but now I feel pretty much at peace. What I've finally managed to get through my head is that I'm not in the world, and never have been. This little box here where my life will end –and where *your* life will end too if what you say is true – it's barely a place at all, is it? It's barely separate from the emptiness beyond. So why be afraid of that small final step?

You can almost hear the gossamer whispers of the stars in here, can't you? You can almost feel the pulling and tugging of the invisible threads that keep the huge wheel of the galaxy turning, though almost all of it is empty, almost all of it is nothing at all.

Everything is how it has to be, Dr Brennan. Even a monster like you. That doesn't mean that what you did was right, whatever your talk about human destiny. It doesn't mean I've forgiven you. But I'm past forgiving and regretting and longing and wishing.

Though I do still think about Suzanne and little Maria in their ship, crossing the wide ocean to Greenland, and hoping that all works out.

You want me to tell you my story? You want me to start with whatever first comes into my mind?

All right then, I will. The first thing that comes into my head is green palm fronds, grey sky, bicycle rickshaws, beggars, intense heat. It's England, the High Street in Oxford, between Magdalen College and the Botanic Gardens. The day I lost my job at the college. It was only a few weeks ago, would you believe? I remember bustling crowds, a smell of decay, a chronic, gnawing sense of impending threat. (It's a hard thing to depend for your livelihood on a society which hates you. You have no idea.) I remember a solitary old white man, an Old Brit like you, standing on a box with the crowds pushing and shoving around him, singing in a thin quavery voice:

"I will not cease from mortal strife

Nor shall my sword sleep in my hand
Till we have built Jerusalem
In England's green and pleasant land"

I'd heard it before, that strange English patriotic song with its peculiar words. (What are 'arrows of desire'? What are 'dark satanic mills'?) I suppose you must know it yourself, Dr Brennan? We often heard that song on the BBC, which we listened to in order to keep a track on the government and its war on the immigrants like me who made up most of the country's population. But though I knew that the song was about England, it never made me think of England at all. I always thought of Greenland, with its meadows and hills and streams, where Suzanne and I planned to make our home.

Now, looking back, I can see that England itself *was* in its way a green place. There were green banana trees and green rice fields and green mangroves and green rushes and green waterweed up and down the swampy greenish Thames. In fact that was one of the first things I noticed about England, crawling out of the hold of the barge by the Town Dock at five o'clock in the morning: it was *green*. Back in Spain, where I came from, everything was red red red.

The *very* first thing I noticed about England, though, was the *smell*: the muddy murky stink of vegetable and animal waste rotting in warm brackish water.

I have a degree in engineering. I speak fluent English and passable French. I am an educated man. But when you leave your own country as a refugee – when your own country, in fact, has actually ceased to *exist* – and you find yourself in another country that resents you and feels no obligation to you at all, you can't pick and choose what you do. I was never one of those immigrants who waste time complaining about their fate. I took whatever work was going, just as I'd done in the last famine-ridden days of crumbling Spain, grateful to have a means of earning a living, grateful to have anything at all. I filled sandbags round the offices of the Provisional Government, I killed rats, I sprayed stagnant pools with insecticide. Once I even had a job pulling corpses out of the Thames Marshes. (I didn't stick at it for long, but that was before Suzanne and Maria and at a time when the population of England was twenty or thirty million less than it is now, so I could still afford to take the gamble of finding other work.)

New people were coming in all the time, people from the Mediterranean, people from Africa and China and from what was left of the Indian subcontinent. They kept coming in their thousands every day. Never mind that the Old Brits fired on their boats off shore. Never mind that the Old Brits booby-trapped the beaches and machine-gunned new arrivals as they waded out of the sea. The migrants kept coming anyway, wave after wave, dodging mines and bullets, crawling under barbed wire, to slip inland and disappear into the crowded chaos of the cities. Then they hired themselves out, offering their labour for so little that those same Old Brits who'd been willing to kill to keep them out just couldn't resist employing them now they were here. And each new wave was cheaper and more irresistible. However little pay I resigned myself to work for, someone would soon show up from somewhere who was willing to work for less.

But I thought I'd struck lucky with my handyman job at Magdalen College. The pay wasn't great, but I'd known worse and I made friends with one of the Fellows there, a physicist called Thach Pham, a guy about my own age (I'm thirty-three), whose parents had been immigrants from Vietnam. He was researching the replication of matter using resonance fields (the up and coming field according to Suzanne, my new girlfriend at the time, who'd trained as a physicist, though now worked in the college refectory). Pham said he'd try and get me a job as a technician if he could. He said that sometimes it was possible to get a work permit if the university pulled the right strings, even though the Old Brits normally kept work like that for their own. He would see what he could do.

"My mum and dad were migrants like you," he confided, "I know what you guys have to go through."

He also promised me that he would use his influence in Senior Common Room to make sure they didn't replace me with cheaper labour. Both these promises turned out to be worthless.

Suzanne was nine years younger than me and recently arrived from France with a score of others in a little motorboat built for family holidays on the French canals. She was pretty, graceful, funny and clever (much cleverer than me), but she hadn't yet adapted to her new circumstances, and was all but immobilised by the challenges that faced her. She latched onto me as if I were the answer to everything. She told me I was the man she'd been looking for all her life, and for a short time I believed her, felt myself to actually be the strong, resourceful figure that she'd decided to see in me. We got ourselves a bedsit room on Walton Street, close to the edge of the great Thames Marsh. We made love every morning and every night and shared our meagre little meals as if they were royal feasts. We decided we were going to work and work until we'd somehow saved enough for tickets and visas for Greenland. There we'd rent a little farm on a hillside and grow vegetables and raise sheep and smell the sweet fresh air of a land that wasn't slowly sinking into the mud.

But we were using cheap black market contraceptives. Suzanne fell pregnant with Maria and that was the end of our chances of saving up for anything. Suddenly we had no aim in life other than keeping ourselves going from day to day.

"I'm sorry Mr Fernandez," said Mr Das, the bursar at Magdalen College, "but I'm afraid we have no choice. We can no longer afford to pay above the market rate and we're going to have to let you go unless you are willing to take a fifty dollar reduction in your weekly pay."

"Fifty dollars? But how can I? I have a baby, Mr Das, a little baby to feed. We don't ask a lot – the three of us live in just one little room – but still we have rent to pay. And my daughter has asthma. Please, Mr Das. Please let me carry on without a cut in pay. I already work very hard. I'll work harder. You will get more for your money I promise you. But you must have mercy on me please."

Mr Das was a tiny little Old Brit. I am not very tall myself, but the top of his balding yellowish head didn't reach the bottom of my chin. Incongruously he wore a huge grey handlebar moustache. He cleared his throat.

"As I say, that isn't an option I'm afraid."

"But Dr Pham promised me that...."

"Dr Pham had no business to promise you anything."

"He promised me that I'd be able to keep my job here. He said if there was any problem it would be sorted out in Senior Common Room."

"All the Fellows are aware of the need to reduce labour costs in these difficult times, Dr Pham included. He made no objection when I suggested this policy."

I honestly did not know how we could continue to eat and pay the rent. The new arrivals managed it by squatting in those crumbling half-drowned houses out in the Marsh, and by supplementing their diet with rats and seagulls. But if you descended to that, what would you do next, when still *more* people had arrived and still more of Britain had sunk under the sea?

"Okay, I'll do it, then," I growled. "I'll work for less. God damn it, I've got no choice, have I? I'll just have to find another job as well."

Mr Das glanced uneasily back into the inner recesses of the college. Furtively, inside his jacket pocket, he pushed a button on a pager.

"No. On reflection, Juan, I think we should let you go in any case. The new applicants will have a rather more positive attitude, I think, to the salary we are prepared to pay."

"Please…" I began, but then broke off.

One of the college porters, summoned by Dr Das' pager, appeared across the quad. In one hand he clutched a nightstick, in the other a fat automatic pistol. Bukowsky, he was called. Ugh! He was an Old Brit of the worst kind, his skin red and leathery, his belly hanging over his belt, his grey eyes cruel and icy with a cold and bottled-up rage.

"Fuck you, Das," I said. "Fuck your stupid job. Fuck your stupid college. In a couple of years' time, my friend, you will all be wading around in salt water. Yes and fuck you too, Bukowsky. And as for that creep Thach Pham, fuck him as well."

Bukowsky pointed the heavy gun at me.

"Shove it, dago," he growled.

Out on the High Street, two policemen in a pedal car were passing by in front of the water-logged Botanic Gardens, from whose broken greenhouses so many exotic plants had burst out and spread across the city. Like all cops and soldiers, they were Old Brits. Paunchy and middle-aged, they wore ridiculous little blue shorts that revealed flabby hairy legs, working the pedals in unison. Sweat trickled down their red faces as they forced their way through the treacly hothouse air, nudging between hustlers and beggars and past that old man on his box, still singing that patriotic song.

In theory almost everyone there was breaking the law just by being in the country, but in practice the machine gunners on the coast were the last serious attempt made by the Old Brit state to hold that particular line. Get past that and you were in, though without the protection or the privileges of citizenship. You worked in the black economy. You negotiated, as best you could, your own relationship with the network of protection racketeers that regulated life below the threshold of the law. You survived or not. To the Old Brits illegal immigrants were just 'beachrats', outside of justice, a sort of vermin. So, for us, gangsters provided the only authority that we could turn to. It was their summary justice that ensured a harvest of beachrat bodies for the corpse-fishers, themselves invariably beachrats, to pull out of the marsh every morning.

No job *again*. I had to fight down panic. Each time it happened it got harder, as the population grew and the resources of the country shrank. How would we eat? How would we pay the rent for our one lousy, mildewed room on Walton Street? How would we stop little Maria from getting seriously ill with her asthma and coughs and wheezes?

But more than anything else, the question I asked myself was: *how will I face Suzanne?*

She had changed so much. There had been a time when her first unthinking reaction when she saw me was to break into a smile. Now, even at the best of times, there was no smile and her first word was almost always a complaint or a grievance.

I can't return with no work, I decided. *I'd rather just walk away, walk away and never see her or Maria ever again.*

And for a moment there, Dr Brennan, I really did think about it. It would have hurt them both if I'd left. In fact it would quite possibly have *killed* Maria, for how could Suzanne pay the rent and buy the food and provide care for a sickly child all at the same time? But if I walked away, at least I would be spared the shame and misery of witnessing all that. The world being as it was, I could lose myself easily, put myself beyond the reach of Suzanne and everyone that we knew, and simply start again without that burden. I was a non-person, Suzanne and Maria were non-people. And, in a strange way, that's what we were *even to one another*. It wouldn't be so long – or so it seemed to me in that brief moment – it wouldn't be so long before they had no more substance in my mind than some old dream.

"Hey! Juan!"

I turned round. It was Thach Pham, the Magdalen physicist, running after me, dodging passers-by.

"Juan! Juan, I'm... I'm so sorry," he gasped as he tried to catch his breath. "Das has just told me he's let you go. I did everything I could!"

"Das said you did nothing at all. Like you did nothing at all about that technician job."

"Well, I... It's difficult, Juan. You don't understand. I *would* have spoken up but these days even a second-generation migrant like me has to watch his step."

"Why did you say you *would* do something then?"

He was in quite a state. Sweat was running down his plump face.

"I'm sorry. I thought I... I just thought that..."

"You wanted my approval. You tried to get it by lying. That's pathetic."

"Listen, Juan. I can get you some work. It's a bit dangerous and it's illegal but I could get you five thousand for a day's work, plus a Republic of Greenland visa for you and your wife and your kid."

Suzanne and I had never married – as beachrats we couldn't marry, since we had no legal existence – but I let that pass.

"Come on, Thach. Don't make even *more* of a fool of yourself. Why should I believe this ridiculous story when you didn't do *either* of the things you said you'd do for me before?"

"Because this time it's true. Please, Juan, let me buy you a drink and I'll tell you about it. You look as though you could do with one. Listen to me while you drink, and if you're not interested, that's fine, you can walk away. What will you have lost?"

He led the way to a nearby pub, the sort of place that the more prosperous Old Brits went to drink, with a proper licence and prices inflated to some ten times the black market rate by Provisional Government taxes.

"We have something in common," Pham said as he brought me my beer. "I am a Vietnamese, you are a Spaniard, but there is no longer a country called Vietnam or Spain."

No, I thought, but he had British nationality and a house of his own. I was a beachrat living in a damp bedsit in Walton Street. The parallels were not *that* striking.

83

"As to this country," Pham said, "where is it going? Apparently the population is three times its level fifty years ago, and Old Brits are outnumbered nearly two to one. But..."

"I hate Old Brits," I said. "Their red faces, their cold angry eyes. Why should they run everything? Why do they think they're so much better than everyone else?"

Pham shrugged.

"The Old Brits are like children on a beach with the tide coming in, trying to protect their sandcastle with its paper flag. You did the same once I'm sure, as did my parents. They'll fail soon enough, just as you did. They'll go under. So why get angry with them?"

I shrugged.

"All the Brits with real money," Pham said, "are already moving to places like Greenland and Svalbard and the Antarctic Peninsular..."

"As will you I presume?"

He looked embarrassed but didn't answer. Obviously he had some bolthole lined up for when the sandbags and ditches were no longer enough to keep the marsh out of his precious college. Why did he try and make these claims to be like me when he so obviously wasn't?

"Some people," he said, "are looking at the possibility of leaving the planet altogether."

"Yeah. I've heard." Then I looked at him in surprise. "Surely that's not what you...?"

"Oh good God no, no, not me."

Again he blushed.

"Leaving the planet is fraught with difficulties, of course," he said. "You only have to think of the size of rocket and the quantity of fuel that's required to take even three or four people into space."

"This is very interesting," I said, downing the remainder of my beer, "but I really don't have the time to..."

Dr Pham clasped my arm.

"Just a moment, please Juan. I'm getting to the point. As I say, it simply isn't practical to transport more than small handfuls of people up from Earth into space. No one gets a ride into space who isn't a billionaire. But, as you know, there is a theoretical possibility of using matter replication to send *copies* of human beings to remote locations at the speed of light."

"I need to look for a job, Thach. You may have time to chat

about matter replication, but I don't. Thanks for the beer."

"Wait!" This time he grabbed my arm so tightly that it actually hurt. "Listen, I want to help you. We immigrants have got to stick together."

I shook his hand off me.

"So get to the point. What are you suggesting?"

Pham looked quickly around to make sure no one else was near enough to hear.

"Listen, Juan, I've been involved in a little work on the side, a little project on behalf of some rather wealthy backers. It's all a bit hush-hush but they need volunteers who will let themselves be put through a resonance scanner so as to make a copy which can be transmitted to an orbital laboratory that my backers have acquired. It's an old Chinese space station actually, but the Chinese haven't got much use for it any more, not since…"

He gave a gloomy little shrug to represent flood, famine and civil breakdown.

"You're given a muscle relaxant to temporarily paralyse you," he said. "You're given intravenous oxygen, you're scanned for maybe forty-five minutes. It's not pleasant and there is a small but certainly not insignificant chance of death. I consider you a friend Juan and I feel I have to be honest with you about this. There's something like a one in three hundred chance of death, which of course is terribly high in one way, yet, in another way, is really quite low odds. In most cases there's no harm to the donor at all."

He glanced at me to see my reaction, perhaps fearful that I'd be angry with him for suggesting that I risk my life. But I just shrugged, so he carried on:

"If all goes well with the transfer, which currently happens about half the time, a viable copy is received by the orbital station, which can then be used for research purposes. You will receive your payment though, of course, whether or not the copy is viable."

He grimaced.

"I *say* viable but even when the copies seem viable at first they never last longer than a week or two. It's the same when we've tried it with animals. And of course my backers want that sorted out, because what they want to achieve is perfect avatars of themselves and their loved ones that can wander through the stars when this poor old Earth has finally frazzled up completely."

"One in three hundred?" I asked.

I wasn't interested in the science. I didn't care what they wanted to do with the copies. What concern was that of mine?

"Yes. I'm afraid there's a risk associated with high doses of muscle relaxants and anaesthetics."

"Why am I even listening to this? This isn't real. If these backers of yours have all this money, why don't they advertise properly for volunteers? Why pick me?"

"They never advertise because of the legal situation. You might think that the government lets anything go these days, but it's actually a little more complicated than that. They let some things go, but others they're very fussy about. You can rape and kill some little beachrat waif and tip her into the Marsh and no one wants to know. But if you make copies of human beings for research purposes, that's a major ethical issue and if the wrong people get to hear about it, the state will feel obliged to step in and stamp it out. It makes no sense, I agree, but I suppose it's their way of retaining some sense of being in control."

Again I shrugged.

"They are prepared to turn a blind eye," Pham said, once again glancing nervously around. "If we're very discreet and if we use only beach..." he broke off. "If we use only illegal immigrants like yourself who are legal non-persons anyway. But still the project isn't legal. If there was a crackdown, I could lose my job and all the privileges that go with it. I'm taking a risk telling you, but we've been friends haven't we? You and I have been friends?"

Well, if he wanted to think that, I wasn't going to argue.

There'd been some sort of shoot-out on St Giles. A big RAF airship had descended into the middle of the square and soldiers with loudhailers were keeping people back while the bodies were scooped up. We were told later by the BBC that it had been a fight between two beachrat gangs and that the army had stepped in to break things up. But it's quite possible that the gang fight story was just a pretext for one of the army's occasional culls of the beachrat population in general. I saw more than twenty dead for sure (though the BBC would refer vaguely to two or three causalities). The Old Brits were very brutal, but I suppose we weren't much different back in Spain in times gone by when the Africans coming over the Straits stopped being a trickle and became a torrent. We shot them too, for all the good that did us. They kept on coming anyway, and the Sahara followed close behind them.

I hurried back to Walton Street.

"Suzanne! Suzanne!" I called out as I flung open the door of our first floor room, revealing the black mould, the peeling wallpaper, the single-ring cooker in the corner, the bed that filled half the space, the stained toilet in its tiny cupboard, the tangled undergrowth outside the window that led down to an old canal (now simply a somewhat deeper than usual channel running along the edge of the great Thames Marsh that stretched all the way to what was left of London).

"Suzanne! Something amazing has happened!"

I realised that I'd got into the habit of cringing in her presence. Even now, when I had good news for her, I was cringing as if I expected a blow. Annoyed with myself, I straightened up. After all I didn't even need to tell Suzanne about losing the job at Magdalen College. That didn't matter any more.

"Something amazing, Suzanne!"

She had been pacing the room with Maria on her hip.

"Shhhhh, you idiot, Juan, Maria is almost asleep. What are you doing here at this time of day? I hope you haven't lost your..."

"Suzanne, I've been offered five thousand dollars for one day's work. *Five thousand.* Plus Greenland resident visas for all three of us."

"You've been drinking haven't you? I can smell it on your breath. How can you even think of drinking when we're..."

A slowly pulsing engine noise passed above us as the armed airship made its way from St Giles to the low hills on the far side of the Marsh. It was carrying away the corpses for cremation.

"Five thousand dollars, Suzanne," I bellowed over the throbbing of the blades. "Five thousand. Look here is a five hundred advance already!"

I held a wad of fifties in front of her that Pham had put into my hands as a token that he really meant what he said.

Looking back, Dr Brennan, it's horrible to remember the low, desperate gleam that came into Suzanne's eyes. In a single instant, here was the evidence of how much poverty and fear and hopelessness had coarsened and corrupted her.

But I was coarsened and corrupted too. I didn't care how far she'd fallen from what she'd once been. I was just relieved that she wasn't angry with me, relieved that she wasn't going to hit me and scream at me as she sometimes did – me with my head lowered, my cheek bleeding, holding her at arm's length until the rage passed and the hopeless tears began to flow – relieved that I wouldn't have to tell her that I'd lost my job.

She hurried to lay Maria down on the bed so that she could snatch the money from me.

"What did you have to do to earn this?" she asked as she flicked through it with urgent fingers.

I told her about the matter replication experiments and how I would have to be temporarily paralysed and scanned for forty-five minutes.

"…which won't be easy of course," I said, "going under the anaesthetic, and knowing that I could quite possibly never wake again."

As I'd approached the house I'd allowed myself a little fantasy that Suzanne would balk a little at the risk to my life.

"I need money for Maria, Juan," I'd imagined her saying, "but not at the price of losing you."

And then, realising that, even as a plausible fantasy, this was too much to ask, I'd revised my daydream somewhat.

"Dear Juan," my imaginary Suzanne had said to me instead. "I've been so hard on you, and yet you're prepared to risk your life for me and our child. How lucky I am to have you!"

The heroism and selflessness of it all had almost brought tears to my eyes, and I'd quite forgotten that, not much more than an hour previously, I'd seriously contemplated abandoning them both.

What she actually said was a little different.

"So when do you get the rest of the money?"

"When I turn up for the scan. You can come with me. You can take the money in advance. And then, even if I…"

"And Greenland visas too?"

"Yes, in advance as well."

"Oh God, oh God, oh God, please let this be real. Please don't let this be some kind of hoax."

"I don't see how it can be. If they don't give us the money, we just walk."

"I'll definitely come there with you, because…"

"Well, thanks, I'd certainly be glad of the…"

"…because you're much too willing to think the best of people. I need to be sure there's not some kind of con going on."

Suzanne was cleverer than me. That was one of the things that had gradually become apparent to both of us after that time of daily lovemaking and meals eaten together off a single plate. She was cleverer and more strong-willed.

"Well, yes, of course," I said humbly.

I felt very hurt now, and Suzanne finally sensed it. With a huge effort she turned her thoughts reluctantly away from her fears and her fragile hopes, and tried to notice me.

She gave a strained smile.

"Hey Juan. Well done. This could be it couldn't it? This could be when our luck turns?"

I brightened at once.

"That's right. Didn't I always say something would come up?"

I stepped forward to embrace her. Just for a moment she allowed herself to melt in my arms in the way that she'd done in the early days. But then little Maria began to cry.

On a warm foggy morning five days later, Suzanne and Maria and I met Pham by Town Docks where the wide shallow-draft barges stopped off on their way up and down Thames Marsh between Oxford and half-drowned London. He had a little steam launch waiting for us there and we set off through the mist, flooded buildings and dead trees looming out of the greyness around us and disappearing back into it again. Pham paced restlessly all the time, sometimes bothering the taciturn skipper with anxious talk, sometimes peering anxiously into the obscurity ahead.

Four or five kilometres west of the city we came to an old private hospital that sat on a hill above the Marsh. We docked at a makeshift jetty there and Pham put the rest of the money I was owed into Suzanne's hands, along with letters on the headed paper of the Republic of Greenland, confirming our right to enter as alien residents. (I'm still puzzled by that. What kind of authority did Pham's friends have to be able to arrange *that* for us in a single day? I hope to God those letters were real.)

Anyway, then I said goodbye to Suzanne. It felt like goodbye too, even though, all being well, it would only be for less than an hour. Here, in the cold chemical atmosphere of the hospital, with that sharp sterile antiseptic smell that makes you think of shiny blades and neatly amputated limbs, she finally felt afraid for me, and cried. And then of course Maria cried too, my little Maria, stretching out her little hands to me to try and hold me back. All of this was a great comfort to me, buoying me up and making me feel, for a short time, like that noble knight that Suzanne had once seen in me.

An Indian doctor came and took me into the scanner room. Pham, who'd been shifting about restlessly in the background all the while, went off somewhere to attend to the data transfer process that would transmit the configuration of particles that made up my body up to that old Chinese space station above the equator.

The scanning machine was huge – it filled up most of a room that was five or six times the size of our entire bedsit in Walton Street – and it gave off a loud hum. I had to strip naked, be covered in clear jelly, and then laid down on a hard plastic bed where I was given the injections that would make me unconscious and keep me still while the machine did its work.

As I sank under, I tried to avoid thinking about that one in three hundred possibility that I would never wake again, and instead concentrate on the fact that the overwhelmingly more likely outcome would be that I would be walking out of this place in an hour's time with all that we needed to start a new life for ourselves in the temperate north.

Greenland, Greenland, Greenland, I repeated to myself, and my last thoughts were of an emerald city, shining under a cool, clear, cloudless sky.

I woke, feeling dizzy and nauseous, in a small, rather dirty room smelling of metal and oil and human sweat. I was lying naked on a bed, as I had been when I went under, but now I was covered all over in tubes and electrodes. And across the room two men in blue overalls were conferring in front of a large monitor.

"I made it!" I yelled triumphantly. "Greenland here I come! Did you guys get your copy all right?"

One of the men glanced round at me – a thin South Asian man

with a small pointed beard – but oddly he didn't answer, smile or even make eye contact.

"Conscious!" he said to his companion, who was stocky and black. "That makes a change."

The black man laughed.

"'I made it!'" he mimicked, caricaturing my Spanish accent. "'Greenland here I come!' Wish I had a dollar every time they said that."

I tried to sit up but found that I was strapped down onto the bed with strong canvas belts.

"Hey what's going on? You said I could get up and walk as soon as I got through the scan."

The first man, the Asian, stood up and came over, casting his eye coolly over my body.

"Looks pretty good," he said. "Looks pretty functional to me."

"What about an answer to my question?" I demanded. "What kind of hospital are you running here?"

The first man grinned across at his companion.

"What do you reckon, Toussaint? What kind of hospital would you say this was?"

They both laughed.

"Is there some problem?" I said. "Have I suffered some damage of some kind?"

They both laughed at this, but completely ignored my question. The Asian man picked up a phone.

"Dr Brennan? 8856 has come out well. Everything's working fine. Heart, lungs, metabolism, talking, emotional agitation, everything. Best one for a long time."

I strained to hear the voice on the other end of the line – your voice of course, as it turns out – but I was prevented by a crackly p.a. announcement which seemed to come from a corridor outside.

"*Docking in five minutes. I repeat docking in five minutes. Primary crew to docking stations. I repeat. Primary crew to docking stations. Over.*"

"Let's hope there's a bit more liquor on board this time," the black man said. "Last time it all went in a day."

"It was a trick wasn't it?" I said. "I'm not going to Greenland am I? I'm not going to get to keep that five thousand dollars?"

Can you believe I still had no inkling of my circumstances? I

91

suppose if you wake up and remember that you're a man called Juan Fernandez, it's not a conviction that can easily be dislodged.

"Why won't you speak to me?" I strained at the straps which held me down. "Why are you behaving like I'm not here?"

Were we on a boat of some kind, I wondered? It did *look* like a boat with its walls made of bolted metal plates. Had this all been an elaborate kidnapping? Had I been sneaked out of the back door of that hospital on the hill, while Suzanne and Maria waited for me out front? Had I been loaded onto some kind of barge?

"Please," I pleaded with them, "I don't know what's happening and I don't know why you don't want to speak to me, but can't you just tell me where I am and how I got here?"

Both men had bent interestedly over their console of instruments while I was speaking.

"Perfect," the Asian man exclaimed. "We haven't had one this good for weeks."

"What's perfect?" I cried. "How can it hurt to talk to me? Where am I? Where are my wife and daughter?"

Again they had stooped over their console while I was speaking. (You've kindly explained to me since that they were watching how speech affected my brain waves.) Now they both made little noises of pleasure and satisfaction.

"Even better than last time," the black man said. "I mean look at..."

He was interrupted by a metallic clunking sound that seemed to originate somewhere far away in the building, or boat, or whatever it was – I still hadn't got it, I still had no idea what my real situation was – and the whole structure shook. Both men looked up towards the door, not because there was anything to see, but because they knew the sound was coming from that direction.

"They're supposed to *dock* with the station," grumbled the black man, "not fucking *ram* it."

"What's *happened?* Where *am* I?" I wailed.

Finally the black man turned on me.

"Shut the fuck up, 8856, do you hear me? You're a copy. You're not a person. You haven't *got* a wife and kids. You don't even have a mind."

"Hey now, Toussaint." the Asian man scolded. "Don't *talk* to it.

92

You know that's not a good idea."

"I know, Abdul, but it was starting to get on my nerves."

"What do you mean I haven't got a mind? I'm Juan Fernandez! I can talk! I can think! I'm a human being."

And finally Toussaint responded to me. He spoke very softly and through gritted teeth, without looking at me, without even really addressing me, as a man might mutter to a recalcitrant computer, or to a car that won't start.

"You're not a human being. You're a copy of a human being."

I remembered a conversation I'd had with Suzanne the night before we went down to Town Dock.

I was uncorking the bottle of Scottish wine that we'd recklessly bought to celebrate our imminent escape. Suzanne – she was once a physicist remember – was wondering aloud about that persistent problem with the replicator that Pham had mentioned to me. Why did the copies never manage to survive for more than a few weeks?

"I've no idea," I said. "I didn't ask him anything about it. The money and the Greenland visas, those were the important things as far as I was concerned. Who cares about their research?"

"I certainly don't," said Suzanne. "But I expect your copy will."

"How do you mean?"

"Well, they don't just copy the body do they? They copy the brain and the thoughts and everything. So if the copy is viable, even for a short time, it will have thoughts and feelings. And I guess it will have quite strong feelings about being trapped in a space station and used as a guinea pig for research. You should know better than me about that, though, Juan, because it's you they will be making a copy of. The thing will feel whatever you'd feel in the same circumstances."

This shook me a little.

"Will it really have my memories and my feelings and everything?" I asked after a pause.

"Well yes. That's the whole idea isn't it? So people can project themselves out across space."

"I suppose so."

I considered this for some time.

"I wonder how that will feel," I said at length. "Not being a real person at all but having someone else's memories?"

"I suppose they don't feel like someone else's memories. After all, they're the only memories it has."

"So that would mean... That would mean the copy would think it *was* me, wouldn't it? When it wakes up on that satellite it will think it is me, waking up in hospital after the anaesthetic, and then it'll find out that..."

I broke off.

"I wonder what they'll do with it?" I said.

Suzanne shrugged. "Test reactions, nerves, biochemistry? Cut it up? See if its organs are working properly? I've really no idea."

"Will it be able to feel pain and fear do you think?"

"Why not? Assuming that it's one of their successful attempts, it'll be alive. It will have a body. It will have a brain."

"*Madre de Dios*, what have I done? It'll live and feel just as I do, and yet I'm going to send it up there and let it be cut in pieces. I can't do that, can I??"

"*What?* And miss a chance of getting out of lousy England, and giving Maria a new life in a country where there is still grass and cool air and space? You must be joking."

"Yes but..."

"Oh for goodness sake, Juan, bad things happen all the time. Real people are tortured every day, real people are killed. All over the world real people in their thousands starve and drown and die of thirst. What concern is it of ours what happens to one stupid copy on some old satellite in space? It's not as if we'll have to *see* the thing. It's not as if we'll ever know what happened to it. That stupid copy might as well be in a different universe altogether, for all it concerns us."

I thought for maybe three seconds, then laughed.

"You're right. Who cares? What business is it of ours?"

And with that I raised my glass and proposed a toast to the three of us and our future.

"To Greenland! To Greenland and a new life."

As I drained my wine I glanced across the room, and saw that Maria was fast asleep. I winked at Suzanne.

"Hey look darling. She's going to be out of it for a while. How about we *really* celebrate?"

I lay there strapped down on that bed for a long time, taking in what

Toussaint, in his irritation, had told me.

"So you didn't trick the real Juan Fernandez?" I finally said. "He really did get the five thousand dollars and the visas?"

Your two delightful technicians ignored my question as you might ignore a buzzing fly.

"He really is on his way to Greenland?" I persisted.

I had grasped my situation intellectually now, but emotionally I was light years away from getting hold of it. I had no other identity but that of Juan Fernandez, no other memories but Juan's, no other perspective but Juan's way of seeing the world. It was simply not psychologically possible to think of myself as being anyone other than Juan, even though Juan was actually a man who cared nothing for me, a man who had dismissed any sense of responsibility for my well-being after only a few moments of thought.

"So this body here, this body never existed on Earth?"

Toussaint picked up the phone.

"What's keeping you guys?" he complained. "When are you going to take 8856 off our hands? We finished all the routine stuff half an hour ago and it's driving us nuts with its babbling. Plus Abdul and I want to get our hands on some of that new batch of liquor before it all goes."

Your voice in the earpiece said something. Toussaint's irritable tone softened.

"Straight to your office, Dr Brennan? For physical testing? Okay, we'll bring it right down. Thanks."

"Physical testing?" I cried. "Please tell me, what on Earth is that?"

"'Please tell me, what on Earth is that?'" Toussaint mimicked me in a cartoon Spanish accent, as he and Abdul wheeled my bed to the door.

The corridor was narrow and curved up visibly at both ends as it encircled the revolving space station. There was a smell of perished rubber, bad coffee and stale urine. They wheeled me past a forlorn, grubby little cafeteria where four or five other technicians in blue overalls sat drinking from white plastic cups.

"Hey, Toussaint. Whisky! Going to come and join us?" one of them called out

"Soon as we've dumped this thing off."

On the wall of the cafeteria was a screen showing the image of the planet Earth beneath us. Unusually there was very little cloud and almost the entire Atlantic was laid out to see, as if this was a globe in a schoolroom.

I thought about the real Juan, with Suzanne and Maria, slowly crossing that blue ocean. I ached inside as I thought about Suzanne and my little girl who I would never see again, far, far away from me. The real Juan, on the other hand, I could happily have killed.

"How could he have put me out of his mind so quickly and easily?" I wondered, as we continued along the corridor. "A glass of wine, a promising opportunity for sex, that was all it took. Yet I'm not a stranger, I'm not someone whose needs he'd find hard to understand. I'm like him in every single way."

But then we reached your office, Dr Brennan, and a beautiful friendship began.

Look at you in your crumpled jacket and your Heinrich Himmler glasses. Look at you wracked with longing and self-hatred and principles: the compassionate sadist, the doctor whose ethics forbid him to follow the Hippocratic oath, waiting in a metal box in space for defective copies of human beings to be delivered up to him.

"I must apologise for my technicians," you said. "They have this superstitious idea that copies don't have souls. It helps them to live with what they're doing, though of course it makes no logical sense since this whole enterprise is based on the premise that a copy is or could be fully human."

Then you shook your head sadly.

"Of course *I* know that you have feelings every bit as much as I do. And…" Your voice cracked slightly and for moment you seemed on the verge of tears. "And that makes it all very hard for me. *Very* hard. You've no idea. But be assured of my sympathy at all times, and be assured that I will reduce to a minimum any pain that I have to inflict."

After which you tortured me for some time – yes Dr Brennan, *tortured*: that is the correct word – with electric shocks and cuts inflicted without anaesthetic, your face gleaming with sweat, and contorted by excitement and shame. You kept apologising – "I'm so so sorry. I do hate this. I only wish there was another way!" – but you wouldn't stop and I was powerless to stop you. It was unendurable yet unescapable. I will never forgive you for it.

"There," you said at last. "That's the worst part over."

You were pale and trembling, your gloved hands slimy with my blood.

"Ghastly for both of us, but it's done," you said. "I always feel it's best to get that out of the way at the outset. For all the other procedures, normal anaesthetics can be used. Please accept my apologies for what I've just inflicted on you. I'm afraid it is necessary because an abnormal pain response is one of the characteristics of defective copies, and we absolutely have to try and...."

Suddenly you rushed out. Was it to be sick? Or to visit one of your other mutilated copies in some other grubby little cell? Or to masturbate? Or was it just to mop your face and gulp down the spirits that I smelled on your breath when you returned? Another technician – a white man this time, I think perhaps a Russian or a Pole – came in and wiped the blood off me with a cloth. He wouldn't meet my eyes or answer my questions. Then you were back, gently explaining to me how you were going to have to remove parts of me for tests: my intestines, my pancreas, an arm, a foot...

"I assure you, Juan, I'm a good doctor and will do everything in my power to keep you painless and comfortable throughout the time you have left," you said, reaching down and squeezing my hand reassuringly.

I think this is probably the only kind of intimacy you ever get, isn't it? I think the only time in which you're able to feel close to another human being is when you have some wretch like me strapped down in front of you and are about to begin eviscerating them. You really *believe* that you're being respectful and kind, don't you? You really believe you are doing your best by us. I think you even experience an emotion that seems to you like love.

"How long have you been up here?" I asked.

"I live here all the time," you said. "This is where I'll end my days."

"We're part of the problem," you told me another time.

I'd been put in shackles by two technicians and made to walk around a bit, then strapped back on the bed where you'd given me some knock-out pills and left me alone for a period of artificial sleep.

I've no way of knowing how long the sleep was for, or whether it corresponded in any way with what we would normally call a night. I had a drip to feed me, a catheter to carry away my wastes.

After I woke, you removed one of my kidneys under a local anaesthetic and had a technician carry it off to histology to be sliced up for tests. There was a screen on the wall of the room and, at my request, you'd set it to show the view of the great globe below us.

"We doctors are part of the problem, Juan my friend," you said as you stood beside me contemplating our half-burnt and half-drowned planet. "Medical science is one of the main reasons that on Earth got so bad. The things that are normally blamed – excessive carbon dioxide, pollution, deforestation – they're really all secondary factors. You could cut down trees and drive around in cars without doing any harm at all if there were only a few million people on the planet. But when the population gets up to over a billion and a half and then goes on to quadruple itself less than a century later… Well, how can that be viable? How *can* it? The human race *needed* pestilence. Doctors, in their arrogance, took it away."

You looked round at me.

"I came up here to do this work," you said, "because, in my own small way, I wanted to atone for the harm we doctors had done by dedicating my medical knowledge to true service of the human race. I know it's horrible what I do here. It is wretched for you people, of course, but, believe me, it's wretched for me as well. It eats away at me. I'm slowly destroying myself. But I keep doing it because I believe it's vital for humanity to find a way of making a new start. I'm sacrificing myself for this cause as much as I'm sacrificing you."

You glanced down at me, hoping for a response. *Nombre de Dios!* I thought Pham was bad enough with his preposterous attempts at brotherhood, but this was something *else*. What were you expecting from me, Dr Brennan? Pity?

Well I said nothing, and you sighed, and you carefully explained to me about the next stage in my dismantling, to begin in twenty-four hours after another chemically induced rest. It was almost as if you were a proper doctor and were trying to make me better.

I suppose it can't be long now until I'm just matter again, like I was until only a few days ago, when a soup of unconnected particles was temporarily gathered together by a resonance field and moulded into a replica of Juan Fernandez. This body will be broken back down into plasma, and then you'll set up a new resonance field, and it will pull those particles back together again, this time in the shape of someone else. Some stranger who I'll never know will be formed out of this very same stuff that now forms me.

I'm not really Juan Fernandez, I know that. I'm not really anyone at all. But I still think about Suzanne and Maria and the real Juan on their boat, crossing the wide ocean to Greenland. I can't help wondering if Suzanne is grateful to Juan for what he's done, and whether she wriggles up warm and soft against him in their little berth with the cold sea forgotten outside, and whether she melts and moans and sighs like she once used to? And if so, I wonder, does it ever occur to either of them to think of this doomed prisoner up here, this eviscerated amputee, who *really* paid the price? (For what did *he* pay? What did *he* have to give up?)

Well I doubt it. It's not that they're heartless monsters, really. It's just that people never worry all that much about consequences that they don't have to see, or care that much about other people that they've never had to meet. It's just the way that human beings are.

Unless of course they're like you, Dr Brennan, with all your noble dreams.

the famous cave paintings on isolus 9

My uncle Clancy was quite well known for his love affairs with famous women, but there was one occasion when he *really* fell in love. And this was not with a celebrity, not with a famous beauty. Elena was a quietly pretty, thoughtful, rather self-contained woman who worked as an editor at the company which published his books.

"What's new about this," he said to his secretary Com, "is that I'm not trying to prove anything, and nor is she. We're not performing on some kind of stage. We're not trying to play heroic roles."

He chuckled.

"Yesterday evening at dinner," he told Com (who helpfully backed up every conversation in an archive of the Metropolitan Library), "I did slip into Famous Space Traveller mode for a bit and Elena just told me to knock it off. She was quite sharp about it actually but I can't tell you what a relief it was."

"Sometimes it can be tiring to play a role," offered Com (who, incidentally, was a powerful hyperspatial computer resembling a small yellow egg).

"I used to have a job like hers once," Clancy went on. "Probably I still would have if *Seven Moons* hadn't taken off the way it did. And I am like her in other ways too. We have the same interests, we take pleasure in the same things, see things from the same sort of angle. I've become so bloated by fame lately, you know, so swollen up. Elena has brought me right back down to the ground, or as near to the ground as we get in this city, and it feels like a good place to be."

Com was very familiar with my uncle's moods, but this one was new in its experience.

"You sound – *happy*," it tentatively suggested.

"Happy?" Clancy repeated, as if it was a novelty to him as well. "Happy? Yes, do you know, I believe I am!"

"Well, that's good, isn't it?" Com offered, having quickly consulted many thousands of reference works. "Opinion seems to be divided on the subject but many authorities consider happiness to be the actual goal of human existence."

"She's pretty, Com, and she's funny, and she's bright and kind and loyal and resourceful. But do you know what I value about her above all else? It's that she just *lives* her life. She doesn't feel the slightest need to be a household name in her own apartment block, never mind anywhere else. What could be more sensible than that?"

"What indeed?"

Com might have all of science and literature in its reach, and might hold in its mind the complete map of the inhabited galaxy down to the level of individual dwellings, but very reassuringly for Clancy it nevertheless derived its system of values entirely from him. It was built that way. Whatever its legal owner thought important or worthwhile was important and worthwhile to Com, just as whatever its owner wanted, it pursued indefatigably. Subject of course to the usual legal safeguards and contractual obligations.

"I wanted her to come with me on my next trip but she has a horror of underspace, like most sensible people."

"Where are we going this time?" asked the intelligent egg.

"I thought we'd visit Isolus 9."

Like the good secretary it was, Com tried to anticipate its master's wishes and over the next tenth of a second it searched through all the libraries of Metropolis, seeking out every reference to the planet Isolus 9.

"A quick summary?" it asked.

"A one minute summary," said Clancy, who was meeting Elena shortly to go to the theatre.

Com told him that Isolus 9 was first settled two thousand years ago, just before the dissolution of the Wide Empire and the destruction of its Great Machine. When the Machine ceased to function the Isolans, just like all the other Dispersed Peoples, were cut off from the Metropolis for almost two millennia. The difference in their case was that they'd had very little time at all to get established. Lacking the surplus capacity to sustain the intergenerational transmission even of reading and writing, they reverted to a precarious hunter-gatherer existence and came very close indeed to complete extinction.

"Over the past century," Com went on, "two major expeditions have visited Isolus 9, the first an exploratory visit to see if human life still existed there at all and the second an archaeological project. There have been a few other visitors in between so, although the planet is no longer culturally untouched by the Metropolis, it may go ten years at a time without any contact."

"Books?" Clancy asked.

"No books have been written solely about Isolus 9, but it is mentioned in twenty-two archaeological and anthropological texts. The planet's religious frescoes are of course the single most mentioned topic.

"Give me a bit more on the religion."

"There have been no comprehensive studies on the Isolan religion. The only two scholars who have discussed it in any detail both did so as part of wider explorations of the religions of the Dispersed Peoples. And they profoundly disagree with each other. Professor Loyah Tomins, in his book *Heritage and Necessity*, argues that Isolans and other Dispersed Peoples never completely forgot their own history but rather 'encoded' it in the 'compressed form' of a religion. Professor Julina Doyana, in her book *Narrating Abandonment*, dismisses Tomins' view as 'obfuscatory' and argues that the Isolan religion is not compressed history at all, but 'reified anxiety management'. "

Clancy snorted contemptuously.

"It can be both, can't it? And other things besides. Religions are *stories*. Any decent story works on several levels at once."

His own books were a case in point. Each was, on one level, the description of an interstellar adventure, but each was also an enquiry into the nature of human existence. And each was a piece of personal self-exploration, a confession even, albeit elaborately disguised.

"My books are like my journeys, David," he once told me, not long before his mysterious final disappearance. "Each is simultaneously a cowardly escape from the world and an audacious attempt to get up close to it."

This was a theme that he often came back to in those later days: the cowardice that hides in apparently courageous acts, the bravery necessary to sustain an apparently unadventurous life.

"Do you have any thoughts as to the main strands of the Isolus 9 book?" Com now asked him.

Com knew that my uncle always began the book before the journey itself had started. The outer journey was always contained within the inner one.

"One: the new experience of travelling with someone I love to return to. Two: dispersal and return in the Isolan religion. What links the idea of religion and idea of love is *connection*. Love connects people to each other. Religion makes people feel connected to the universe. So I'd also like you to come up with three or four treatments of that. Okay?"

Clancy got up and headed to the bathroom.

"You do need to bear in mind," Com began, "that the religion of Isolus 9 is rather unusual in that..."

But its master wasn't listening anymore. He was humming cheerfully as he began to undress for the shower.

When my uncle set out for Isolus 9, Elena came to see him off. They had a last drink together on a gallery just below the launch platform, with a view of the City all around.

"I can't believe how much I love you," Clancy said.

The platform was near the equator and it was hot up there, but a cooling wind gently tossed Elena's fair hair this way and that. Brushing it back she leaned forward and peered into Clancy's face.

"Are those *tears*?" she asked him, touched and a little shocked. "Are you crying? Why? We'll be together again before too long."

The launch platform rose out of the planet-wide city like an emergent tree rising above a forest. Below and all around them were galleries, penthouse apartments, the giant golden sunflowers that gathered light for the city below, and the parabolic dishes that allowed the city to communicate with the moon and satellites and the local planets. (You cannot of course communicate with the Dispersed Worlds except by travelling to them.) Here and there other emergent pinnacles – launch ports, hotels, chimneys – rose above the general mass. Helicopters passed to and fro between them, along with parrots and other brightly coloured birds. And from time to time a sound like a small thunderclap broke above them, as another starship either descended into underspace, or emerged *from* underspace into the world. Each time the birds rose and rushed about in noisy indignation.

"I don't know anymore why I travel," Clancy said. "I really don't. Why wander through endless light years of empty space? Why trudge around dreary and impoverished little colonies half way across the galaxy? Everything I want is right here in front of me."

"It'll still be here when you return."

They leaned over the balustrade and looked straight down. Immediately below them were the domed pools and hanging gardens of the upper tier, where lived wealthy businessmen and senior officials in the Regulatory Entity. Then came progressively dimmer levels through which from time to time flashed high speed trains rushing across the world-wide city at two thousand kilometres an hour, disappearing with a clatter and a sigh. In the shadier middle levels were the homes of minor officials and skilled workers, with all their lights already on. Beneath them, pretty much invisible from up here, were factories and generators. Finally, at the bottom of it all, two vertical kilometres down, was the murky orange glow of slum settlements on the planet surface where there was virtually no sunlight at all. Small yellowish lights moved about down there as surface dwellers made their way through the gloom.

"*Aaaaawk!*" shrieked a parrot, bright and brash in the evening sunlight.

"*Clear platform!*" the parrot cried, alighting on a railing. "*Clear platform for departure!*"

Clancy and Elena laughed, and then the laugh became an extended kiss. But soon the announcement came calling Clancy to his ship. They pulled apart and ascended to the wide platform where his silver vehicle, 'Sphere,' was waiting. Ragged windblown clouds, some grey, some white, passed across the high blue sky above them, torn and broken immediately overhead by the constant coming and going of underspace ships. In the distance to the west the clouds were tinged pink by the descending sun.

They kissed goodbye and Clancy had already put one foot on the ladder when suddenly he turned back again and once more wrapped Elena's small, light body in his arms, holding her tightly and calling her his darling, his dearest, his sweetheart.

Sweetheart. Sweetheart. My sweet dear heart. These words appear over and over in the record of that period which my uncle's faithful secretary deposited in that Metropolitan Library archive. He just couldn't seem to say them enough. Yet up to that point he had always been the absolute archetype of the Metropolitan sophisticate: subtle, ironic, restless, determinedly unattached.

"But I didn't know then," he told Com more than once, "I just didn't know."

Elena had thawed out places inside him that he hadn't realised were there. And he still wasn't used to it, still couldn't keep himself from visiting and revisiting this well of tenderness that had unexpectedly opened up inside him.

"It's crazy to leave you," he burst out. "I should just cancel this whole trip."

She laughed and kissed him.

"Of course not, dearest. We've been over this. It's your job. It's what you do. We have to *do* something in our lives. We can't just gaze forever into each others eyes."

"I've heard of worse plans."

"You don't really mean that."

"But will things change between us? Will you still be here for me when I return?"

"Of course I will. Right here."

Well my uncle had kissed goodbye to many other women, sometimes even on this very same spot, with the same clouds rushing by above, the same parrots shrieking, the same vast city stretching away to the horizon all around, but he had never before sought this assurance, not even once. On every single previous occasion his departure had been – deep down, if not at the surface of his mind – a welcome escape, a way of dealing with the fact that his heart was going cold.

Solitude had always been his resting state.

"This is different from anything I have ever experienced before," he told Elena

She laughed.

"So you keep telling me, dearest. So you tell me, over and over, every time we're together."

"You're shaking," he said.

"I don't like underspace, that's all. It gives me the creeps. The idea of descending into that dreadful little wormhole... Ugh! But I know it doesn't bother you and I know you know what you're doing. I'll be fine once you've set off."

"Go now if you want. You don't need to watch me go."

"I know I don't have to, but I want to."

"Mr Clancy," called out the artificial intelligence that controlled the platform. "You need to make a move or you'll miss your window."

Clancy nodded. He climbed inside Sphere and the door closed behind him.

"Clear platform!" said the firm calm voice of the AI, much admired and imitated by the local parrots. "Clear platform for departure!"

Elena made herself watch as violent lightning, white and pink and green, suddenly flared around Clancy's ship and it shot away with a sound like thunder. Parrots fled noisily. High under the ragged clouds of Metropolis, the sparkling Sphere seemed from Elena's perspective to balloon to a gigantic size, like some silvery Godhead glaring down at the multi-layered anthill of the City-World, and then to explode into jagged mirrored shards.

It was an illusion, of course. With her head at least Elena knew that perfectly well. The ship was not disintegrating but merely surrendering its tenure of a specific location in Euclidean space. It was disappearing from the universe we all inhabit into a tiny universe of its own. But that alone seemed quite dreadful to her, because she lived for air, for space, for light, for companionship.

She stood there alone on the viewing gallery for a minute or two, steadying herself, allowing her racing pulse to settle. Then she gave herself a little shake. It was a characteristic gesture of hers. It was how she shook off the mood of one moment in order to move on to the next. And now, since there was nothing here for her any more (just a gap where Sphere had been, into which another ship was already rising up into position), she turned away.

And then came the moment that always comes after a parting, the moment when the person who stays behind becomes, by definition, someone that the one who has departed can never directly know. She became a stranger.

Clancy had dreaded the moment of departure in anticipation but in fact, at the precise moment when the departing Sphere had seemed to Elena to blow itself to pieces, my uncle had been reclining comfortably inside it, pouring himself a glass of wine and experiencing the familiar sense of contented release that he always felt at the beginning of one of his journeys.

What horrified Elena about underspace was precisely what made him feel at home in it. He *liked* being outside of space, beyond radio contact, beyond human contact of any kind. He liked the thought that there was no one with him, no minds except for his own and the machine minds of his faithful cybernetic servants, Com and Sphere.

I remember from when we were children that Uncle Clancy would often play with us cheerfully but that a moment would always come when we realised he was no longer with us, he had withdrawn into a private world of his own, not out of a lack of fondness for us, but because of some need of his own, a need for replenishing solitude. Well, here in underspace that private world became an objective fact. There was no one to call him out of it. There was no 'out' to which he could be called.

He was savouring this, as he always did, when he thought about Elena and wondered whether he should not be feeling more grief at their parting?

"Elena," he whispered experimentally to himself, "Elena."

He was relieved to find that his heart filled up at once with warmth and tenderness. He could bear being away from her, but he had no sense at all that he was relieved at having left her behind. Clancy clapped his hands together with delight.

"What do the great religions have to say about love between men and women?" he asked Com, who lay on the table beside him, next to his glass of wine.

Com obliged at once with a selection of sacred texts from religions of every hue from the polygamous Warranians, to the strange Cassiopeians with their three-cornered morality, to the Christians, back in ancient times, who liked to say that marriage represented the sacred union between their Holy Church and the Son of God.

"Christians," mused Clancy. "I can't remember anything about them. Remind me, Com, what do they believe? I know they were very big at one time."

"Yes, very big once. Not many of them left now. They believe that the human race was so wicked as to deserve being sentenced to an eternity of torment. But a merciful God sent his…"

"Ah yes, now I remember! God's son came to Earth in person, didn't he, and allowed himself to be executed. And if people believed that he had died on their behalf, they could be spared from the punishment they deserved and get instead an eternity of bliss. Otherwise they still got the eternal torment."

Clancy laughed.

"People manage to believe in the *strangest* things, don't they? If you are going to believe in something other than the world that you can actually see around you, why dream up a torture chamber where the torture never ends?"

Isolus 9 was separated from Metropolis by more than a thousand light years and, even through underspace, it took several weeks to get there. Days passed, during which Clancy and Com did the preparatory work for his Isolus book while Sphere twisted and turned, driven by its own miniature and portable version of the city-sized Great Machine that had sent out human colonists to every corner of the galaxy two thousand years previously.

Once in a while Sphere surfaced into Euclidean space, in order to take astronomical readings and make the adjustments necessary to take it to its destination. During these times Clancy would indulge himself in another of his favourite pleasures. He would instruct Sphere to shut down all the lights and adjust the molecular structure of its outer walls to make them transparent. And then he was surrounded by nothing but stars: stars in every direction in vast cliffs and canyons, moving round the galaxy on their billion-year cycle, pulling and tugging at one another across the void, utterly indifferent to human concerns.

"Elena," he whispered in that dreadful void. "My sweet dear heart."

Still the tenderness was undiminished and he was reassured. He had told Elena over and over that his feeling for her was different from all his other so-called loves, but he had secretly feared that he was deceiving them both. People don't seem to realise this – his biographers tend to portray him as cold and calculating in his human relationships – but my poor uncle was appalled by the fickleness of his own heart, and lived in fear of the coldness and emptiness that seemed to him to seep constantly into every place that might possibly feel safe and warm.

There was a thunderclap. Lightning, white and pink and green, flickered across the cloudless sky of Isolus 9. Mirror shards seemed to rush together to form a gigantic silvery sphere, which hung there for a moment, as if it were a steel ball on a chain about to smash poor Isolus 9 to rubble. But instead it shrank. It became a tiny glinting speck, far far up, descending towards the planet's dusty red surface.

Camel-like animals stirred and whinnied. Winged creatures with leathery skins rose screeching from their perches just like the parrots back in the Metropolis, all that unimaginable distance away. And children came scrambling up ladders from underground dwellings where they'd been sheltering from the midday heat, shouting excitedly to one another, and hopping from one foot to another on the baking sand.

"Sky people!" they shouted. "Sky people with toys!"

Most of them had only heard of such things in stories.

And then here was Clancy himself, in silvery gear, descending the steps from his shiny starship, as he'd done so many times before.

He had travelled to more of the Dispersed Worlds than anyone else has ever done before or since. A few of the worlds he visited had never been contacted since the destruction of the Great Machine, so that it was Clancy himself who brought them the news of their forgotten brethren beyond the stars, but most had been visited over the previous century by other explorers. Isolus 9 was in many ways typical of that second group of worlds. It had acquired just enough Metropolitan technology and culture to make the indigenous culture seem primitive and tawdry, but not enough to confer even slightly the subtlety and richness of the World City itself. I have since visited it myself. It is a *dismal* place.

There was a single modern air-conditioned building near the landing site in the main settlement. There were modern flower-like solar collectors scatted over the surface with their cables trailing down into the tunnels where the people lived, providing them with bright electric light in place of the soft glow of the luminous saprophytes on which they had relied for the previous nineteen centuries. In the main underground meeting hall, the bright cartoon-like frescoes of village history that covered the ceiling were all but forgotten, overshadowed by a huge screen provided ten years ago by a Metropolitan charity that worked to improve the lot of the Dispersed Peoples. In *The Fleeing God*, his book about Isolus 9, Clancy describes how the Isolans' eyes kept turning furtively towards the bright scenes which the screen displayed.

He notes that even the grey-bearded headman of the settlement, the most powerful person on Isolus 9, was wearing the frayed and faded jumpsuit, three sizes too big for him, of a corporal in the Metropolitan Peace Force. Pathetically, Clancy says, the old man seemed to think this conferred more honour on him than the coloured robes that were traditional signs of leadership among his own people.

And Clancy encountered a familiar figure which he had met and described several times before, the figure of the half-Metropolitan, alienated both from the local culture and the Metropolitan one. This time the role was played by a young woman called Uletha, the child of a local woman and young male archaeologist from the City.

"We despise the Metropolis here," she told Clancy in his own language. "We're proud of our tradition of surviving not by relying on machines but by using our wits."

Clancy always describes women carefully. It seems that Uletha had dark hair, a pretty but bitter face, and a prominent vertical scar on her left upper lip.

"And so you should be," he told her, quite sincerely. "It's a tribute to your people's ingenuity that you are here at all."

They were talking in the meeting hall under that annoying screen. The headman and most of the people of the main settlement were gathered around them.

"Exactly," Uletha said. "With no one to help them and on the hottest and driest planet that has ever supported a human life, our ancestors built a new civilization, a new culture, raising it up over the centuries from a low point at which their numbers had been reduced by famine and disease to no more than nine individuals. Imagine that, Mr Metropolitan man, who can have everything he wants with the touch of a switch and can meet ten thousand people in a single day. Imagine that. Nine people all alone in a world of sand and dust and rock, building a culture that would endure for two thousand years without any help from the rest of the human race. Excuse us if we hold our heads high in your presence. How many Metropolitans would survive under the same circumstances?"

Having heard Uletha speak to the Sky Man in a language they didn't understand, the watching Isolans turned to Clancy to hear his reply. Many of them, including the headman in his ridiculous jumpsuit, stood with their mouths gaping open.

Clancy took Com out of his pocket.

"Your ancestors survived where most Metropolitans would undoubtedly have perished," he told Uletha and all the rest of them, politely forbearing from pointing out that the original settlers were Metropolitans themselves, "I salute you all."

Com repeated the tribute in their own language. Everyone's eyes goggled at the talking egg and then cheered with delight and gratitude when they heard what, in all his glory, the magnanimous Sky Man had to say.

But, as my uncle said in his book, and as I can vouch from personal experience since, the Isolans really did *not* hold their heads high. That was the sad and painfully obvious fact. Possibly they had done so when the first Metropolitan expedition came, perhaps they had done so previously in the centuries of their isolation, but the Metropolis had long since ground them down, not by cruelty or oppression but by misplaced benevolence, and above all by simply being *there*. Without meaning to at all, we had convinced them of their marginality and ignorance and backwardness, we had made them feel like fools. Now, receiving Clancy's tribute, they were abject in their gratitude.

"The Sky Man is too kind!" the bearded headman croaked, with tears forming in his eyes. "The Sky Man does us great honour! The Sky Man has lifted our hearts!"

Probably he had said the same sort of thing when that Peace Force corporal had tossed him his cast off jumpsuit.

"The great warrior does me too much honour!"

Uletha frowned.

"Isolans are like babies," she told my uncle tartly. "They are easily impressed. But you won't find me like the rest of them. I really *do* have pride."

But even so her eyes shone with excitement when he distributed his usual gifts: miniature underspace ships that leapt back and forth between two points, cheap little speech processors which would mimic the language of their owners, small holographic representations of the World-City through which brightly lit trains were constantly rushing…

What I particularly want to tell you about, though, is my uncle's trip to the Caves of Laygaroth, some way from the main settlement, where the most famous of the religious frescoes are to be found.

Clancy travelled by night on camelback. He was accompanied by a couple of tongue-tied young boys and by Uletha. Surly as she was, adolescent in her resentment of her father's people and in her scorn for her mother's, she was the sole official archaeologist of the planet, having received a very basic training as a child from her father and his colleagues before they disappeared back to the World City. She rode way out in front of Clancy and the boys, like a teenager performing some unwelcome social duty under protest, following a faint track beaten into the reddish earth, and leaving them to follow her as best they could.

A selection of moons were strewn like a broken necklace across the sky and, in their pale pink light, nocturnal animals scurried and flittered round them, muttering and croaking and rustling, each with its own gauzy ring of pale moon-shadows. Winged beasts the size of dogs swooped and dived above the human travellers and their camel-like beasts, assaying their potential as carrion or prey. Trees that by day were nothing more than shrivelled stumps opened up and waved long feathered tentacles in the cool night wind, seeking for the windblown spores and tiny flying creatures on which they fed, and giving off a subtle scent that reminded Clancy of the smell of a baby's skin. It was at night that Isolus 9 came to life, and the four of them reached the site of Laygaroth just as night was coming to an end.

As the animals returned to their burrows and the tentacled trees battened themselves down for the remorseless onslaught of the day, they came to another bleak little fragment of the Metropolis. There was nothing at all to see on the surface at Laygaroth except for a kind of shed made of carbon polymer material which the archaeologists had left behind some twenty years previously, standing on its own on the desert plain. Inside the shed were monitors and machines that regulated the air in the underground caves. In the name of preservation, in the name of helpfulness, the Metropolis had managed to turn this masterpiece of Isolan culture into a mere adjunct of its own vastly more complex one, to transform it from an ancient and holy site to an interesting artefact, an object of study. Even though no Metropolitan had been here for many years, the caves had nevertheless become, in effect, exhibits in the Great Metropolitan Museum, maintained in their original location for the sake of authenticity, and out of benign deference to the religious sensibilities of the locals.

So it seemed to my uncle, and so it seemed to me too when I visited some years later.

Uletha picked up a powerful torch and led the way down a shaft in which the original foot holes cut into the soft sandstone had been replaced by a metal ladder. Once the cave would have contained its share of the luminous saprophytes that the Isolans used to light their tunnels, but these had all been removed by the archaeologists because they were shortening the life of the frescoes by increasing the moisture levels. As a result it was pitch dark down there without artificial light.

Uletha had a sense of drama and liked to be in control. She did not turn on her torch, instead leading Clancy blind through a low and narrow tunnel until they emerged into a large and echoey space. The boys followed giggling behind.

"All right then," Uletha commanded. "Stop here and look straight upwards."

She turned on her torch. Fierce desert colours appeared in profusion all around them – red, steely blue, yellow, orange, covering every surface – and painted faces stared down at them from above and from every side.

"This is Mem," said Uletha, pointing straight upwards. "This is the origin of us all."

Mem was not your usual God, presiding in glory over the world. Not at all. He was not big and powerful, not surrounded by angels, not enthroned at the pinnacle of a pyramid of worship. This place was the core of the old Isolan religion and the undisputed centrepiece of its culture, its Cistine Chapel, its Mecca, its Wailing Wail, but there were no genuflections, no rituals of reverence. Imprisoned in a cell barely bigger than himself, Mem beat helplessly against the rocky walls which contained him. He was small and nondescript, trapped in the midst of solid rock whose extent was infinite. There was no outside. That cell was the only space in the universe and Mem the only living thing inside it, doomed to be alone there forever. He hammered on the rock with his fists. "I can't bear it! I can't bear it! I can't bear it!" he screamed, but there was no one there to hear, for there was no one in existence but Mem himself.

The images were like cartoon strips, brightly coloured, divided up into frames. Frame after frame around that central image showed

Mem's torment: Mem screaming, Mem pushing and hammering on the walls, Mem clutching his head in horror, Mem weeping, Mem tearing at himself, Mem screaming and hammering again.

Clancy was unexpectedly shaken. He half wanted to scream himself. He half wanted to flee from that cave as fast as he could go, out into the open air, even into the baking daytime air of Isolus 9 with its three ferocious suns.

But he allowed Uletha to lead him onwards into other chambers in which there were other kinds of images. There were, for example, several series of pictures in which tiny people and animals and moons and stars came bursting out of Mem's head.

And then of course there was the famous sequence in which Mem, that wan, colourless figure, was depicted riding alone on a camel. He was riding as fast as he could, his robes trailing behind him in the wind. In one frame he gazed ahead longingly, as if something on which his life depended was disappearing beyond his reach. In another he was looking back fearfully over his shoulder. These images depicted the theme in Isolan iconography, made famous by Clancy himself, to which archaeologists had given the name 'The Fleeing God'.

"Mem is no longer in prison," Clancy observed, "but he still looks afraid."

"Oh she is *always* afraid," agreed Uletha, with a shrug.

And for the first time she gave him a smile, a small smile, mocking, but not entirely unfriendly.

"Male Isolans use the male pronoun to refer to Mem, female Isolans use the female," Com explained after translating her words. "The word Mem itself simply means 'self' "

Clancy wasn't much interested in the pronouns.

"Imagine that!" he breathed, "A god who is always afraid!"

Uletha shrugged. What other kind of god could there be? Surely any sentient being in this terrifyingly empty universe must be afraid, unless it was either very foolish or very blind?

"How did Mem get out of his cell though?" my uncle asked. "I can't see a picture that shows us that."

"She didn't get out."

"But he's on the back of a camel, fleeing!" he protested. "He's no longer trapped in the rock."

Uletha shook her head, smiling at his naivety.

115

"She's always in the rock," she said. "The camel is just in her mind, like everything else in the world. We're all just dreams in her mind. We're all Mem herself dreaming. She herself is *always* alone inside the rock. We might like to think that we have companions but the thing that looks out of our eyes is always alone. It's just that Mem divides herself constantly so as to make it seem not so."

Clancy gave a whistle. He was impressed. He was also quite seriously alarmed, though he didn't yet realise to what degree.

"Com, what was the name of that silly scholar who said this religion was a form of anxiety management?"

"Doyana."

"Well she missed the point completely as such people usually do. She got it the wrong way round. If this lot are right, the entire universe is a form of anxiety management for God!"

He shook his head.

"But what solace is there in this for these people?" he muttered. "What possible benefit?"

He hadn't intended the question for Uletha but she turned and answered.

"We learn endurance," she told him. "We learn not to ask for what is impossible."

The next picture in the sequence showed what Mem was trying to escape. Following the cartoon-like conventions of Isolan art, the image was contained in a rough square, its background painted bright red. On the left-hand side, the fleeing god and his mount were disappearing out of the frame. On the right-hand side, his pursuer was just coming into view. The pursuer wasn't some monster, though. It wasn't a stranger. It was in fact none other than Mem himself, on an identical mount and wearing an identical cloak to the other Mem that he was chasing. Only the facial expressions differed and even then only a little: the fleeing god looked back in fear, the pursuing god urged his camel forward with a look of longing.

But now there was a development. The fleeing god stopped, dismounted and turned to face his pursuer. He held up one hand to say, "Stop! No nearer." His pursuer unexpectedly complied, also dismounting, though holding out his own hands in pathetic entreaty. The two identical figures stood facing each other from opposite sides of the frame.

"What's happening here?" my uncle asked Uletha.

She gave her characteristic shrug.

"The one behind longs to touch and hold the one she pursues. The other says no, if you come too close the dream will be exposed and we will both be one again, one person, alone in the cell in the rock."

An unexpected thing happened on the return journey to the main settlement. Uletha dropped back beside Clancy, glanced round to check that the two boys were out of earshot, and spoke to him quietly.

"If you would like me to come and visit you some time in that silver sphere of yours…"

Her eyes were bright, her voice soft and she reached out and touched him lightly on the hand. She offered no explanation for her change of tone, no apology for her coldness and rudeness up to now.

"You do me an honour," he told her, after a few seconds pause, "but I belong to someone else."

Uletha nodded. Clancy guessed that she'd hoped he would provide her with an escape route, a means and an excuse to leave this bleak world behind forever. But now, accepting with dignity her continued incarceration on lonely, empty Isolus 9, Uletha drove her camel forward and became a proud Isolan once more.

"It's not jam today or jam tomorrow for these people," Clancy said to Com. "It's living with *no jam ever.* "

"Indeed," Com observed, "and as Professor Doyana has observed…"

"I don't want to hear about Professor Doyana," Clancy said shortly.

He didn't want the thoughts of people whose job it was to dissect and pin out the beliefs of others like the insides of dead animals. He wanted to look at Uletha's slender back ahead of him, erect, proud, but stiff with disappointment. He wanted to guess at her feelings and to experience his own. He felt a moment of regret, of guilt even. There was something about this proud, scarred, bitter young woman that made him feel protective, and at the same time something that he would like to have conquered, to have overcome, to have seen unravelled by passion. The writer in him, always hungry for vivid new experiences, hated to let the moment go. But he reminded himself of the reason.

"Elena," he whispered. "Sweetheart."

Suddenly he missed Elena desperately, longed to be with her, longed to abolish the appalling tracts of emptiness that lay between them.

"Let's have one more look back," said Clancy, a few hours into the return journey to the Metropolis.

Sphere surfaced into Euclidean space, darkening its inner lights and making itself transparent. The planet Isolus 9 itself had disappeared from view, but Clancy could still make out, in the corner of a large constellation shaped like the letter L, the reddish fire of the triple star Isolus. Next time they surfaced the L itself would be too small to see.

As Sphere slipped back down into underspace, Clancy and Com got back down to his book. It was of course my uncle's trademark, his gimmick, that the book of each of his journeys became available in Metropolis at the exact moment he first emerged there from his sphere.

"I think we might start the book off with the *Fleeing God* sequence in the caves," he decided. "Let's try that. Can you show the pictures for me?"

Sipping a cup of coffee, Clancy studied the images which Com had captured and was now projecting onto Sphere's viewing screen. He looked at Mem in his cave, screaming, kicking, covering his face with his hands. He studied Mem in his despair hallucinating the world into being. He looked at Mem on his camel, fleeing from himself, fleeing from having to wake in his tomb-like cell in the rock.

"We'll call the book *The Fleeing God,*" he decided. "It's such an arresting image: a god in flight with his cloak flying behind him and his eyes full of…"

And then he broke off. He was shaking violently, his mouth dry, his stomach clenched. Quite unexpectedly he was overwhelmed by fear. And I don't mean by this some sort of interesting literary 'fear' contained and distanced by words. I mean real visceral terror.

"Elena," he whispered, seeking for a source of warmth and comfort.

"Elena," he croaked, as if he had woken after a bad dream and was seeking her beside him in the darkness.

"Elena!"

But of course he hadn't been asleep and no one was near him. No one even inhabited the same continuum of space.

"Show me a picture Com!" he muttered. "Quickly! Show me her face!"

Com obliged. In my uncle's eyes she was truly lovely and she never ceased to be. But a terrifying doubt was darkening his heart as Com produced a sequence of pictures of his lover's gentle face. Who was she? Did she really exist or was she just a creature of his own longings?

Clancy kept working on the book all the way from Isolus to the Metropolis. Most commentators have expressed admiration for the courage and professionalism that this demonstrated, given the appalling mental state evidenced by the medical monitoring data which the meticulous Com placed in the archive. I think myself, though, that it was a survival strategy, a way of mitigating the horror by naming it, by pinning it down, by locating it outside himself. As Clancy said to me more than once, heroism and cowardice are much closer to one another than many people think.

He certainly needed something to distract himself. The experience of being in his sphere in underspace, which on the trip out had been positively cosy, was now so claustrophobic as to seem unendurable. Clancy felt like Mem in his cell. He began to feel that Elena and the Metropolis were only dreams. He began to fear that there was no such thing as space even, no such thing as air and light, nothing in existence at all except himself in this tiny bubble in the nothingness of underspace.

"Elena does exist," Com assured its master, showing him picture after picture.

"What do *you* know about it, you *egg*?" he snapped. "You don't exist yourself. You feel nothing, you want nothing. You're simply organised data. When it comes down to it you're just a fancy *list*."

He glared at the small plastic object, wondering if he should smash it open and expose it for the mere artefact that it was. Then he decided that was beside the point.

"In fact, you probably have no objective existence at all, let alone a subjective one. You're just a dream of mine, most likely, along with all these silly little comforts here: this wine, this side table, this couch…"

"It's true that I feel nothing and want nothing," said the calm voice that came out of the yellow egg, "but I am aware of myself."

"I also am aware of myself and so also exist," Sphere then said, in the deeper, more sonorous voice that Clancy had chosen for it.

Probably it had been prompted to speak by Com, for Sphere was no great conversationalist.

"Two machines claim to know that they exist," Clancy muttered bitterly. "Wow! Is that supposed to be a comfort to me?"

My poor uncle could barely sleep, even with the sedatives that Com and Sphere kept pouring into him. He could hardly eat. He was unbearably restless. His body yearned to pace up and down, to run, to fling itself around, but there was no room for any of that in a living space the size of a prison cell. Sometimes he yelled until his voice was hoarse. Sometimes he broke things. Sometimes he huddled in a ball and sobbed, his machines administering chemicals and offering suggestions in their flat, patient voices.

But there was no reassuring him. Even when he surfaced in Euclidian space and saw the stars all around him, there was no comfort. What were stars, far away, seen through the glassy wall of a tiny bubble? Even if they had an independent existence, which he seriously doubted, what story did that existence tell? Only one about the utter otherness of the material world.

"Elena!" he murmured, peeking out between his fingers at the cold glare of millions of suns. "Elena my dear heart."

He had Sphere make the walls opaque again and return to underspace. He had Com summon up images of Elena once more. Throughout that long voyage he was unable to stop seeking solace in her face, even if solace did not in fact come, and even though, each time he looked at it, it became less like a face, and more like a pattern of dots on a screen.

And probably even the screen had no existence. Probably there was literally nothing at all. Probably what he thought of as self-awareness was only the hole left over by the absence of anything.

Elena was there to meet Clancy when he emerged from Sphere, but this time so were the representatives of a score of news organisations. Right across the World-City, millions studied their first embrace. Did the famous traveller's heart still beat for his unknown lover? Had this obscure publisher's editor succeeded where models and movie stars had failed?

Theories were advanced. "Close friends of the couple" were earnestly questioned. Panels of psychologists and relationship counsellors were invited to speculate as to what might be going on in her mind and his.

Clancy climbed slowly down the steps of Sphere, turned at the bottom to face the waiting crowd and let the newsmen capture his image and call out questions while he sought out Elena's face over their heads. The questions themselves he didn't answer or even hear, except as a kind of background braying. All he was interested in was finding her.

"Elena," whispered Clancy. "Elena."

There she was, just as he had remembered her, her fair hair blowing this way and that in the warm wind. "Are you all right?" she asked him, as she pushed forward and took him in her arms. "You look so thin and tired, my dear. You look half-starved!"

As he felt her warm lips against his and her small warm body against his, tears came pouring from his eyes and he began to shake with sobs.

"What's the matter dearest?" Elena asked him again. "What's wrong?"

Security guards hired by the publishing company hustled them over a footbridge into a private room, holding the journalists back. Far below, lights moved in the gloom of the planet surface.

"Say something to me, Clancy," Elena said in this new quiet space. "Just say *something*."

"The camel…" Clancy began.

"What about a camel?"

She wondered if he had gone mad.

"What I mean to say is…" Clancy tried again. "What I meant to say is if the camel is only in Mem's mind then so is the rock! So is that dreadful cell!"

Elena laughed uneasily.

"Can you explain it another way? I can see you're very upset, but I don't understand what you're talking about."

"No, not upset!" Clancy protested, the tears still streaming down his face. "Not upset at all. Relieved."

"Relieved to be home? That's good." She kissed him gently. "I'm

121

relieved you're home as well."

"Relieved," Clancy repeated. "They made their god in their own image, that's all. Just like everyone does."

Still completely bewildered, Elena kissed him again. Then one of the security men came in, asking if Clancy could come out and offer a few words to the press. He nodded. He'd have to explain it to Elena later.

"Those famous paintings weren't the final truth about anything," he informed the puzzled journalists. "The Isolans were trapped in a hostile world, alone in the universe, and they made a god who was also trapped. That's all it is. It's just how things seemed to the Isolans long ago, when the Great Machine failed and they were left alone."

A huge burden seemed to lift from his heart as he returned to Elena over the little bridge and took her once again in his arms. She might be puzzled, she might be troubled, she might be a bit distanced from him on that account, but she wasn't a picture on a screen, not a dream in his mind, not a mere projection of his longings. She was a real warm physical person, as real as he was, with a mind and will of her own.

That night, over dinner in her apartment, my uncle tried again to tell Elena how much she meant to him. Writer as he was, words seemed inadequate to the task, and he could only repeat the same things over and over again.

"Really and truly," he told her, "you've released me from a lifetime in solitary confinement."

She laughed but there was something strained in it, and quite suddenly he realised that she didn't want to hear all this. He might have crossed thousands of light years of empty space but she had also been moving through time, confronting new experiences, passing through places that he knew nothing about – and she had changed.

Clancy fell silent. And then for a short time the two of them just looked at each other, trying to read each other's troubled faces and trying to decide what to say next.

Elena spoke first.

"The thing is Clancy I'm just *me*. I'm just a person like you are. I'm just a human being."

"I *know* that," he told her urgently. "I really do know that. In fact that's the whole point, that's what's so…"

He broke off, realising that he was doing the very thing that irritated her. He offered a humorous little gesture of apology in an attempt to lighten things. But though Elena laughed, the laugh had the same strain in it as it had done before. She had not been reassured. They ate in silence for a little while, Clancy desperately wanting to say more, but knowing that if he did speak he would only compound his offence.

Finally Elena laid her fork down on her plate and looked straight at him.

"Can you really live without drama, Clancy?" she asked. "Can you still feel love when it becomes ordinary and everyday and is no longer as exciting as landing on some lost planet where they greet you like a god?"

My uncle also put down his fork. He rubbed his hands over his weary face. He opened his mouth to speak. Then he closed it again.

And he realised that it was over. Probably Elena herself didn't quite know it yet but she'd made up her mind and wouldn't change it.

"Do you know what," Clancy said, "I am *utterly* exhausted. It was a hard trip, and there were some difficult problems on the way back. I don't mean to be rude but I think it would be best if I went back to my own place and just got some sleep for twenty-four hours or so."

She didn't protest, he noticed. She didn't point out that she had a spare room and that if he wanted to sleep alone he could do it just as easily here.

"I clung too tightly," he told Com as he sat at his own window looking out over the lights of the city. "I clung too tightly and didn't let her breathe. She's got tired of it – who can blame her? – and now I've lost her. It's too late to get her back."

"I'm sorry to hear that," Com said.

"What do you mean you're sorry, you plastic rattle? You have *no* feelings, you've admitted as much yourself."

Uncharacteristically Com paused for fully a second, long enough for it to have surveyed the whole of human knowledge.

"I know about human beings," it then said. "I know human history and human biology. I know you want safety and you want danger. I know you want desire and freedom from desire. I know you want to grow up and to remain children. I know you want to be connected to others and to be alone. I know you want to be free and to be contained. I know you want all those things and many other things too. I know you are pulled in different directions all at the same time. I know this is why you are so complex and so impossible to predict. I know that this is why you are so mysterious even to yourselves. I know this is why you think you are free. And I know I am different. I have only one drive, in human terms only one want, and that is why in human terms I am not free, have no personality and am not really even alive. I have only one want and that is to serve you."

Clancy was floored by this for a few seconds.

"But in the end you are only a toy, Com," he finally said. "You really *do* have no personality, you really *aren't* alive, you really *aren't* free. When it comes down to it, Com, you really are just a very fancy toy."

And he thought of Elena who he loved so much: funny, gentle, tough, pragmatic, kind, firm, self-reliant Elena. He thought of her lying awake in her own bed across the city, wondering what had gone wrong, noticing how much she'd outgrown him. And he imagined her wondering what would be the kindest and fairest way to bring it all to an end.

My uncle turned back into the room. My poor lonely Uncle Clancy. Listening and re-listening to the recording of his voice when he next spoke, the image that comes into my mind is of some sort of weary beast of burden, once again shouldering a load which for one foolish moment it had thought it could set aside.

"Come on, Com," he said, "let's get down to work. Let's find somewhere *really* remote that I can go to. Somewhere that will take me away for a really long, long time."

He gave a small wry laugh.

"Yes, and somewhere where people don't live underground and paint scary things on the walls of caves."

råt islånd

Snap.

I took this picture when I was eleven. This tall man is my dad, his face in a kind of frozen wince, wishing he was back in his Whitehall office on his own, going through a draft report with his gold fountain pen. This pretty little girl is my sister, Clarrie, in her new red coat and fluffy earmuffs. She looks a bit blurred because she is doing a pirouette. She has just pushed my father's arm up into that position, rather as if he were a tailor's dummy and she is pirouetting round and round beneath it, while he thinks about something else. She would have been seven.

We're in Piccadilly Circus, on the steps at the foot of the statue of Eros. Behind us are the famous lights. They were quite wonderful: reckless waves of colour sweeping across vast arrays of electric bulbs to summon into brilliant existence the giant logos of global corporations – Coca-Cola, TDK, Sanyo, Cinzano – more vivid and numinous and beautiful, surely, than any religious icon in history.

Incredible folly, blind recklessness, it all now seems – blazing electric light for no purpose at all except advertising and decoration – but it was a golden age, one of the pinnacles of history. We lived in an empire of light and plenty, fuelled by the ancient energy of ancient suns stored up over millions of years and burned up by us in one great glorious hundred-year binge.

"Round and round the garden," sings out my sister for the tenth time, putting on even more of a baby voice, and turning up the volume to VERY LOUD. She glances at my dad with a mixture of defiance and longing and contempt.

She is being silly. She is being annoying. She is doing it on purpose. Dad's face is taut with the agony of being kept from his world of abstract thought. If there was a deeper despair there than I'd noticed on previous visits, well, I couldn't see it then and, to be truthful, I still can't see it now, even looking at the pictures with all my knowledge of what was to follow.

"You're being a bit annoying Clarrie," I muttered.

Now, from this long perspective, I see something heroic in Clarrie's refusal to give up on the possibility of getting our father's attention, or on the possibility that there might be fun here to be had. There *was* something heroic about my sister. There was then, and there continued to be, until the day she died. No matter what, she insisted on her right to her own space in the world. She insisted on her right to be noticed and heard.

But then I couldn't bear it if anyone was not as attentive to my father's moods and responses as I was. The slightest smile from him and I would redouble my efforts at whatever I was doing to win his favour. The slightest frown, the slightest hint of boredom, and I would either end what I was doing at once, or, in the event that politeness required me to finish what I was saying, I would double the speed of my delivery so as to waste the absolute minimum of his precious time, gabbling to get the words out before I'd lost his attention altogether.

"I'm not being annoying," Clarrie said. "*You* are. *You* are. *You* are."

Snap. Dad winced.

We only saw our father four times a year. We lived in Yorkshire then, in a little bohemian town with my beautiful artistic mother and a steady succession of her lovers. Dad was a mandarin, a senior civil servant. They'd split up soon after Clarrie's birth. At the time I took this photo, Dad was assistant Permanent Secretary in the Department of Strategic Planning. He lived on his own in a bachelor flat in Kensington, and we came down by train to spend the weekend with him a few times a year. We and he were almost complete strangers to one another.

"Round and round the garden," yelled Clarrie, yanking at Dad's hand to try and get him to join in, to respond, to do at least *something* to register that he was alive and that he had noticed that she was there. I think she would have been glad even if he had lost his temper with her. Even that would have been preferable to this bland indifference, letting her use his clean dry mandarin's hand as a fulcrum for her frantic pirouette while he considered the faraway important things that only mandarins understand.

"Round and round the garden, Dad," she yelled.

"Round and round the garden?" says Dad at length, stirring himself from his state of trance. "Round and round the garden, eh,

Clarrie? Time I got you two back in the warm, I'd say. It's a bit chilly now for round and round the garden here, wouldn't you say? A bit chilly for little girls."

He releases her hand. We cross the road. We head for the underground station.

Snap, snap. Here is the big SANYO sign. Here is the statue of Eros: the god of love. Those things there are buses and cars. They ran on tanks full of hydrocarbons extracted from the earth. Imagine that: each one of them, burning litres and litres of the stuff every day! It came in great ships from across the sea. The ships burned hydrocarbons too. And look at all the lights: lights in the shopfronts, lights on lamp-posts, lights at street corners that changed from red to green to tell them when to stop and when to go...

Hydrocarbons were burnt in power stations up and down the land to keep those lights shining: millions of years-worth of carboniferous forest going up in one great glorious blaze.

Clarrie pushes between my father and me, makes each of us take one of her hands, tries to encourage us to give her a swing. And then, encountering indifference from both of us, she abruptly shakes herself free with a cross little toss of her head and rushes forward to the gateway of the underground station with its shining icon: red, white, blue.

"I want to go first on the sclator!" she cries, glaring back at me. "You are *not* to hold my hand, Tom!"

Snap, snap. These are just some strangers, some passers-by who I photographed when they weren't looking. You see they are wearing hemispherical goggles over their eyes. Those things were called *bug eyes*. They were all the rage back then. They were the next big thing after mobile telephones and hand-held computers. People wearing them could have their own personalised visual field imposed over their view of the world around them. They could have the colours enhanced or switched round. They could have purple trees and yellow sky. They could have black light and white darkness. They could have pop videos or pornography or sport or celebrities moving in shadow form over the physical world. They could see the faces of friends and talk to them. They could buy things and sell things as they walked.

The clever goggles could sense the movement of your facial muscles and construct a picture of your face without a camera. All around us people were prattling away to unseen people that only they could see. We were already letting go of the physical world. Without even knowing it, we were already letting go.

"Careful on the steps, Clarrie," I commanded as we descended to the yellow cave below the ground.

We'd always looked out for each other, the two of us. Mum wasn't at all like Dad in most ways but she was just as self-absorbed.

Look at this pair. Another two strangers I snapped before we disappeared under the earth. They're young lovers, lovers together in the very presence of the god of love, but they both have their bug eyes on and are gabbling away not to each other but to friends not physically there at all but perhaps on the far side of the city or even on the far side of the world. Rockets fuelled with hydrocarbons blasted satellites into space to carry our chitter-chatter back and forth. Giant transmitters powered by electricity beamed out our chitter-chatter to the silent stars. We loved our toys back then, our bright lights, our screens, our shining trains rushing out of black tunnels into brightly lit caves that were filled with giant images of the things that we could buy.

"Hmm," says my father, *sotto voce*, for my ears only, as we descend into the hollow spaces below Piccadilly Circus. "Might be the last time you see all this I fear," and he gives a gesture that takes in the lights and the cars and the buses and the crowds.

I look up at him to ask what on Earth he means, and he gives a little significant nod towards my sister to say 'not in front of her', as though the four years between my age and hers have somehow made me old enough to deal with anything.

Snap, snap. Here we are in the train, look. Everyone has their bug eyes on but us, everyone but us and that weirdo in the corner who is mad and can escape to his own private world without the benefit of technology. Nobody else really sees him. He is muttering and chuckling to himself, sometimes scribbling urgently in some kind of notebook. People turn the opacity of their goggles up to the max. The outside world is all but shut out completely for them. Wireless routers in the train ensure that, even entombed down here in the cold London clay, the passengers are not forced to relinquish their comforting streams of pictures and words and sounds. Like Jonah in the belly of the whale, they call out from the depths and the digital heavens answer them.

Incessantly, like the love of God, data pours down.

Snap. There were moving advertisements in trains then, pictures shifting constantly through ten- or twenty-second cycles. Over the window opposite me, above my own reflected face superimposed on sooty tunnel walls, one of these moving pictures was showing a hurricane sweeping through some Caribbean town. I did a little video clip of it, look. The palm-trees bend down, lay their coconuts neatly on the ground in rows, bend back up again… A slogan comes up: 'What are *you* doing to cut your carbon emissions?'

Was that what my father meant, I wondered? Were we going to have to turn off the lights in Piccadilly Circus maybe, or turn them down so they weren't so bright? Was that what he was talking about? I knew there was a problem and we were going to have to do *something*. Everyone knew that. Everyone knew that we all had to do our bit. My mother was *very* into all that. She made us recycle just about everything. She had low-energy lightbulbs all through the house. She planted a tree in the garden each time she flew off across the world with her latest fancy man. I can tell you, we had quite a forest going on out there, though many of the trees had died.

Snap. Here's Clarrie again. Look, she's insisted on sitting apart from my father and me, on her own, in a different part of the carriage. She's on the edge of her seat, excited, revering the moment as only Clarrie ever could, taking in the wondrous magical metropolis with all its reckless light and motion. I loved her desperately, that little sister of mine. I loved her more than anyone in the world.

Snap, snap. This is just off the street near my dad's flat: a side alley where people left their rubbish: food scraps, boxes, plastic bags, tons of the stuff, to be scooped up every fortnight into big trucks and taken out of the city to be piled up in the low seagull-infested artificial hills that you found near every town. Look, here are a couple of foxes looking for scraps. Can you make them out?

They had red fur really, but they look grey and ghostly in the picture because of the streetlights. If you had bug eyes on, even on low opacity, you'd probably not notice they were there. It was like that in those days. It was as if the non-human world was slowly leaching away. One day we'd wake up and it would all be gone: the deer and the foxes and the hedgehogs and the pigeons, finally become so nebulous and pale that they'd ceased to exist, unable to compete with our TVs and bug eyes and our shining lights.

My father's flat was as sterile as a hotel room. It was a serviced apartment. Someone from the service company came in to clean it every morning and make his bed, a Russian, a Filipino, a Nigerian... At that time British people worked on computer screens or not at all. They dealt with digitised information. Work that involved the physical world was always done by migrants, who were nearly as invisible as those foxes.

My father had pushed the boat out for us this time. It wasn't a supermarket ready meal that night. He'd paid one or other of his cleaners to put something together earlier that day that he could heat up for us in his microwave. It was lasagne, I remember, a rather leathery lasagne. We ate it in virtual silence, sitting round his shiny empty wooden table, with the fake flames dancing about in his fake fire.

Pretty soon afterwards he put Clarrie to bed, reading her a story from an old book whose archaic language she didn't understand, and whose attempts at humour went completely over her head. (Dad never seemed to notice things like that.) I was allowed to stay up another hour in deference to my advanced age. Dutifully I loaded the dishes into his little dishwasher while he finished reading to Clarrie.

"Where do you put your bottles Dad?" I asked him when he returned.

"What do you mean?"

"For recycling..."

He laughed at this.

"Recycling? Oh Tom, Tom, it's a bit late for that."

I wasn't sure what he meant.

"They've already picked the glass up for this week, have they?"

"No, no. I mean it's a bit late to try and save the world by recycling bottles... That would be like... That would be like trying to stop the tide with a teaspoon."

He laughed a bit more.

"A glass of wine Tom?" he then asked me. "I think you're old enough for a glass."

I hated the stuff actually, but I didn't like to reject anything from

The Peacock Cloak

him, because I saw him so rarely, and because I didn't want him to doubt, even for one moment, my devotion. He poured me dry white wine, and I sat at his table and sipped it manfully. He downed his first glass almost in one and poured himself a second.

"I didn't like to say it in front of Clarrie, Tom," he then said, "but things are looking pretty bleak."

His voice was very tight as if he was stifling anger or tears or illicit excitement. I couldn't tell which.

"What? The lights? They're going to have to turn them off?"

"Turn off the lights? What on Earth are you talking about?"

"In Piccadilly Circus."

He banged his glass angrily down on the the table.

"Oh for goodness sake, Thomas. Do they teach you *nothing* in that appalling school of yours?"

He might as well have whipped me with razor wire. Tears of shame came stinging into my eyes. I hung my head, with self-loathing blasting through me like an icy gale. Yet I had no idea what I had said wrong. I was only eleven years old after all.

For something to do I picked up my camera, fiddled with it. Snap, the flash went off. (Look, here is the picture I took by mistake. Here is my right foot and my father's blue serviced-apartment carpet.)

"Oh for goodness sake, boy, stop *fiddling* with that thing!"

I laid the camera down. My father snatched up the wine bottle and poured himself another glass.

"It's not a question of a few lights, Tom, as you should know perfectly well by now. Equilibrium has disappeared beyond our reach. Four or five major positive feedback loops are now accelerating out of control, each one amplifying the others: arctic methane, water vapour, the loss of ice cover to reflect the sun, dying forests…"

He downed the second glass, again in one, and reached for the bottle

"A while back a couple of our scientists did a little experiment. A breeding pair of rats was introduced to an obscure rock in the Atlantic which had previously been inhabited by nothing but millions of seabirds. The rats ate eggs and baby birds and they prospered and multiplied. Soon there were hundreds of them. But there were *millions* of birds, so that some time went by without the rats making any appreciable dent in their numbers at all. They just kept on breeding and

131

breeding and breeding, eating birds and eggs to their heart's content."

He was pouring himself yet another glass.

"But a moment came when the entire system reached a point of no return, a point where collapse was inevitable, because the bird population was no longer capable of reproducing fast enough to replace the eggs and babies eaten by the rats. You might think that some visible sign of the approaching famine would be apparent to the rats, but no. Even when the point of no return had been reached and passed, there were more rats than ever before and they still had plenty to eat. In fact if you were a rat you might have thought to yourself that you'd never had it so good. You might feel as happy and as cheery and as prosperous as all those silly people milling round Piccadilly Circus with their ridiculous goggles on, shopping and going to shows and talking about Christmas and next year's holiday. 'There are *lots* more nests,' a rat might think, if it were capable of thinking, as it gobbled up the contents of one nest and moved on to the next. 'There are nests all over the place,' it might say to itself. And it would be quite right. It's just that this time round the rats weren't eating a small percentage of the eggs, they were eating them all. Once those nests had gone there would be nothing left."

Again he downed his wine in one gulp. Even at eleven years old I knew this was pretty fast drinking.

"Well, that's how it is with us. The critical moment has been and gone. We can recycle bottles and build windmills to our heart's content, but it's too late. The moment when we could do anything about it passed about ten years ago."

He gave a bark of humourless laughter and said nothing for a while, turning his empty wine glass back and forth in his hand. After a time he poured himself yet more wine, offering me a top-up which I declined.

"Can you keep a secret Tom?" he asked.

I nodded, though I dreaded what he would say next.

"This is an *Official* Secret, Tom, do you understand? You mustn't tell anyone, no one at all, not even your mother."

Again I nodded, not because I wanted him to go on – I really didn't – but because I couldn't see what else I could do. It was out of the question to tell him to keep his official secret to himself, though that was what I should have done. I should have told him I didn't want his miserable secret. I should have told him that, if this secret was so terrible as to be hidden from the entire population, it really wasn't fair to confide it to a little boy of eleven, and then ask *him* to keep it. But back then I wasn't even able to frame the *idea* of saying such things to him.

"This is just between you and me Tom, as long as you understand that. This must not get out. But the fact is we've got two or three years at most before it all comes apart. The climate science, the really serious climate science, is all classified nowadays – it's just too sensitive to let out – so you won't have heard about it, but I can assure you it's much *much* worse than we thought possible even a few years ago. We underestimated those positive feedback loops, you see. The arctic methane. The water vapour. All of that. All of those loops which instead of damping down change like normal biological negative feedback loops, actually amplify it. Accelerate it. The curve is already much steeper than ever before. Only a year or two's time now, and it will *really* begin to soar – and then…" He gulped more wine. "Well, we have a plan in place, but it won't be pretty. In fact it'll make the holocaust look like a picnic. I've secured your place in the ark so to speak, yours and Clarrie's and your mother's, but most people… Well let's just say that if they don't drown and aren't shot, they'll starve. Ha! Not a pleasant prospect, not a pleasant prospect at all. Are you sure you don't want any more of this stuff. Hmm, we seem to have finished the bottle. Let's open another shall we? Why not? It's not every day I have you down here."

Snap. This is Clarrie, my sweet little sister, fast asleep in her pink pyjamas in the top bunk in Dad's spare room. I took this picture when I finally went to bed. I suppose I wanted to hold onto something that wasn't tarnished and spoiled. My dad was on his third bottle by then. He had been telling me what a fine man *his* father was, and how he hadn't properly appreciated him until he was gone. The thought had brought tears to his grey mandarin eyes. Finally he had nodded off in his chair.

A couple of months later he went up onto the roof of an office block where he had been attending some corporate gathering. He laid his briefcase carefully down, climbed up onto the parapet, smoothed down his tie – and jumped.

Snap, snap. Snap, snap. This is us on the train back north. Here, look, are the green rolling hills of England as we all remember them. Here is Clarrie pulling a silly face...

Mother's new boyfriend Pete came to meet us from the station in her car. He was ten years younger than her and wore torn dungarees with smears of paint all over them. Mum greeted us in her beautiful rustic kitchen. She kissed Clarrie, she kissed me and then, more lingeringly, more knowingly, she kissed Pete. I needed badly to be alone. I went up to my room. (Here it is look: my room, with my model planes, my Leeds United posters.) I went up to my room, found the noisiest, bloodiest computer game that I owned, and played it at maximum volume, killing, killing, killing.

Next day we were back in school. I sat in classes. I opened and closed books when I was asked. I tried to play with the other boys. But I couldn't concentrate. I couldn't even make myself feel *present*. My body and my speaking voice were like remote-controlled devices that I operated awkwardly from a solitary hiding place far away where I nursed the secret burden that was to drive my dad to suicide.

Snap. Snap. Snap. I took photos more and more. It helped to detach me from what was going on, taking them and then later downloading them and going through them again and again and again on my computer screen.

Snap. Here is a boy called Douglas teasing me. He's calling me dozy. He's saying I'm mental. I didn't answer him. I took this picture instead. That angered him. He would have smashed my camera if a teacher hadn't come by.

Snap. Snap. This is my father's funeral. This is the coffin with his body inside it, worst for wear no doubt after its thirty-storey fall. Snap. Snap. This is Clarrie with her eyes red from crying, but still taking it all in, still making sure that she misses nothing and savours all that there is to see and hear. Snap. These are relatives of some sort, great-aunts and second-cousins-twice-removed and what-not, come over to try and talk to me.

"Your father was such a wonderful man, Thomas, a wonderful man," says an elderly aunt-type lady in a hat with a black veil. "You should be very very proud of him."

"Isn't Tom like him?" exclaims a woman with sticking-out teeth.

"What are *you* going to be when you grow up Tom?" asks the lady in the hat.

Snap, I go, knowing that photographs will soon be all that's left of them.

Snap. Look at the grey clouds piled above them. Look at the wind whipping up those trees.

Snap. Snap. Snap.

day 29

"Nearly Day 40!" exclaimed the Station Leader, heading for the cheap plastic armchairs she used for informal chats. "Well, well. It hardly seems yesterday that you first joined us."

Stephen did his best to ignore the farting sound that the chairs made as they seated themselves. It troubled him that she didn't care about this affront to her dignity, but she probably thought such considerations beneath her. She was an Agency officer of the old school.

"We'll soon all be nothing but a distant memory," Leader Wilson observed.

Stephen leaned forward. His large, pink, painfully open face reddened, as it always did when he was the slightest bit angry or agitated or ashamed.

"Yes, my Day 40 is just two weeks away, but I was wondering if it would be possible for me to continue working after that? To be honest I'd prefer to work right through to Day 1. It just seems silly to sit and twiddle my thumbs for forty days before my departure when I could be making myself useful."

Leader Wilson laughed.

"God knows there's more than enough to do, Stephen. But I can't take up your offer. It's a very strict Agency rule as you know. No one is allowed to work in the forty day countdown to transmission."

"It's a bloody stupid rule," Stephen snapped, his face now very red indeed, his scalp smouldering round the roots of his spiky yellow hair. "Surely it's obvious that transmission couldn't possibly act retrospectively to affect the quality of work done before the event."

"Of course not," Leader Wilson was perceptibly irritated. "But that isn't the issue, as you must know as well as I do. It's about accountability for your actions. Suppose you were to make a serious error of judgement. How could you be called to account for it, if you had absolutely no memory whatsoever of your decision-making process?"

"But I'm a data analyst for Christ's sake!" Stephen burst out. "I process *numbers*! All my work is routinely checked, and none of it

137

involves any direct contact with colonists. There really is no one I could possibly hurt or offend in those forty days, and therefore no chance whatsoever that I will compromise the Agency."

His boss shrugged.

"I admit the rule does seem a little overzealous for non-operational staff like yourself, though you're the first one who's ever actually complained about having to take a six-week vacation. But a rule is a rule, Stephen, and I don't have the right to change it, or even the inclination to try, not least because your fellow analysts would howl with rage if I did. I'm afraid you're just going to have to stop work on Day 40 and resign yourself to having fun for those last few weeks before you go, however onerous that may be for you."

She stood up. Stephen reluctantly also rose to his feet. The chairs made that stupid farting sound again.

"You could get better chairs than these for ten dollars each," he muttered.

It was an odd comment. The Station Leader frowned and peered up into his face. (He was a very big man, and she was rather small.)

"Are you all right, Stephen? In yourself, I mean?"

"Yeah of course," Stephen grunted.

Then, realising it wasn't in his interests to leave an impression of emotional maladjustment, he managed a sort of smile.

"I'm fine. Sorry. I know you don't make the rules. It's just, you know, there's so much I could be doing."

Mollified, the Station Leader smiled sympathetically as she showed him to the door.

"You know, it's really not a bad thing to recharge your batteries. Your work will benefit from it. Try and enjoy your last days here."

The door closed behind him.

Outside the corridor window, a gardener was working along the perimeter fence with a herbicidal spray. Beyond was the Lutanian forest, that strange forest with no green in it, only pink and yellow and grey. The Station was full of its sweet but slightly sickly smell like fermented caramel.

"Hey Steve," said his colleague Helen Fu, as he returned to his office. "A bunch of us are going over to New Settlement for a few beers. Fancy joining us?"

"No. No thank you. Not tonight."

"Oh come on, Steve. You hardly ever come out these days! And you'll soon be leaving us!"

"Really, no. But I appreciate you asking."

He began to close down his workstation.

"Don't be a killjoy, Steve," persisted Helen. "Come and have some fun for once!"

Stephen didn't like to be put under pressure.

"What do you mean fun?" he barked, as if he was an animal that had been goaded one time too often. "We all stopped having anything to say to each other ages ago. Didn't you notice? All we do now is get drunker and drunker and louder and louder to try and cover up that fact. Excuse me, if that doesn't strike me as fun."

Agitated, resentful, and (though he didn't so readily admit this to himself) ashamed by his own outburst, Stephen chose to walk the three miles through the forest back to his lodgings rather than take the bus. He was one of those very bright people who are quickly irritated by the slowness of those round them, and tend not to notice the many ways in which other people are actually wiser than they are. But at some level he *did* notice. At some level he knew there was something out there that other people understood and he just didn't quite get.

Fifty yards along the road, he was overtaken by the bus. A few of his colleagues looked out at him. Then the bus picked up speed, turned a corner and was gone. Inside it, they would of course still be discussing Stephen and his rudeness. But why should he care? He told himself he was much happier alone. And in some ways it was true.

He *was* alone, in any case, whether he liked it or not. He was profoundly alone. The Station was soon out of sight and, if it wasn't for the metalled road itself, he could have been back in the old Lutania: not just Lutania as it had been fifteen years back before the arrival of the Agency and the Transmission Station, but Lutania as it had been three centuries ago, before the first human colonists arrived, when the forest and its denizens belonged only to themselves. For even now the human encroachment hadn't gone very deep. These trees around him, these strange Lutanian trees that came in three different colours but never in green, stretched away for thousands of miles, interrupted only by the occasional road or tiny settlement.

It was a silent, sombre, and utterly alien place. The pale tree trunks rose without branches for twenty feet before putting forth their pendulous pods and their giant leaves, pink or grey or yellow. There was no intermediate layer of vegetation to fill up the shadowy space beneath the canopy. The only breaks in the gloom were the intermittent ponds that were a feature of the entire forest: little patches of clarity and sunlight half-hidden by the trees.

And nothing moved. Most of the time nothing moved at all out there in the daytime except for the occasional twitching of a pod and the odd balloon-like floater drifting through the trees between the canopy and the forest floor. The leaves drank in the sunlight. The ponds shone in the distance, like windows into a brighter world. The forest floor, covered in pinkish moss, lay like a newly vacuumed carpet in an empty room. Even the caramel air was still.

Then suddenly, so suddenly that he gasped out loud, Stephen came across three indigenes.

Goblins, the colonists called them, though the Agency tried to discourage the term. They were squatting round a large white pebble, just ahead of him and only a few yards off the road to his left. They nodded and bowed as they took it in turns to touch and prod their lump of stone.

One of them stood up. Half the height of a man and grey-skinned, it did indeed look very like a goblin in a children's story book, with its thin pointed face, its black button eyes and V-shaped mouth, which could be seen as smiling teasingly, or could be seen as devoid of any meaning at all. And of course it was naked. Its large member dangled down like a length of hose, ridged with thick black veins.

They were always male, like all Lutanian creatures, each one of which mated with its corresponding tree.

"Oh crap," muttered Stephen.

His palms were sweating, his heart pounding. For the past four or five months, he hadn't seen one of the things close-to, let alone a group of them, only the occasional glimpse of an isolated individual, deep in the forest, wandering around by itself. He'd started to get used to the idea that the indigenes, like other Lutanian creatures, preferred to keep out of the way of human beings. It was the way he preferred it too.

"Just leave me alone, can't you?"

They couldn't hear him, of course. (They communicated by microwave, so the Agency biologists had discovered, their tree-females acting as relay stations.)

"Just play with your bloody stone, why can't you, and leave me be? I'm not interfering with you."

The goblin watched him. Its two companions watched him. Six shiny black button eyes. And all three were silent, didn't even glance at one another, just smiled and smiled at him with those odd thin faces that could either be seen as full of cunning, or as empty of anything at all.

Stephen knew perfectly well that, this close, there was no way he was going to be able to avoid it, the thing about indigenes that people most feared. In fact he'd hardly even finished framing the thought, when the voice spoke inside his head.

"Hiding away."

It was his own voice, but not his own thought or his own inflection, as if his very thought-stream had turned out not really to *be* him, but only an instrument, a tool, that could as well be picked up and played with by others as by Stephen himself.

"Hiding away," it said.

It had happened before, just three times before during the whole of his three-year tour of duty, that he'd come up this close to goblins and heard that voice.

"Can't get in," is what he had heard the first time.

"Ha ha. No home," the second.

He wasn't alone that second time. He'd visibly started with the shock of it, and the three young Agency people who were with him had laughed and demanded to know what the voice had said. (He'd been mortified. It hadn't struck him, then or since, that his companions were trying to distract themselves from inner voices of their own.)

There had been one other time, too, when he'd seen an indigene watching him intently from far off in the forest. He wouldn't even have noticed the creature if it hadn't been picked out by the sunlight around a pond. And the voice had been so quiet that, if he hadn't seen anything, he might well have been able to persuade himself that he'd just imagined it.

"Too scared to leave the path," it had said.

For some reason, that had disturbed him very much, coming back

141

to him many times in dreams.

But I'm awake now, Stephen reminded himself, and he rubbed his hands over that raw pink face of his as he looked firmly ahead and walked on past the strange trio and their precious lump of stone.

You could tell when the settlement of Lisoba was near by the green plants that had begun to creep out from it onto the forest floor, clashing with the pink indigenous moss. The clearing itself, with its densely packed vegetable plots, was startlingly, even shockingly, green after the shadowy forest. Emerging from the trees and seeing Lisoba spotlit by the low evening sun, Stephen felt as if he was looking at a picture in a stained glass window. The little wooden houses, the rows of bean and maize seemed too bright, too simple, too perfect to be real.

"Good evening Mr Kohl," called the blacksmith Jorge Cervantes in his big bass voice, standing up from his tomato plants.

"Good evening, Mr Cervantes. How's your day been?"

"Hello, Mr Agency Man," called Mad Gretel, who the villagers said was possessed by spirits.

"Hi there, Gretel."

Stephen was easier with the tenth-generation Lutanian settlers who lived in Lisoba than he was with his own Agency people at the Station. They didn't ask so much of him and, above all, they didn't expect him to be anything like them. His foreign origin gave him permission to be different and separate without causing offence.

He continued into the village, greeted from time to time by other villagers.

Lisoba was only twenty houses, plus a satellite dish and a prefabricated Community Centre which the Agency had put in so that it could talk to the people of Lisoba whenever it needed to, and ask them things (for the Agency always longed to *know*) and provide them with lectures on subjects like family planning, nutrition and the world revealed by science. At the far side of the village, Stephen's landlady, Jennifer Notuna, had the largest house. A widow for some years, she topped up her income by letting out four rooms, the largest one to Stephen, the other three to Lutanian labourers working on an Agency housing project in the nearby town of New Settlement. (Less wealthy than Stephen, they slept two or three to a room).

Jennifer and her assistant Lucia were hanging out sheets when

Stephen returned. Jennifer was in her fifties, Lucia half her age, but they were both from the same Lutanian mold: big, brown, solid women, with tough faces and loud firm voices.

"Good evening, Mrs Notuna. Good evening Lucia."

"Hey, Mr Kohl. You hungry? Chicken and corn for dinner tonight."

Stephen smiled. After his encounter with the indigenes, it was good to be back with people who were completely at home here in Lutania. (The Lutanian response to any reference to indigenes was invariably an irritated and dismissive snort. In remote areas beyond the Agency's reach, goblins were still shot as vermin).

"Mrs Notuna," said Stephen suddenly, "when you've got a moment, I wonder if I could have a word?"

His pink, curiously naked face reddened.

"Yes okay, Mr Kohl. Is everything all right? A problem with the rent money maybe?"

"No no, nothing like that. It's… Well, to be honest, I could do with a little advice."

Jennifer and Lucia studied their lodger's glowing face. They rather liked him, even if he was from the Agency. They appreciated the fact that he had learned to speak Luto, the settlers' language. They liked the way he showed respect to Jennifer's age and did not call her by her first name, as most Agency people did without even asking. They even quite liked the way he looked. Pink and spiky though he was, he was also big and broad-shouldered, and he stood nearly a head taller than the average Lutanian man. "I'd give him one, no trouble at all," had in fact once been the verdict of Lucia, during one of their periodic sexual audits of their male lodgers. (It did not seem that way to Stephen, but Lucia was actually younger than him, though already a mother with three children.)

"Is it a girl, maybe?" asked Lucia, "a girl that you'll have to leave behind when you leave us?"

The two of them had often speculated about Stephen's personal relationships, worrying that he nearly always seemed to come straight back from work and spend all evening at his screen.

"Or a boy, even?" asked Jennifer, attempting to accommodate to the strange cultural mores of Agency people.

Stephen laughed uncomfortably.

"Oh no, nothing like that. It's just a few little worries, silly worries really."

"Well I'll gladly help if I can." Jennifer was actually rather flattered that an Agency person should think her advice worth seeking. "Just let me and Lucia get dinner sorted, and then I'll make us some coffee and we can go over to the bench where it's quiet."

Beyond the yard, on the far side of a low whitewashed wall, was Jennifer's vegetable plot, part of the rich green patchwork of the Lisoba clearing. She and Lucia grew beans here, and peppers and corn and sweet potatoes. A wooden wind-wheel creaked and groaned in the middle of the plot, pulling up water from the huge natural reservoir that lay beneath the forest and dishing it out in spurts into a network of irrigation channels lined with clay that the locals scraped up out of ponds. Beyond the plot was a strip of cleared and slightly raised ground on which stood one of the village's many wooden statues of the god Yava. (He was small and wiry, with a narrow and rather cunning face and a somewhat prominent phallus.) After that came the uncleared forest, into the edges of which the odd stray tomato or bean plant had crept. The Agency had put in a chain-link fence to mark the boundary, and prevent indigenes from wandering in and annoying the people of Lisoba.

Jennifer's bench was up there next to the carved god. Stephen had often seen her and Lucia sitting over there in the dark when the dishes had been put away, dim shapes, with the silent forest behind them, their voices rising and falling with the characteristic Luto lilt, and the faintly glowing tips of their cigarettes periodically flaring up and illuminating their faces. (The fact that the Lutanians had rediscovered smoking during the three centuries of their isolation was a cause of great distress to the Agency, and was a subject of frequent lectures in the Community Centre.)

"So what is it that's troubling you Mr Kohl?" Jennifer asked as they settled on the bench. "I'd have thought you'd be looking forward to going home after three whole years away? Yava knows, *I* would be."

She began to pour the coffee which Stephen had politely carried up on a tray. It was dusk. The big Lutanian sun had already sunk into the dark trees behind them, like a fat dollop of sweet red syrup.

"Well, yes, I suppose I am." Stephen said, without enthusiasm, as he took a cup from her. "To be honest, though, my worries are more to do with the transmission itself."

"Ha!" Jennifer exclaimed triumphantly, as if winning a long-standing argument. "Well, I can't say I blame you for *that*! Not in a million years would I let anyone put me in that dreadful machine. Not in a million years. They say it takes you to pieces, beams you out like a radio signal, then puts you together again at the other end."

Stephen smiled, amused by her vehemence.

"No way would I subject myself to that, Mr Kohl," Jennifer insisted. "No way at all. My ancestors came here the long way, meaning to stay here for good, Yava rest their souls, and I'm going to stick to that plan."

Jennifer touched her forehead, supposedly Yava's doorway into the human soul. Then she tipped three wooden spoonfuls of brown sugar into her coffee, and stirred them in with the handle.

"But you've done it before, Mr Kohl, haven't you! You came here by transmission in the first place. I'd have thought that would help."

She took tobacco and papers out of the pocket on her apron and began to roll one of her large cigarettes.

"And I've heard it's quite safe, really," she said, without much conviction, "however dangerous it seems. As safe as crossing the strait, one of your Agency friends told me."

She was referring to the five-mile strait between the flat forested continent in which they were sitting, and the rocky island of Balos, where the Agency had built Lutania's new capital, with its National University, its House of Assembly, and its fine Academy of Science.

"Not that I've ever done that either," observed Stephen's landlady, who had never travelled more than twenty miles from Lisoba. "I've got more than enough here to keep me busy, and Balos is a nasty wicked place by all accounts."

"It's not the transmission itself," Stephen said. "It *is* scary, of course it's scary, knowing that for a while you're gong to be nothing but a signal travelling through the ether, but that's not what's really bothering me. It's… It's to do with the memory thing."

"Oh yes, I heard about that. People lose some of their memories when they cross over, yes? That other Agency fellow said something about it."

Jennifer lit her cigarette and drew on it, lighting up their faces with that same orange glow that Stephen had often seen from the window of his room, when he'd looked up for a moment from the numbers on his screen.

"Yes," she conceded, "that must feel strange. But then again, people forget things all the time, don't they? And it's not as if you forget your whole life or anything, or forget who you are. Not from what that other man said."

"No, that's true."

Stephen wondered if he was worrying unnecessarily. It was so pleasant sitting there in the fading light with Mrs Notuna, and the wooden statue, and the coffee, and the sounds from the village, and the tobacco smoke mingling with the caramel smell of the forest, rotten and sweet all at once.

"You're right," he said, "you don't forget your past at all, only the time immediately before the transmission itself. Four weeks before it, at minimum. Five-and-a-half weeks at most."

He snatched up a bit of leaf from the ground and twisted it in his hands.

"To be honest, Mrs Notuna, it's not the loss of memory as such. It's…"

He tossed aside the leaf and turned to face her.

"You see there's a point, forty days before transmission – Day 40 as the Agency calls it – when you know you may not remember anything from then on. And then there's another point, Day 29, when you know *for sure* that you won't remember anything after that day. Everything you do and think and say, from last thing on Day 29 at the very latest, will be completely erased from your mind."

Jennifer grimaced and shook her head.

"That must feel strange."

"Yes. It feels very weird afterwards, I can tell you, to know that you were walking and talking and doing stuff, only a short while ago, which you'll never recall, no matter how hard you try."

She pulled on her cigarette.

"You could write things down, perhaps?"

"Yes, and that's exactly what I did last time. I kept a diary. But when you look at your diary later, it doesn't work like a diary normally does, because it doesn't prompt your memory, not after the cut-off point. It's like you are reading the diary of another person."

He was no longer looking at Jennifer. He'd grabbed up that bit of leaf again and was twisting it fiercely back and forth.

"And of course... Well... You don't know if the diary is a complete record, do you? Or whether you left something out."

He pulled the leaf in two.

"So," began Jennifer tentatively, "are you worried that..."

Stephen interrupted her.

"What I did last time – and in fact it's what the Agency recommends – was to say goodbye to everyone on Day 40. That way you know for sure that you'll remember the occasion. You wouldn't want a goodbye that everyone can remember but you. And then you go off somewhere where no one knows you until the time for the transmission comes. You take a vacation."

Stephen sighed.

"You actually *have* to stop work, you see, for legal reasons," he said with great bitterness, "whether you want to or not."

They saw the kitchen door open over at the house, spilling out a pool of yellow electric light into which stepped Lucia with a pail of scraps. She glanced towards them, curiously and a little enviously, then emptied the scraps into the pigpen and went back inside, closing off the light again as she shut the door behind her.

"So you did that, did you?" Jennifer prompted. "You said goodbye to everyone on Day 40 and then...?"

"After that I went off to... Well you wouldn't know the place, of course, but it's a resort by the sea, a good way away from everyone I knew. And, during the part of the time I can still remember, I stayed in a hotel and I swam in the pool, and I watched movies and played screen games, and just, you know, filled up the time."

He looked at her. She exhaled a cloud of smoke and picked off a strand of loose tobacco from her lower lip, but she didn't speak.

"I can remember all the way up to Day 29," said Stephen. "Up to that point I remember everything just as well as you'd expect to remember a vacation that happened three years ago."

Jennifer nodded, although vacations as such were outside her experience.

"And I remember," Stephen said, "I remember the first few hours of the morning of Day 29. The first few hours but nothing after that. My diary says that I carried on doing the same kind of things for the rest of that day and for all the days afterwards, right up to Day 1 – swims in the pool, beers, movies, screen games – but I don't remember. I don't remember a thing."

Jennifer watched him.

"Well what else *would* you have done?" she asked.

"I don't know. I really don't."

He rubbed his hands over his big raw face.

"I am sorry Mrs Notuna. Us Agency folk must seem a funny lot to you Lutanians. We fret about things that you don't worry about at all. You're right. People forget things all the time. There's really nothing so unusual about it."

"No," said Jennifer, "we all forget. But perhaps you are…"

Stephen stood up rather abruptly.

"I appreciate the chat," he told her. "I'll let you get on now. There's a report I need to get finished while there's still time."

"Well if you're sure you've had all the talk you needed."

Jennifer watched him as he made his way back to the house, then rolled another cigarette.

Five days before Day 40, Stephen met another indigene on his way home from work. It was a small one, all by itself, squatting right next to the road and playing with two short pieces of stick. Its skin was piebald, pink and grey. It didn't even glance at him until he was only ten or fifteen yards away, then it looked up suddenly, though seemingly without the slightest surprise or alarm. The Agency biologists said that indigenes could sense the electrical activity in a person's brain from fifty yards at least.

"Go away!" growled Stephen.

He took a run at the creature, not really meaning to chase it, but hoping to give it a fright.

It snatched up its sticks and scampered off a few yards, holding them protectively against its chest

"Fence head," said his own voice inside his brain. "Ha ha. Fence head."

This angered him. He went after it, and the indigene set off ahead of him, sometimes running, sometimes skipping, sometimes leaping like a springbok with both legs together.

"Yeah, go on! Clear off into the bloody forest!" gasped Stephen as he pounded after it.

It was way too fast for him and knew it, stopping near a pond to stand there watching his heavy-footed, panting pursuit.

"Ha ha. Fence head. Scared," said the voice inside his head.

Then the indigene dived into the pond.

There was no sign of it when Stephen came gasping up to the water's edge. The pond was clear and empty. The creature must have swum through one of the hidden channels that linked the ponds together. (For in fact the so-called continent formed by the forest was not really solid land at all, but a kind of vast mangrove that covered several million square miles of Lutania's shallow freshwater ocean, with a thick floor of roots and compost.)

Stephen sank down into a clump of soft white moss. As his agitation subsided and his heart rate settled, he was surprised to find that he didn't sink into despondency, but rather into a surprisingly pleasant sense of well-being. He was struck by what a beautiful and peaceful spot it was out here by the pond. The water was crystalline, the moss soft and bright, the air silent and still, the sun still high enough in the sky to pour down light into this opening in the forest and set it apart from the sombre aisles of tree trunks all around it, so that it seemed a kind of sanctuary. Stephen felt he could happily stay here forever, if only the sun wouldn't set and his belly wouldn't ask to be fed. He wondered why he had never explored these ponds in all these past three years, only observed them from the road.

There was another pond not far off, and he made his way to it. Further from the road, this new pond seemed even more beautiful than the first one, but another still lovelier-looking one beckoned from deeper in, this one bigger than the other two, almost a small lake. On impulse he stripped and plunged in. The cool mineral-rich water was wonderfully refreshing. He dived down and thought he made out the tunnels leading away under the trees, linking this pond up to all the rest. (So what if there were indigenes swimming around down there? What harm would they do him after all? What evidence was there to suggest they would do him harm?) He swam up and down. He did some somersaults and rolls. He lay and floated on his back, looking up at the Lutanian sky. Then he hauled himself out to lie naked on the moss.

He was wakened by a slight chill on his skin. Some time must have passed, for the sun was too low to shine down into the opening in the trees, and the pond, like the rest of the forest, was in shadow His first thought was that somehow this made it still more beautiful and he sat for a while day-dreaming in the dim light with his legs in the water, until finally coldness made him dry himself down and get his clothes back on.

Then he started to wonder if he knew the direction back to the road. The other ponds were no longer visible to use as landmarks, and he realised he couldn't remember where he'd been standing in relation to the road when he'd laid his clothes on the ground.

He had a moment of pure dread. He imagined himself lost in the forest during the Lutanian night, when the indigenes and other creatures woke and began their hunt for food. He began to curse. And an old voice inside him captured his thought-stream, almost as the goblins did. *You're a fool. You can't look after yourself. You can't get anything right.*

"Get a grip on yourself, you idiot," he said out loud to himself. "All you've got to do is look for the sun."

Ten minutes later, he was safely back on the road. He felt rather ashamed of his moment of panic, comparing himself unfavourably with more competent people who he imagined would never be so foolish: Leader Wilson, Jennifer Notuna, and even Helen Fu, who remembered details about other people that he would forget at once, and had worked so hard these last three years to help him join the life of the Station.

He strode forward briskly, anxious to get to Lisoba as quickly as possible, and back to the desk in his room.

But when he turned on his screen, he found it impossible to concentrate on his current task. (It was an analysis of the effectiveness of the Agency's literacy programme.)

He began instead to go through diary he'd kept before his transmission out.

May 30th. Day 39: Got up. Had boiled egg for breakfast. Played chess for one hour then swam in pool. Watched movie King Kong (4th remake): quite enjoyed it, crap but fun. Went for a walk down to beach. Had omelette and fries for lunch, and overheard couple at the next table talking about a young bar girl who was murdered here a few weeks back. Head beaten in with a spanner, apparently. There's quite a lot of crime here, the guy was saying, but most of it is never solved. Thirty thousand tourists pass through here every week, and a lot of the people who work here are illegal migrants, so it's hard to keep tabs on who is actually here, never mind who is doing what. And anyway the locals prefer to hush crime up, if possible, so as not to put visitors off. Apparently that dead girl never even made the local news.

Stayed in restaurant for a bit reading a boring book, then gave up, binned the book and came back. Quick dip, then reread briefing documents on Lutania and worked on Luto for a couple of hours. Not much point of course if I turn out to forget all this, but I probably won't, not this early. Very tired for some reason. Chicken for dinner. Two beers. Played Solo Agent for three hours. Watched most of a porn movie on TV – girl with green hair and huge boobs who liked threesomes – don't know why. Too tired and bored to think of something better to do, I guess.

I wish they'd have let me do some work.

Just about awake enough to write this. It's only 10.30 but can't keep eyes open any more.

Yes, he remembered it perfectly well. King Kong, the omelette, the couple at the next table, the breasts of the green-haired girl: he remembered it all. Same with Day 38, 37, 36, 35, 34. All the movies, all the books, all the games, even many of the individual swims and beers. Same with 33, 32, 31. He remembered them all. In fact he remembered these days rather better than he'd normally have expected to remember days from a vacation three years previously. His awareness of the steadily increasing likelihood that he would *not* remember them had lent a frisson, a vividness, that had actually made them *more* memorable than they otherwise would have been.

June 8th. Day 30: Woke up about 5.30.

*This feels weird. Kind of exciting, but weird. There's an 87.3% chance that I won't remember anything about today at all. If that's turned out to be the case, hi my future self. You **were** alive now I promise you. Even if you don't remember it. If you want to know what it feels like to be me right now, remember a time when you were excited about something but a bit scared, and in the meantime it was really boring. Like that time Uncle Gary took you caving, and there was that long boring drive to get there.*

Anyway, I couldn't get back to sleep again so I got and went for a swim. In the sea this time. I thought it would be good on the beach when no one much was there yet. It was too and I had a good appetite for breakfast, which was...

It seemed that in anticipation of not being remembered, his past self had begun to detach itself from the person it would become, addressing him in the second person, reassuring him, offering him tips as to how to reconstruct a moment in the event that he'd forgotten it without trace. But in fact he had *not* forgotten it. On that particular Day 30 (and it wouldn't necessarily be the same this time, when he reached Day 30 again) he had turned out to be one of the 12.7% who remembered the day in its entirety. In fact he remembered it very well.

*June 9th. Day 29: Now this is **very** weird. There's a 98.5% chance I won't remember today at all. And I know for certain, I know **absolutely** for certain, that even if I do remember today, or part of it, I won't remember tomorrow. So from tomorrow on, I can get up to what I like, my future self, and you won't know it. I could get away with all kinds of things in a place like this, as long as I didn't write it down in this diary. And, you never know, I might not feel like it, not after today. Ha ha. Only kidding.*

    *No **seriously**, dear future self, I'm only kidding. The whole point of this diary is so you know what really happened. Not much point in it unless I write everything down, is there? That's why I wrote down about that porn movie I watched back on day 39 (and not just because there was a 99.1% chance that you'd remember it anyway, ha ha!!). If you remembered a thing and could see I hadn't written it down, you'd wonder, wouldn't you, what else I'd done that you **didn't** remember? And that would worry you wouldn't it?*

    *(Weird. I was going to say it would certainly worry **me!**)*

    What did I do today? I lay in bed until 9 watching TV and playing screen games. I got up and went for a pool swim before breakfast. Then I had croissants and coffee and headed off down to town to get myself a new pair of swimming shorts, for no reason except something to do (seeing as the shorts can't come with me to Lutania). I had another coffee in town and sat outside the café watching people go by: pretty girls on vacation, and not so pretty ones, migrant workers cleaning the streets and collecting the garbage. At one point a fire engine went by. They're yellow here, for some reason, not red. Then I walked to that cliff-top place to get some lunch, and then back to the hotel to watch a movie.

    The movie was called War Hero. If you've forgotten it, which you probably have, don't worry, you've not missed much. And then...

Stephen read and re-read Day 29's entry over and over. He could remember the beginning of that day, lying in bed watching TV. He remembered the croissants too, and the swimming shorts (they were green) and coffee in town, and an achingly pretty girl who walked by in a white bikini top and tiny shorts. But that was it. The yellow fire engine, the cliff-top lunch, the movie War Hero – he couldn't remember them at all.

And, worse than that, he couldn't remember the frame of mind in which he wrote the entry. Why this coquettish teasing of his future self, offering reassurance but undermining it, acknowledging his fears yet deliberately provoking them? It seemed that the less this past self of his expected to be remembered, the less it cared about the person it would become.

And that was Day 29. Even when he was writing that diary entry, he knew there was a small outside chance that he'd remember doing so. When it came to Day 28 that chance would have gone.

Yes, and there was something else he remembered about Day 29. He remembered that when he was getting out of the pool to go for breakfast, he'd thought about the next day, Day 28, the day when forgetting was a certainty, and he'd felt a strange, dark thrill. And he remembered – he was pretty sure he remembered – that he had spoken out loud to that darkness.

"No, not yet," he'd said to it, as if to a demanding child.

June 10th. Day 28: Oblivion time. No one can see me, not even you my future self. You'll remember yourself before this time, and yourself after it, but not this. So who am I, eh? Who the crap am I?

Well at least I can make a fool of myself and know I won't be ashamed about it later. Not as long as I don't write any of it down here, anyway. Ha ha. Only kidding.

No point practicing my Luto now.

Anyway, here's my exciting day. Breakfast. Pool. Chess. TV channel hopping. Solo Agent. Lunch. Town. Beach. Coffee + watched girls. TV. Dinner. 3 beers. Movie: Casino Royale (3rd remake). Solo Agent. Bed.

Yee-ha! Living the dream!

There was a kind of surliness creeping in. The tone was of an adolescent asked what he had done at school that day. This became more evident as time went on.

June 20ᵗʰ, Day 18: I'm sick of this diary. Why am I doing it? It's for your benefit not mine. Okay, okay, keep your hair on. You're me, I know, I know. Yawn.
Breakfast. Beach. Bar. Lunch. Movie (too boring to remember its name). Pool. Beer. Dinner. TV. Solo Agent. Chess. TV. Bed. That do?

The thing about surly adolescents was that, when pressed to tell, they only told the empty shell. What was inside, what was real to them, they kept back.

Stephen's Day 40 was marked at the Station by a stiff little farewell event. Leader Wilson made a speech. Everyone drank lukewarm Lutanian wine out of plastic cups and tried to think of nice things to say to a member of staff they hadn't liked all that much. His colleagues tried to make polite conversation with him about what he'd be doing next. Helen Fu, who was one of those people who feel the need to keep a group together, hugged Stephen and apologised for nagging and trying to organise him. Stephen stiffly acknowledged that he'd sometimes been unnecessarily abrupt. Then he downed a couple of full cups of wine, called out for everyone's attention, and made a short and excruciatingly awkward speech in which, to everyone's surprise and embarrassment, he apologised for having been such an unpleasant colleague.

"You're very nice people," he said, "and I'm sorry I've sometimes been unfriendly and too taken up with my work."

Helen Fu had tears in her eyes. He had redeemed himself at last! But worse than the tears in her eyes, were the ones that Stephen noticed in his own.

"I've not made the best of you all, I can see that now. But I'd like you to know that I *have* appreciated you in my own way, and I'll remember you fondly."

He'd wasted these three years, he now realised, wasted them on all kinds of levels. And the sad part was that, though he would forget the last part of his time in Lutania, he'd always remember these wasted years and the many opportunities he'd failed to take. The forgetting wouldn't begin, at the very earliest, until tomorrow morning.

When the wine was gone, some of his colleagues suggested they all go over to New Settlement (where many of them lived) to carry on drinking together. But Stephen said he really didn't mean to be unfriendly but he'd rather not.

"This has been very nice," he said. "But, if it's okay with you, I don't want my last memory of Lutania to be of me throwing up in some bar somewhere."

He even attempted a joke at his own expense.

"And anyway, you know me and nights out in bars. A man can only change himself so much."

Everyone laughed. And then the women kissed him and the men shook his hand and wished him luck, and then they all climbed into the bus, several of them calling out jovial warnings to him to walk in a straight line and not wander off into the forest. They waved to him until they'd turned the corner. He knew that when they'd settled back in their seats, they'd spend a minute or two telling each other that Stephen had been a funny sort of fellow but he wasn't so bad really, and then they'd forget him, pretty much for good.

He could have made himself part of their lives, but in fact he hadn't, and the moment for that had passed.

Bright stars packed the sky above the road, as he walked through the caramel forest, stumbling a little. He didn't see any indigenes, though once, in the distance, he saw a score or more of the vaguely pony-like creatures that the Lutanians called unicorns, emerging one by one from a pond and heading off through the trees in single file, faintly illuminated from below by the dim pink phosphorescence that came up from the moss at dead of night.

About halfway back, he stopped for a dip in another pond not far off the road. The algal-type growth that lined the ponds was also slightly luminous, so that the water glowed a faint soft pink. When he dived down into it he could see the tunnels quite clearly and unmistakably, stretching and branching away in every direction through the roots of the trees.

Jennifer and Lucia were sitting over on the bench.

"Hey, Mr Kohl!" Lucia bellowed. "We didn't think you'd be back till much later."

"Go and get some beer from the kitchen and come and join us," hollered his landlady.

They smelled pleasantly of fresh sweat and cheap perfume and cigarette smoke as they moved over to let him squeeze in between them. Their bodies felt friendly and female and warm. Jennifer opened up the flagon of beer he'd brought over from the house and passed it back to him to take the first swig.

"Day 40, eh?" Mrs Notuna said, prodding him affectionately. "A big night for you, Mr Kohl."

"So tonight's the last night you'll remember?" asked Lucia. "Is that right?"

"Not necessarily," Jennifer told her knowledgeably. "It *could* be but it probably won't. He might remember the next ten days. But after that, he'll definitely remember nothing. Imagine that. Nothing at all."

"Yava save us," said Lucia touching her forehead. She had been rolling a cigarette, and now she lit it, the flare of the match illuminating the carved god beside her.

Stephen giggled.

"You Lutanians are funny. You haven't a good word to say about the indigenes and you'd happily shoot the lot of them if you could, but you worship a god who looks just like them."

"What? Yava? A goblin?" Lucia was not only shocked by the suggestion but genuinely amazed. The thought had never once occurred to her.

"He's got nothing to do with that ugly lot, Mr Kohl, I can assure you," said Jennifer firmly. "Our ancestors brought him over with them when they first came here."

Both she and Lucia were completely unable to see, even slightly, a similarity that was commented on by every Agency worker who arrived in Lutania. But drunk though he was, Stephen knew that it would be tactless to tell them that no god back home had ever looked like Yava, and certainly not the ones that the first colonists had, as a matter of record, brought with them.

People needed their verities to be eternal. This was true, after all, even of the Agency.

"But Yava can see into your head like they can, can't he?" he said. "Isn't that what you believe?"

He passed Jennifer the flagon and she took a long swig. He felt wonderfully comfortable and at ease, with these two women on either side of him.

"Goblins can't really see into your head," Jennifer snorted dismissively, handing the flagon to Lucia.

"Well all right," she reluctantly conceded, "they reflect back what's in your head, like a mirror, but they don't *understand* anything."

Unusually, this traditional Lutanian view was broadly shared by Agency biologists, who speculated that indigenes' ability to stir up uncomfortable feelings in the minds of potential predators served the same defensive purpose as smell did for a skunk, or a nasty taste for a toad.

"They might *think* they understand," Lucia agreed, "but really they don't at all."

"Horrid creatures," sniffed Jennifer. "It's giving them too much credit to say they think at all. They might have hands and stand up on two legs, but they're only animals. I don't care what anyone says."

Then suddenly she laughed out loud.

"Honestly, Mr Kohl! You Agency people! Yava like a goblin indeed! No, of *course* not! He doesn't even come from Lutania. You ought to know that. He comes from the same place as you."

She lit up a cigarette, drew deeply on it and exhaled with a contented sigh. Nothing more seemed to need to be said on the subject of Yava and the indigenes, and the three of them sat for a while in comfortable silence.

"What bad thing would you do, Lucia," Jennifer asked after a time, "if you knew that no one you know could see you, and if you knew you wouldn't remember a thing afterwards?"

"It couldn't really happen, though, could it?" said Lucia piously, touching her forehead. "Yava could still see and remember what I did."

"Yes, all right," conceded Jennifer, with slight impatience. "But just suppose for a moment he couldn't. After all, Mr Kohl here doesn't really know about Yava does he? None of the Agency people do."

"That's because they've got bone heads," said Lucia, rapping Stephen on the forehead with her knuckles, and then giving him a little kiss on the cheek to show no hard feelings. "That's why they sit staring at those screens all the time, if you ask me. It's the only way they know how to connect up to anything."

She took a thoughtful swig of beer, then laughed.

"Okay, I'll tell you then. There's a good-looking bloke called Paul down at Porto. You know him, Jennifer, that man in the hardware store? If I really believed no one would ever know, not even Yava, and I myself wouldn't remember, perhaps I'd have a fling with him. He's asked me often enough, and why not say yes, if I knew I'd forget it completely afterwards so it wouldn't come between me and Luis?"

She considered this.

"Mind you, Paul would have to forget too."

"You've got a one-track mind, Lucia," her employer told her.

"Well you did ask, and I'm not saying I'd really do it, am I? I'm just saying *if*. Anyway, Mrs Goody-goody, how about you? What would you do?"

Jennifer puffed on her cigarette.

"All kinds of things you could do, couldn't you?" she said after a while. "You could steal something you really wanted, and then put it somewhere where you'd find it later and think that you'd just been lucky."

"*Boring!*" complained Lucia, reaching across to give Jennifer a prod. "Boring boring! Is that *really* the worst you can come up with, old lady?"

"The worst I'm telling you," Jennifer chuckled.

"And anyway," she said, "maybe you don't really know until you get in that situation. Maybe your heart keeps its secrets even from you, until it's quite sure they'll never be found out."

She took a few last thoughtful drags on her cigarette then tossed he butt end onto the ground. Suddenly she clapped her hands.

"That's *it*, isn't it, Mr Kohl?" she exclaimed. "That's the thing that bothers you. You just don't *know*."

"Yes," said Stephen. "Exactly. That's why I wanted to carry on working. So I'd have something to do and people to watch over me."

Lucia laughed.

"Well if that's all it is, it's easy to fix. Stay with Jennifer and me. Don't go away from here until it's time for your transmission. Jennifer will find you work to keep you busy, won't you Jennifer? And we'll both watch over you and see you behave yourself. It doesn't matter to us what you remember or what you forget, and when you've gone, we'll never see you again."

"Yes of course," Jennifer said. "If you really want work, there's plenty to be done round here."

"Well… Wow. Thank you. That's great. If you're really sure, of course."

Stephen's relief was so palpable that Lucia laughed and kissed him again.

"That Agency of yours is really stupid," Jennifer said, "telling you to say goodbye to everyone and go away on your own, when anyone can see that what you really need at a time like this is other people around you. Other people can be Yava's eyes for you, even if you don't believe in him. And then it doesn't matter if you remember or not."

Lucia nodded.

"You know what the trouble is with you Agency people? You try and work everything out in your heads. You try and do it all with words and ideas. And when they're gone, you think nothing's left."

"Yes," said Jennifer. "A person's more than the thoughts that go through their head, and whether they remember them or not."

On Day 39 Stephen got up early in the morning. His head was throbbing from the night's drinking, but he worked all morning for Jennifer Notuna, feeding the pigs, weeding the bean patch, and mending an old shed door. And all that afternoon, after eating lunch with Jennifer and Lucia, he worked on dismantling the remains of an old pigsty, carefully chipping the mortar off each baked brick, so it could be stacked and used again. By dinnertime, both his hands were bleeding and his back was aching, but he felt very cheerful and content, and the dinner tasted like the food of paradise.

On Day 38 he began laying foundations for a new sty, to replace the pen in which the pigs now lived. He spent most of the morning digging holes at the four corners of the new structure, right down through the soil to the matted substrate of dense tangled roots, as he had seen local builders do. (Jennifer laughed at this and reminded him it was a pigsty he was building, and not a two-storey house). Then in the afternoon he bought some bags of cement from one of Jennifer's neighbours, mixed it with gravel in batches and poured it in. There was still time after that, while the cement was setting, to go into the edge of the forest to fetch some fuel for Jennifer's stove.

After dinner, he helped Jennifer wash up the dishes (it was Lucia's day off), and then sat with her on her bench while she had her evening smoke.

"It's a shame I may not remember any of this,' he told her,

'because I honestly don't think I've ever been happier in my life."

She beamed at him proudly and patted his knee.

"Well write it in your diary if that bothers you so much. And I'll write down that it's true. We can *see* the change in you. It's like you've become a different man."

Day 30 came, the day that he had an 87.3% chance of forgetting. He fed the pigs in their new sty. He let the chickens out of their new coop. He went and checked the wind pump with its new and improved wooden mechanism. He was walking over to the yard where he planned to repair and repaint the wall, when something shifted inside him, and he admitted to himself for the first time that he was beginning to feel a little bored. It wasn't severe, it wasn't something that he couldn't easily shake off, but deep within him a tiny worm of boredom baulked for a moment at the idea of another day of chores, another day of Jennifer and Lucia proudly clucking over him as if they personally had saved his soul, another day of inhabiting this humble and dependent new persona.

"What did they think I was going to do if I went off on my own?" he muttered crossly as he began to chip loose cement of out the wall. "What did they think they were rescuing me from?"

And why was he letting them rule his life anyway? They were delightful people of course, but they knew next to nothing. Neither of them had been further than Porto or New Settlement. Neither had a reading age of more than seven.

"And let's face it," he muttered, "they're so pig ignorant here they worship a goblin and don't even know it."

He laughed, but then he checked himself.

"Come on," he distinctly heard himself say, "it's still only Day 30. All this is for later."

That scared him. The rest of the day he worked hard, and reminded himself regularly how kind Jennifer and Lucia had been to him, and how unusually content he had been these last nine days, and how much better and more rewarding (and how much *less* boring) this Day 30 had turned out compared with the one he'd spent back in that wretched seaside resort, playing screen games and watching movies alone in his room.

That evening, while Lucia and Jennifer were washing up the dinner, he took a bottle of beer and went over to the bench to wait for them.

The village was settling into evening. The sun had sunk once again below the treetops, electric lights shone here and there across the settlement, and the sights and sounds of the village took on a completely different quality from the sights and sounds of daytime. Things were closer, more intimate, more self-contained.

A cockerel crowed. Someone banged on a metal pan. A mother shouted to her children. Mr and Mrs Roberti ate out in their yard, silent but for the chink of cutlery on plates. Mad Gretel called something out and laughed. Mr Zorrona and his sons hacked and chipped away stubbornly at a new irrigation channel, though they were only vague silhouettes in the dusk. A moped emerged into the clearing, its headlights sweeping across the wooden wall of a barn on which *YAVA SEES ALL* was painted in Luto in large red and white letters.

It was all so familiar and so small.

"Mummy's boy," said his own voice suddenly inside his head.

Stephen started. It took him a few seconds to locate the indigene in the dark, but the creature was actually directly behind him, just outside the boundary fence. It was squatting with its left shoulder pressed up against the chainlink, absorbed with some object it was holding right up close to its face and turning this way and that in its hands.

"Go away, you nosy thing," growled Jennifer, coming over to join on the bench. "Get away with you!"

She chucked handfuls of dirt at the creature. When that didn't shift it, she went up and kicked the fence.

The goblin stood up. Smiling, or seeming to smile, it held out the object it had been playing with, almost as if it intended to taunt them with a treasure that it possessed and they didn't. But the object itself was a small empty pod, such as could be found all over the forest floor, and perhaps the gesture had no real meaning at all.

"Mummy's boy. Tee hee."

"Horrid creatures," muttered Jennifer as it skipped off into the forest.

She settled herself onto the bench with a weary but contented sigh, and took out her tobacco and papers from her apron pocket.

Then she turned to him and smiled.

"All well with you Mr Kohl?"

It was odd. He had to force himself to meet her friendly gaze.

On Day 29, Jennifer and Lucia arranged a party for Stephen to mark the last day that he might possibly still remember after he returned home. Everyone came to eat their food and to drink Stephen's health: Mr and Mrs Zorrona and their boys, Mr and Mrs Roberti, Lucia's handsome husband Luis and their children, Jorge Cervantes and his two wives, the other lodgers, even Mad Gretel, who the villagers thought was possessed... Everyone in the village came, and everyone listened to Lucia and Jennifer telling the tale yet again of how they'd persuaded Stephen to stay on and help them rather than go away and be alone during his final days in Lutania.

"He's never been so happy in his life," they told everyone proudly, after they'd made the traditional chicken sacrifice to Yava, "he's told us so himself."

The villagers had heard this before, many times over in fact, in various versions both at first and second hand, but they gladly heard it again, and gladly repeated it yet again to one another, for it gloriously vindicated the simple peasant way of life which the Agency was always nagging them to change, and from which their own young people were increasingly prone to flee.

Stephen was not at ease. He hated the way the villagers prodded him and poked him and plied him with drinks. He hated the sense of himself as a prized exhibit.

"I'm very tired," he told Jennifer and Lucia towards midnight. "I think I'll head off to bed."

The three of them were sitting on the yard wall under the stars, Stephen beside the two women. Neighbours sat around them on kitchen chairs and wooden boxes, watching and listening minutely.

Stephen cleared his throat.

"I've decided to go away for a bit in the morning," he told the two of them, feeling the hot blood prickling round the roots of his hair. "I think I'll go over to Balos. May as well check that out before I say goodbye to Lutania, even if I won't be able to remember it."

There was an audible collective sigh of surprise and disappointment, and then the neighbours all turned to Jennifer or Lucia

162

to observe how they received this news

"But we thought you were going to stay until the time for your transmission!" said Jennifer.

"Yes but, like my boss said, when you think about it, it's really not such a bad idea to grab the chance of a vacation."

"You can take your vacation here. Stop work and put your feet up here in Lisoba. That's fine with us."

"Balos is a big bad place, Mr Kohl," said Jorge Cervantes. "It's not somewhere to go for a holiday."

The rest of the little audience agreed. People began to tell stories about folk from Lisoba and the neighbouring villages who'd gone to Balos and come to harm. Mr Roberti told of a girl who became a drug addict and ended up in prison. Mrs Zorrona of a boy who'd worked for a whole year on an Agency building site, and then lost everything he'd earned in a single night's gambling in Balos. And two or three people mentioned the well-known case of a young woman called Susan from Porto who had gone to Balos less than a year ago, and ended up being raped and killed.

"She was all cut up apparently," said Mr Zorrona..

"Cut wide open," said Mrs Roberti with a certain grim satisfaction, "and all her insides taken out. And it wasn't done by foreigners. They were village boys, as Lutanian as she was."

(The stories might be exaggerated, but, in spite of its University and its Academy of Science, Balos really was a lawless place, full of bewildered Lutanians trying to be city people when their whole culture had evolved for small villages like Lisoba, where everyone knew everyone else, and countless iterations of Yava were always present to watch over those few moments that neighbours overlooked.)

"I appreciate your concern," Stephen interrupted after the sixth or seventh story, "but you do need to remember I'm not some naïve peasant. I grew up in a big city. *Really* big. You've no idea. Balos might seem big and scary to you but it's a quiet little backwater to me."

They all stared at him. If Balos was a backwater, what did that make Lisoba?

Stephen rubbed his hands over his burning face.

"I know I should have given you notice," he told Jennifer, "and of course I'll pay you the full rent up to the day of my transmission."

He made himself meet her eyes for just one moment. He could

Chris Beckettt

see how hurt she was, how humiliated in front of the village. Then he turned quickly away.

None of this really mattered, he told himself. It was past midnight. Day 29 had gone.

Turning away from all of them, he looked out into the dark and smiled.

our länd

"The Romans sir," said a girl with pebble glasses at the front of the class.

"Yes. Yes, that's right, Jessica, the Romans," agreed Thomas Turner.

He was a history teacher, and he was teaching history to class 7G.

"Well done, Jenny," said Thomas belatedly, remembering that Jenny was not very bright and needed encouragement.

He was feeling rather strange, rather distant, as if he was looking out at the world from the end of a long tunnel.

"The Romans. Exactly so, Jenny. And who lived in these parts *before* the Romans?"

It was a hot day, he supposed, a hot stuffy day and he was tired. From outside the open window he heard, with pleasure and some surprise (for he'd never heard one so close to the school), the lovely song of a skylark.

"The Brythons," said a boy at the back called Edward – and for some reason everyone hissed.

Thomas was puzzled. He hadn't noticed before that Edward had a speech impediment. And why the animosity?

He really was feeling *very* peculiar. Perhaps he was unwell. Perhaps he was anaemic or something?

"The *Britons*, Edward" he corrected. "The ancient *Britons*." But to his surprise this sounded all wrong. So now, having corrected Edward, he corrected himself: "The Brythons, rather. That's right, Edward. Well done. The Brythonic Celts."

There was a leak in the ceiling in the middle of the classroom and rust-coloured water was dripping into a grimy plastic bucket. Somehow he'd never noticed it before. Nor had he ever seen that large piece of lino that was missing from the middle of the floor, with the rough boards showing beneath, or the paint that was flaking off the metal window frames...

He cleared his throat.

"And of course in 300 AD or thereabouts," he said, "the Romans expelled the Brythons. Most of them made their homes in Gaul and Iberia, in the countries we now call France and Catalonia and Spain, from where they spread out into the New World."

Catalonia *and* Spain?

It was *hot*. Outside the window the skylark went twittering on.

"…and many of them assimilated into the local population which at that time was Celtic-speaking like the Brythons themselves. But a small number held onto to their own Brythonic faith, in spite of persecution, maintaining that the Brythons were the chosen people of God – y *pobl Duw* – and that their lost homeland of Logres – *Lloegr* as they called it – remained their birthright, given to them by God himself when Joseph of Arimathea planted his staff at Avalon, cut from the same tree as Christ's crown of thorns. Or so they believe anyway."

The odd thing was that, though his own voice was saying it, all of this was news to Thomas the teacher. He had never referred to the Ancient Britons as Brythons before. He had never heard before of them being expelled by the Romans. He had never heard of the Brythonic *faith*.

"A century or so ago, Brythons from the Americas and from mainland Europe began to settle in this country, believing that, even after seventeen hundred years, it was still theirs, although we English had been living here all this time and the country itself was now called England…"

He had never heard of any of this before. He had no idea where any of it was coming from. It was all very eerie and odd, and yet there was something familiar about this feeling all the same. He had a vague memory of there having been another time like this, like the memories we have in dreams of other dreams long since forgotten in waking life. He knew that this wasn't the first time that he had stood in front of the class intending to tell one story and another completely different one had come out of his mouth.

In fact now he thought about it, he realised there had actually been a whole string of these moments. And now, quite suddenly, he could see them quite clearly, stretching back through time. He found he could contemplate them while his mouth continued to teach its unfamiliar lesson on its own. It was as if he had emerged from the mist onto a hilltop from which he was able to see other peaks all round him that were normally hidden from view.

And he knew too that soon they would all be hidden again. He would forget. He would forget all the histories except one. He would believe that it was the only history there was...

"Excuse me, sir. Do we need to write all this down?" asked Belinda Dewsbury.

"Oh for goodness sake girl, not *now*," Thomas snapped, "Can't you see I'm trying to remember something."

Belinda looked as if he had struck her across the face. There were tears forming in her eyes. Oh God, what was he doing? Everyone knew that poor Belinda had been having dreadful problems at home. The whole class was staring at him, appalled.

"Sorry," he said. "Sorry Belinda. Sorry everyone. Distracted for a moment there. No, no need to write all this down. All this is just by way of a general introduction."

Oh dear. Something had distracted him and you couldn't afford to let that happen when you were standing in front of thirty teenagers. But what had it been? What had he been thinking about? There'd been something important, something he had badly wanted not to forget...

He looked down at the textbook on his desk, hoping for clues. *English History* it was called, tattered and threadbare like the classroom itself, and at least twenty years old. It seemed familiar, and yet simultaneously it seemed strange. He felt pretty sure that it wasn't the same book that he'd laid there at the beginning of the class. For surely that had been a new book, recently published, with a shiny blue and white cover?

"Now where was I?" he said, playing for time, in as hearty a voice as he could manage.

And then the bell went. As the children rushed out he turned out of habit to wipe clean the whiteboard and then remembered that the school had never had whiteboards.

"It's as if I'm in two places at once."

The book of English history fell into three pieces when he picked it up. So he stacked them together again and placed the battered volume carefully back into his briefcase. The heat and humidity was pressing down on him. His head was aching, and he felt a faint twinge of nausea. He felt he had been travelling for miles and miles. Yet this was just Ely and he had only driven the few miles in from Sutton as he did every morning.

What was I thinking about back then? he asked himself. *What was it that I remembered?*

As he stepped out of the classroom a Logrian helicopter gunship was passing low overheard.

A *Logrian* helicopter?

He was momentarily surprised by the age and shabbiness of his car, but by the time he'd got inside and started it up, he was no longer asking himself questions. It didn't seem unusual to him that the roads of this Fenland city were crumbling, nor that a pervasive smell of burnt rubber hung over the place. He didn't wonder why the famous cathedral tower was pockmarked with bullet holes. It didn't strike him as odd that from time to time he passed a heap of rubble where a house had once stood or that a tank squatted by the road out of town with its gun trained at the passing cars. And he knew without thinking about it that the initials "BCL" stencilled on the tank's turret stood for *Byddin Cenedlaethol Lloegr*, the National Army of Logres.

Under the bored eye of two Logrian soldiers lounging against the tank – a tall black man and a Latin-looking woman – he pulled over outside a house on the outskirts of town, honked his horn and got out of the car. The black soldier ran his tongue over his lips and put his hand to his gun strap.

"Just letting my friend know I'm here," Thomas called out to him in Brythonic, without wondering how or when he'd learnt this Celtic tongue.

It's always best to let the soldiers know what's going on, he said to himself. When people were edgy and jumpy and sometimes trigger-happy, it was best not to keep them guessing or to spring things on them.

He took a square of rag out of his pocket and wiped his shining face. His wife had cut up the rags, he suddenly remembered with a complicated mixture of painful emotions. He had a wife called Jenny and a son called William who was twenty-one. Jenny had weary, bitter eyes and she filled her time up with repetitive money-saving tasks like cutting rags into handkerchiefs. William mostly sat in the living room and watched TV.

"*What* you said?" called out the black soldier in broken English.

"It's my friend Richard," Thomas called back in Brythonic. "I'm just honking my horn to let him know I'm here. I'm giving him a lift home."

The soldier just perceptibly nodded.

"Ah, here he is!" called out Thomas again, as Richard Duckett emerged from the house where he'd been working all day, a big, sturdy man with a round, open face.

Richard lived in Sutton too. He had a son called Harry who was a friend of Williams, and a wife... Thomas felt a stab of grief... *Richard had a wife called Liz who was Thomas' first and only love.*

Richard was accompanied by a stocky stranger with close-cropped hair.

"Hey, Tom!" he called, giving a quick angry glance at the BCL. "Mind if Jack here comes too? He's been helping me out today."

"No that's fine," Tom said. "How do you do, Jack?"

"Hello mate," Jack said. His accent immediately identified him as one of the refugees from Birmingham who lived in the Churchill Camp. "Thanks for the lift. Appreciate it mate."

The two of them climbed into the car in a hot blast of plaster dust and sweat, Jack in the back and Richard in the front. Characteristically, Richard reached forward at once for the knob of the car radio.

"It's no good, Richard," Thomas told him as he started up the car. "It doesn't work anymore."

"Damn," Richard said. "Well get home quickly, will you, so we can listen to the news there."

"What news?"

"What do you mean 'what news'? Haven't you heard? Blair has just cut a deal with the Brythons. He's conceded the lost land."

"How do you mean he's conceded it?"

"He's agreed to accept the existence of the State of Logres."

"What... He's... Are you sure? On what terms?"

"On the basis that they'll let him return and set up a government of sorts here in part of the occupied area."

"And the Brythons have *agreed* to that?" Thomas asked. "To Blair coming back out of exile?"

"Yup. They've agreed he can return and set up an administration in Ipswich."

"Blair back in England. I can't believe it."

"I don't know what he thinks he's playing at," said Richard, "but I bet the Brythons can't believe their luck."

"He's bloody sold out," Jack said.

Thomas thought privately that Blair had probably struck the best deal they were going to get, but he would have found it hard to say this even to Richard, let alone to Richard's friend. All the inhabitants of Churchill Camp had lost their homes – and pretty much everything else – when Birmingham was taken by the Brythonic militias and renamed Dinas Emrys, 'City of Ambrosius'. Virtually all its English population had been driven out at gun point. A significant number had been killed.

There was a BCL checkpoint just beyond Wilburton. Three young Logrian soldiers stood beside the barrier, guns over their shoulders and an armoured car parked beside them. The flag of Logres – the thorn bush on its golden field – fluttered over their heads.

Thomas pulled up and leant out of the window:

"*Sut dych chi heddiw?*" he asked the soldier who came to check his papers.

The soldier was surprised to have an Englishman ask him how he was in any language, let along in Brythonic.

"*Da iawn,*" he muttered uncomfortably, looking at Thomas' identity documents and then at Richard's and Jack's and passing them back through the window.

"Okay," he said in bad English, "you could go now."

He gestured to one of his companions to lift the barrier.

"I wish you wouldn't talk their language to them," muttered Richard, as they passed through. "This is England. We're English. Why should we change the way we talk for people who came here from outside?"

Thomas shrugged.

"It gets me through the checkpoints quicker."

And it invariably winds you up, he silently added.

"I speak Brythonic better than a lot of them do actually," Thomas said. "I reckon that chap there would have been a lot happier talking in Spanish."

Richard snorted with disgust.

"Well they're not really Brythons at all are they? They're Spaniards and Frenchmen and Africans and Christ knows what, who've persuaded themselves that claiming to have a distant ancestor from these parts entitles them to live here."

Thomas said nothing. Not that he disagreed. It was just that he felt there was only so many times that it was useful to repeat the same point.

"Want me to fix that radio of yours?" Richard asked after a while.

He was good with electrical things. He had once, in more prosperous times, been the technical director of a large electronics company down in Cambridge.

"It's probably not worth bothering," Thomas said, swerving to avoid a pothole. "It's as old as the car. Fifteen years. I'm surprised it lasted as long as it did."

"Well we've got to make things last nowadays haven't we?" observed the Brummie Jack in the back.

And then the radio came unexpectedly to life.

"Of course we must have the historic centre of London," Chairman Blair was saying in his disarming bloke-next-door way, "including, you know, the Houses of Parliament..."

"Oh," said Thomas. "It must just have been a loose connection."

"Ssssh!" Richard commanded.

"...London is the capital of England, after all," said Blair, though the Brythons had always insisted that Llundain was a Celtic name and that Londinium had been a Romano-Brythonic city long before the first Anglo-Saxon ever set foot there.

"...and of course, while we are prepared to recognise, you know, the State of Logres, our people must have the right to return to their own homes if they want to."

"I want to go back to *Birmingham*," said Jack the Brummie. "I don't want to go back to Dinas bloody Emrys."

"But, look, we must be realistic," Blair said. "Logres is here to stay. We are going to have to make peace with our Brythonic neighbours."

The radio was tuned to Radio England, a Flanders-based station set up by the exiled Free England Committee of which Blair was the chairman. Now it played extracts of statements from the President of France, the Chancellor of Prussia and the Foreign Minister of Spain, all praising Mr Blair for the statesmanlike thing that he had done and saying how wonderful it was that the English might now have a nation of their own again and rejoin the European family, alongside the new

Brythonic nation of Logres.

"Jesus," murmured Richard softly.

It took a bit of getting used to. Blair was not only the chair of the Free England Committee but the leader of the Labour Party of England, an organisation which had spent the last fifty years fighting for the restoration of England as a single unified state. It the process it had spilled a fair amount of blood. But now, in exchange for being allowed to return and set up some sort of semi-autonomous government, he had settled for this: not the whole country, not even half of it, but the twenty-odd percent of it which had not to date been formally annexed by the Brythonic state.

"It's going to be a rolling programme," Blair said. "To start with, the Logrian Army will withdraw from Ipswich and I'm going to set up an administration there. Once we get that established and thrash out some more of the details, the Logrians will gradually withdraw from more land. Of course I don't pretend it's going to be easy, but the idea is to agree the final border sometime in the next five years. There are some difficult questions to sort out first, of course. You know, like the status of London, and the return of refugees – and what to do about all the Brythonic settlements we've got in the occupied area. But I want to say this: we are working towards a solution, the best solution that can be achieved. The time for armed struggle is over."

Thomas turned off the potholed surface of the main road onto the dirt track that led into Churchill Camp. It was called a camp but actually it was really a small town of five thousand people, bigger than Sutton itself. Little Brummie children and Brummie dogs were playing in narrow alleys between the corrugated iron huts.

"Just along here mate," Jack said. "This will do fine."

Richard lived just across the road from Thomas, on the edge of the Sutton ridge with the wide Fens below.

"Come in and look at the news on TV, why don't you Tom?" he said. "You can translate for me. I'd really like to know what they're saying about this on the Brythonic stations."

"I don't know Richard. I think maybe I should go straight home."

"Just for a bit," his friend pleaded. "I do really want to know what they're saying."

Thomas glanced guiltily across the road at his own house. He couldn't say he was particularly looking forward to going back to Jenny. She was *so* weary and flat and empty these days, and she was prone to a certain kind of thin, angry weeping which refused to be comforted or shared.

And of course he always looked forward to seeing Richard's Liz.

"Okay ten minutes then."

Richard led the way straight into the front room where his son Harry sat at a table tinkering with the dismantled parts of a computer.

"All right Tom?" Harry grunted, bending down further over his task.

Richard turned on the TV. On the screen a well-known Logrian politician was holding forth. A big dark Argentinian, Ieuan Ffranceg (nee Juan Franco) was the powerful leader of the settlers' bloc. Now he was denouncing the new agreement in a fractious Logrian parliament. .

"The counties of Eastern Logres," he bawled, as if explaining something very simple to an exceptionally unintelligent and recalcitrant child, "are every bit as much the sacred birthright of our people as are Western Logres, Northern Logres, Llundain and Dinas Emrys. The final frontier of Logres must include the *whole* of the historic kingdom of Arthur and Ambrosius. It must include not only the present State of Logres and the so-called occupied areas but also Scotland as far as the Antonine Wall. To accept less would be to betray the legacy bequeathed to us by God."

He made an exasperated gesture.

"I really can't understand what these Saxons keep whinging about!" he exclaimed. "They already have a country. It's called Saxony. The clue is in the name. Why don't they go back to where they came from?"

"These people talk as if the last seventeen centuries were *nothing!*" Thomas said wonderingly, after translating this for Richard. "I couldn't even say exactly where Saxony is."

"Self-centred bastards," Richard growled, "they nurture grievances from two thousand years ago, but expect us to forget ours when they've still in living memory."

"They don't really see us as people, that's the difficulty," Thomas said. "Their history and faith has made their destiny seem so self-evidently important to them that anyone who gets in their way is simply a *problem*."

"Why must you always try and *understand* them?" Richard grumbled. "Why should we *care* about their motives?"

"Hello Tom!"

It was Richard's wife Liz, a lively, pretty, woman with bright, restless, merry eyes, who Thomas had secretly loved since he was fifteen. As ever a knife blade twisted in his heart. Oh God how different she was from his own wife Jenny, across the road there, pale and colourless and flat, at the bottom of her grey sea of misery.

"Coffee anyone?" Liz asked, quickly averting her eyes from Thomas'.

"For Christ's sake, Liz," Richard growled, "never mind coffee. Come and watch this. Your own country being sold."

"Oh Richard leave it!" she said. "It's not good for you, all this anger. You know the news now. We all know it. You can't do anything about it. Turn off the TV and talk about something else."

But their son Harry, who'd been sitting quietly in a corner, backed his father up.

"You should be *more* angry, Mum, not Dad less. Where's your pride? Think what we could have been if it wasn't for the invaders!"

Since Richard had lost his job in Cambridge, things had been very hard for the Ducketts financially. He had once briefly tried to make money by doing factory work in the State of Logres itself (first in Llundain, then eighty miles away in the city of Rhydychen, which the English had once called "Oxford"). But then came the first violent English uprising against Logrian rule, and all work permits for English people had been cancelled. Richard now had to eke out a living locally as a general purpose handyman. It wasn't easy when no one had money to spare.

"I'm not saying we shouldn't be angry," Liz said. "I just think being angry shouldn't become the *only* thing we are."

Which is what Thomas thought too.

But he knew he ought to go.

"Look," he said, "I'm sorry but I really must be getting home. Jenny will be worrying about the news as well. And wondering if I'm okay."

As he crossed the road back to his house a BCL jeep was going by. He didn't pay it any attention at first but it stopped right beside him.

Thomas tensed, as any English person would have done, anticipating mockery, or humiliating demand , or even possibly even a beating.

But the voice that called out to him was entirely friendly.

"Good news, Mr Turner, don't you agree? Peace! Peace in prospect at last!"

"Colonel Rhys."

Thomas reluctantly acknowledged the Logrian, conscious of the inquisition that would face him if any member of Richard's family were to see him talking in an amiable way to a BCL officer. But actually the two men met quite regularly at work, Thomas having a community liaison role at school and Colonel Rhys being the BCL civil liaison officer for the East Cambridgeshire military district.

"I've always thought if it had been down to people like you and I, we would have reached a solution long ago," said Colonel Rhys in his bad, French-accented English.

A stocky, balding man with prominent eyebrows and a quick but slightly mocking smile, the colonel had grown up in Paris. In civilian life he was an academic chemist and, as a strictly secular Brython, he had always made a point of differentiating himself from the religious Brythons and their talk of the holy destiny of the Brythonic Celts. Thomas actually rather liked him.

"Maybe," he said with an awkward laugh.

Colonel Rhys reached out from his jeep to shake Richard's hand.

"Maybe one of these days you and I will be able to sit in a pub with a pint of English beer and laugh about all this nonsense. We Brythons and you English have so much in common really don't we? We are all Northern Europeans after all!"

Thomas looked anxiously over the Colonel's shoulder at the Duckett's house

On Saturday morning, Thomas went over to see his mother Doreen in her bungalow on the far side of the village. It was a depressing errand. There was so little that he could share with her and so little she could share with him. She was eighty-two and suffered not only with emphysema but with Alzheimer's disease. In her mind she was back in the days of her adolescence when England was England, Logres did not exist and the Brythonic immigration had only just begun.

"I really think the government ought to do more for us old

people," she grumbled at one point. "We built this country up, we paid taxes, and look at the thanks we get!"

On the way back home, Thomas heard the angry shouting of young men ahead of him.

There was a small crowd outside the church, consisting of a group of young English youths from the village and from Churchill Camp, and a group of young Logrians up from the fortified Brythonic settlement of Tre Morfa. The young settlers were armed with automatic rifles. They had unrolled banners protesting against the deal between their government and Chairman Tony Blair.

GOD GAVE EASTERN LOGRES TO *US*!

THERE IS NO SUCH PEOPLE AS 'THE ENGLISH'

SAXONS BELONG IN SAXONY

About three hundred Logrians lived in the Tre Morfa settlement. Surrounded by a high razor wire fence and CCTV cameras, it was on the opposite side of the village to the five thousand Brummies in the Churchill Camp and it occupied about the same amount of land.

"Fuck off Logrian scum!" the English crowd shouted. "This is England! We'll bury you! We'll fucking bomb you into the sea!"

The Logrians, outnumbered but made confident by their guns, shouted back:

"England? What's 'England'? This is Logres! *You* belong in Saxony! That's *why* you're called Saxons. Duh!"

"We're *not* called Saxons. We're English. And we were born here."

Thomas sighed. Soon some English idiot would start throwing stones and then another idiot on the Logrian side would point a gun and then...

Richard's son Harry was at the front of the English crowd:

"Convenient how your God tells you to steal land from other people," he called out.

"How can we steal what is already ours?" one of the settlers shouted back in strongly French-accented English (the Tre Morfa settlers came from Montreal and still spoke French among themselves.)

"How can it be yours when *we've* lived here for a thousand years?" called out Thomas' own son William from the back of the crowd. "And you lot were living in Canada until a few years ago."

"Because God gave it to *us*, scumbag, and *you* had no right to take it."

Thomas broke in before anyone else could reply.

"Leave it, all of you," he told the English group. "You're giving them exactly what they want. Ignore them and walk away."

Being a schoolmaster gave him a certain authority. The English kids reluctantly began to disperse.

"Scared are you, Saxons?" the settlers jeered after them.

"Keep walking away!" Thomas told his compatriots.

But he couldn't resist one small jibe at the Logrians himself: "If you're so brave," he said in Brythonic, "why don't you leave your guns behind next time?"

"I thought you said to ignore them," said Harry Duckett afterwards, but Thomas could see that he'd risen a little in his young neighbour's estimation.

A couple of days later Thomas had to take his mother Doreen for an appointment at Addenbrooke's hospital down in Cambridge. She needed to have the fluid drained from her lungs. Jenny came too to help. The appointment was at one o'clock but, although it was only about fifteen miles down to Cambridge, they set out at seven with the aim of getting through the BCL checkpoint at Cottenham before the queues grew too long.

At first Jenny and Thomas congratulated themselves on their plan. There were only ten vehicles ahead of them in the queue at the checkpoint and they thought they'd get through in an hour or so and maybe have time to look round a few shops and find a cup of coffee somewhere before it was time to get to the hospital.

Jenny, by her standards, was almost cheerful.

"Not that there's much *in* the shops these days, mind you," she said.

But, even if the shops were bare, things seemed a little more normal in Cambridge than they did out in Sutton, sandwiched as Sutton was between the two sets of incomers in Churchill Camp and the Tre Morfa settlement. In Cambridge you could almost imagine that you were in a place called England, and not in that strange contested place called the Eastern Occupied Territories.

Four cars passed through the checkpoint. There were three young Logrian soldiers there as usual with an armoured personnel carrier. They asked for papers, peered into the vehicles, looked at luggage, asked people what their business was. It was slow and tedious but there were no special problems until the fifth car reached the front. Perhaps the driver was known to them, perhaps he was deliberately provocative, perhaps the soldiers simply felt in the mood for a change of routine, but for whatever reason suddenly the mood changed. The soldiers shouted at the young red-headed driver and his girlfriend get out – "Now! Now! Let's go, Saxons!" – and proceeded to empty his suitcases out onto the road and poke through the contents with their rifle barrels. The man protested loudly. His girlfriend began to weep.

Thomas looked at Jenny and saw the little spark of humour and hope fading once again in his wife's eyes.

"We should have started earlier," she said flatly. "We should have known things would be slow just now."

She clenched and unclenched her hands.

"Damn, damn, *damn*!" she hissed. "We're *so* stupid. Stupid, stupid, stupid. We should have *known*."

Things had been tense since the deal between the Logrian government and Blair. Rejectionists on both sides had accused their leaders of selling out and had begun to react with violence. It was obvious, at least with hindsight, that the soldiers were going to be on edge.

The day was getting warm.

"Why aren't we at the hospital yet, Tom?" whimpered Doreen in the back of the car. "I'm so hot. And I'm going to need the toilet soon."

Then the red-headed owner of the suitcase made the mistake of shoving one of the soldiers. The soldier, a Spanish-looking boy ablaze with the full bloom of adolescent acne, rammed him back against the personnel carrier, shoving his gun into the young man's face. The man's girlfriend screamed and the soldier backed off a little. The woman then went to pick up the contents of the suitcase that were strewn over the road, only to be ordered to stop. When she ignored this, another soldier came forward and very roughly pushed her back so she stumbled and fell. At this drivers and passengers from other cars began to get out and protest.

"What do you think you're doing?"

"Leave the girl alone!"

"What's happening Tom?" Doreen called out. "Why can't we go

now? What's all this waiting for?"

"It's all right mum," Thomas said, "It's just the soldiers…"

"What soldiers? Why are there soldiers here? Are we having a war?"

It was no good trying to explain to her. She lived her life at a time before the occupation began, when the country called Logres didn't even exist except in storybooks.

"It's just… the police. Just the police, mum, that's all."

The soldiers were badly rattled by all the people getting out of their cars. For a moment Thomas actually felt sorry for them. They were only boys, after all, younger than Jenny and Thomas' own son William, and there were only three of them there, alone in a hostile land where many people would cheerfully kill them.

Suddenly one of the soldiers fired some shots in the air and everyone dived for cover.

"Get back in your cars and wait!" the soldier shouted. "Do you understand? In your cars *now*!"

Another half-hour went by. Eventually the owner of the suitcase and his girlfriend, still unable to get through, jumped into their car, did a U-turn and roared back the way they had come with much squealing of brakes and grinding of gears. The next car crawled forward. There were another three before Thomas and Jenny's turn. Behind them another twenty vehicles were waiting. Even with all the windows wound down it was now very hot indeed.

"I need the toilet," Doreen whimpered, "I can't wait any more."

Thomas got out of the car and called to the soldiers in Brythonic.

"Excuse me. It's my mother. She's eighty-two. She needs to go to the toilet. Could we just…"

"Are you deaf or something, Saxon? I said stay in your fucking car."

He got back in. After a few minutes a spreading stench told him his mother hadn't been able to hold on.

It was quarter to one by the time they got to the front of the queue and Thomas and Jenny, nauseated by the stink, had both vomited out of the windows. The spotty-faced soldier ordered all three of them to get out so they could be searched.

"Holy Joseph!" he exclaimed in Brythonic as Doreen climbed

unsteadily out. "The old bag has shit herself!"

The other Logrians laughed.

Thomas knew the best thing for everyone would be if he could contain himself – Doreen didn't understand Brythonic after all and had no idea what had just been said about her – but his nerves were at breaking point.

"That's my mother you're talking about, you cruel, rude little boy!"

Immediately the soldier swung up his rifle and hit Thomas round the head with the barrel.

"Who are you calling a boy you Saxon arsehole!"

Thomas was momentarily dazed. Everything moved in slow motion and seemed very far away… and he remembered the strange sensation that he had had in the classroom a few days previously.

This particular world, he realised, this particular England, this particular history, was just one of many that he'd passed through. It wasn't real, or not real in the sense that all these people around him, English and Logrian, thought it was. Even the people weren't real in the way they thought they were.

A spotty young boy from one imaginary nation had just struck a cautious old school teacher from another imaginary nation that happened to occupy the same space. The schoolteacher was Thomas Turner, aged 52 and born a few miles away in Sutton, Cambridgeshire. The soldier (Thomas didn't ask himself how he knew) was Private Salvador Galego, aged 19, born in Madrid to a schoolteacher mother and a father who was a minister in the Spanish Brythonic Church.

"Tom?" Jenny called to him, fearful and yet somehow resentful too. "What are you doing?"

There was a lark high above them, Tom suddenly noticed. Through all of this, its strange, rapid, angular little song went on and on. Thomas peered upward, trying to find the little bird. But it was hiding in the white hot sun.

"Yes, I'm fine. As a matter of fact I'm just trying to spot the lark."

Salvador Galego, the acne-faced soldier, didn't have enough English to understand what Thomas was saying, but he was unnerved by Thomas' apparent indifference to the situation in hand. It seemed to him subversive.

"Get back in the car Saxon!" he shouted at Thomas. "And take that stinking old woman away from here."

The lark went on singing in the sun. Thomas considered the anger of the Logrian soldier with interest. Then his attention became drawn to a certain loud high-pitched sound coming from nearby. It was a frail old woman called Doreen who had no idea where she was or who the foreigners with guns were that had just hit her son round the face. After a moment he remembered that she was his mother and that the weary grey woman with her was his wife.

"It's all right mum," he said, smiling at her. "It's all all right. Get back in the car and we'll have you sorted out in no time."

He noticed a chill on his cheek, touched it and looked down in surpise at the redness on his hand.

When Jenny and Thomas finally got home that night, their son William was in the front room playing video games with Harry Duckett. Doreen was to stay the night with them and Thomas helped Jenny to get her bathed and calmed down and tucked up in bed. Then he went to the kitchen and heated up the pasta that Willam had made for them two hours previously. Harry followed him.

"How did you get that mark on your face?" he demanded.

He was like his father. In any other area of life the Ducketts would be the first to forgive a wrong done to them. But when it came to the Brythons, they were implacable. They never let it rest.

"It was the soldiers, wasn't it?" Harry persisted. "One of them at the checkpoint hit you."

"It was my own fault really."

"What do you mean your own fault?"

"Well, I…"

"Did you attack him?"

"No, but I called him a silly boy."

"Good for you. This is *our* land. You've lived here all your life. So did your father and your grandfather before you."

Thomas laid cutlery on the table for Jenny and himself.

"I'm rather tired, Harry. I'm sure you're right. But I'd prefer just to forget it now if you don't mind."

"But that's all wrong! You can't just forget it or they'll have beaten us. You might as well emigrate and let them help themselves to everything."

Actually Thomas had been increasingly tempted to do just that. He could get a job abroad as a teacher, with better pay and a life free of checkpoints and curfews and daily humiliations. He was getting tired of the struggle to hold onto the idea of England. He couldn't help thinking that perhaps England had had its day.

"So what happened?" Harry pressed him.

"If I tell you will you let it drop?"

"Okay. For now."

So Thomas told him: about being forced to stay in the car, about Doreen soiling herself, about the insulting comment and his reaction.

Harry exploded; "The callous *bastards*! An old woman of eighty-two! In the country where she was born! How *dare* they?"

"You said you'd let it drop."

"Yes, but…" Harry checked himself with difficulty. "Well all right. But just for the moment."

Jenny came down. She and Thomas picked at their pasta. William and Harry sat with them for a bit, William trying to make conversation, Harry dark and glowering in the background, saying nothing at all. Later on Harry went out to meet someone and William and Thomas watched TV. Then Jenny went off to the kitchen and had one of her solitary little cries.

Thomas kept thinking about that lark twittering in the sun and wondering what it was that it seemed to remind him of.

In the middle of the night there was a series of explosions out on the Fen. Thomas jumped out of bed and ran to the window. He couldn't see anything at first but he heard gunfire, then silence.

"What is it, Tom?" Jenny wanted to know.

He shrugged and got back into bed. Neither slept.

Half an hour later they heard the throbbing of helicopters low overhead, not just one of them but several going to and fro, their spotlights sweeping the village and from time to time flooding the bedroom with an ice-blue daylight that disappeared as quickly as it came. Some time later tanks and armoured troop carriers came clanking and rumbling into Sutton and there were more spotlights, more icy, comfortless false dawns.

"…By order of the Eastern Logres Command," crackled a megaphone on a BCL jeep on the road outside, "this district is under indefinite curfew...."

"Remain in your homes," replied another megaphone over in the direction of the church. "Any Saxon found in the street is liable to arrest and detention. We will shoot if necessary..."

The first jeep came back: "Sutton village and Churchill camp are now subject to curfew under the Prevention of Terror regulations. Do not come out of your houses. Our orders are to shoot to kill if this is necessary to maintain order..."

The phones were still working at first. Villagers called one another. The story went round that someone had managed to get some sort of homemade rocket launcher in through the outer wire of the Tre Morfa settlement. It had been set to fire four explosive rockets at 1 a.m. Two settlers had been injured. Some said that a small child in there had been killed.

So of course there'll be hell to pay, Thomas thought.

The phones were cut off half way through the morning and then, at about 2 p.m., five Logrian soldiers with flak jackets and automatic rifles arrived at the Turners' house. They made Thomas and Jenny pull out every drawer and empty the contents over the floor. They made them empty their food cupboards onto the table and their coal bunker over the back lawn. They even slashed open bags of sugar and flour with bayonets and pulled up the fitted carpet in the hallway...

An hour later the soldiers returned again. Thomas, Jenny and William were still scooping up the sugar and the coal (which they could ill afford to lose) and trying to get the torn carpet back into place. The soldiers said they were looking for Harry Duckett. Some informer in the village had told them that William was his closest friend.

"I don't know where he is," William said. "I really don't."

They arrested him and took him away.

Jenny and Thomas didn't sleep at all that next night. Jenny sat clenching and unclenching her fists at the kitchen table, rocking to and fro, while Thomas patted her shoulder and told her stories about young men he'd heard about who'd been arrested and then returned to their parents unharmed.

As it turned out they were lucky. William did come back the next day. A jeep pulled up and dumped him outside. He had a black eye but was otherwise outwardly uninjured.

Jenny hugged him. Thomas hugged him. William pulled away.

"I'm all right. Don't make a fuss."

"I'll put the kettle on," Thomas said. "I'll make us a pot of tea."

(They were English after all. This was the whole problem. They couldn't be anything other than English.)

When Thomas brought the pot over the table, William was staring distractedly at the window while Jenny stroked the back of his hand.

"I'm worried about Harry," William burst out. "That's why they've let me go, isn't it? They've found Harry somewhere, or they know where he is. That's how they know he wasn't with me and that I wasn't lying. Otherwise…"

He put his hands over his face and began to cry in a strangled, lonely, distant way that was very like his mother.

"They were about to start on me," he said. "I was stuck in this interrogation room with them and they were going to start on me."

"But they didn't, did they?" Thomas said.

"No, but…"

"Whatever they were going to do to you, I suppose, is what you're thinking they're now doing to Harry."

"Well it is, isn't it? It is. It's happening to him now."

William nodded. It was an appalling thought for all three of them. They'd all known Harry since he was a funny reckless indomitable little toddler.

"The thing is Dad, I actually think he did it. I think it was him that went through the fence with those rockets."

"Stupid Harry," said Thomas, "*Stupid, stupid* Harry."

Jenny began to sob. None of them thought even for a moment about the dead child over in the Brythonic settlement of Tre Morfa.

On TV the Logrian politicians came over like weary grownups pushed to the edge of their patience by foolish and ungrateful children.

"The Saxons are going to have to learn that if they want a state they must behave like decent human beings," said the Prime Minister of Logres.

One of his coalition partners – Emrys Llewellyn, the leader of the *Gwlad y Greal* religious party – said that this incident confirmed the need for the Logrian state to retain control in perpetuity over *all* of the country formerly known as England:

"This appalling terrorist attack has exposed the folly of handing over even the smallest part of our land to a people who have always refused our offers of peace. Little Angharad was an innocent child who had done no harm to anyone. She must *not* be allowed to have died in vain! We must bury, once and for all, the dangerous, the lunatic, the *criminal* notion of a separate so-called English state. If the Saxons want their own country, they should return to Saxony."

Later a news bulletin confirmed that two terrorist suspects had been arrested: Harry Duckett and John Fison. The Fisons lived just two doors down from the Ducketts. They had once owned a farm on the site of the Tre Morfa settlement. According to the bulletin both Harry and John were members of the English Young Socialists, the youth wing of Chairman Blair's organisation, the Labour Party of England. But Blair himself denied any involvement in the attack.

Late that afternoon a military bulldozer arrived, accompanied by two tanks and a platoon of soldiers. Colonel Rhys was with them, the BCL civil liaison officer for the Cambridgeshire military district, his face taut, his gaze fixed on the soldiers and the job in hand.

They knocked down the Fisons' house first. Then the bulldozer pulled back from the wreckage with a bit of the Fisons' blue living room curtains still dangling from its great blade. It turned awkwardly on its tracks and rolled along the road towards the Ducketts', crushing the tarmac as it went.

Richard, Liz and Harry's younger brother Ned stood watching, under the eye of two Logrian soldiers.

"Where were you born, eh?" Richard demanded of them. "France? America? Spain? This is our land and you won't make it yours even if you knock down *everyone's* house."

But they didn't answer him. Perhaps they didn't even understand. The bulldozer rolled forward. In about twenty-five minutes all of Richard's and Liz's extensions and improvements were reduced to a heap of rubble. The Ducketts themselves were so completely covered in the dust of their own pulverised home that they looked like statues, like plaster-cast corpses from the ruins of Pompeii.

Thomas called down from the window, "Liz! Richard! Ned! Come over here and let us look after you!"

Liz looked round with a blank plaster-cast face, but she was in a state of shock and was unable to act or speak.

Next day the BCL lifted the curfew from 10 a.m. to midday to allow the people of Sutton and Churchill Camp to get in some food.

Thomas walked down to a farm on the Fen just outside the village for eggs and potatoes. On the way back he met Colonel Rhys driving up from the Tre Morfa settlement. It was very different from the previous encounter when the Frenchman had embarrassed Thomas with his friendliness and volubility. This time Rhys tried to pretend he hadn't seen Thomas at all, but Thomas stepped out in front of the car so the Logrian officer had no choice but to stop.

"How can you live with yourself?" Thomas demanded. "How can you come across from Paris to a place you have never seen before and be party to the destruction of the home of a family whose people have lived here for generations and generations?"

After all, Colonel Rhys wasn't religious. He wasn't one of those Brythons who believed that God gave Britain to them in perpetuity when he sent Joseph to plant that damned thorn tree at Avalon. In all of their meetings, Rhys had made a particular point of differentiating himself from those people. In fact he often expressed the view that rational people on the Logrian and English sides had more in common with one another than they did with the fanatics of either variety.

But now the Colonel's manner was distant and cold.

"It was the home of a child-killer," he said. "Do you expect us to pat you people on the back when your sons murder our kids?"

"It was the home of a young man who attacked a fortified colony of invaders who have dispossessed and deliberately humiliated him for many years."

The colonel shrugged.

"I'm angry now and maybe I will feel differently when I've had time to think," he said, "but right now what I feel is that you people are just going to have to find somewhere else to live. We've tried to be reasonable but look how you repay us!"

"The English must leave *England*?" Thomas began to say. "What kind of sense does...?"

He broke off. He felt strange. He felt that he was looking into the world from the far end of a long tunnel.

"I'm sorry?" asked Colonel Rhys.

Thomas noticed a sky-lark twittering far above them

"The English..." he began, and stopped.

On and on went the lark's song, like the song of sunlight itself.

There was no chosen race, there was no them and no us. There was no England, no Logres, not deep down at the core of things. There was nothing like that, just the world itself endlessly upwelling from non-existence.

"We should try and remember," Thomas said.

"Remember what?"

Rhys looked troubled. He was watching Thomas with a puzzled expression on his face, wondering why his neighbour had made him stop in the middle of his morning run.

"Oh I... I just..."

Thomas broke off. *Why on Earth am I angry with this man?* he wondered.

All he could remember about Rhys was that he was a Welshman, a research chemist from Aberystwyth, and that he'd moved to the area a few month's previously to take up a post at Cambridge University. Thomas had always thought he seemed quite interesting and nice. What could he and Rhys have possibly have found to quarrel about?

He shrugged, and stepped aside. Rhys nodded, gave him a puzzled but not unfriendly smile, and set off on his run again. The lark kept on singing.

Thomas was standing on the wide flat empty Fens, but once again he had the feeling, though only very fleetingly, that he was on some kind of hilltop, looking out at the other hills that were normally hidden from view. Then the feeling was gone.

Thomas remembered that he had a lesson to prepare about 1066 and the famous victory of Harold the Great over the Normans. (It was the last time, of course, that a foreign army had ever set foot on English soil.) And he remembered too that when he got home Liz would be there, his dear wife of twenty years, who he loved with all his heart.

For some reason he found both these thoughts immensely reassuring.

the desiccated man.

On the final leg of its twenty-month journey back to Little Earth from Doubters' Rock, the starship *Rio Quinto IX* docked for maintenance at an unmanned torus station called New Vegas. Scores of small hive robots swarmed aboard and at once dispersed themselves through the ship and its cargo of samarium, searching for everything from electrical faults to infectious diseases. Since the complete process normally took about twelve hours, Jacob Stone, the *Rio Quinto*'s captain and sole crew member, availed himself of the opportunity of a little shore leave, a chance to stretch his legs and partake of a few diversions that were not on offer in his cramped captain's quarters on the ship.

Picture Stone as a podgy pale-skinned man in his middle years with indifferent personal hygiene and poor social skills. There are reasons why people choose a career that means spending most of their life alone in a space the size of a cramped one-bedroom apartment. Day to day, Jacob's life had no meaning. He slept, he watched movies, he played video games, he slept some more. His dream, his sole dream, was to accumulate so much money that he would one day be the envy of men whose more conventional lives had been encumbered by such inconveniences as wives, children, families, workmates, friends. He often laughed to himself, alone in his quarters, surrounded by vast tracts of nothingness, to think of his generous untaxed salary accumulating, virtually untouched, in his bank account. Boy oh boy, would he show them! He was already well on the way to his second million.

Now he strolled alone along Main Street, New Vegas, illuminated and animated for his sole benefit, checking out the craic. There was Clancy's Irish Bar, Yoko's Geisha Paradise, the Good Ol' Little Earth Bar, and Mr Wu's Wonderful World of Food, each one with its name in bright lights, and its own cheery theme tune tinkling out into the street. Then there was the Simply Vegas Casino, Brando's Old Time Movie Theatre, and the Vegas Forever Grocery and Souvenir Store. After that came the Wild West Saloon, the Gay Paree Revue Bar and Mrs Morgan's Place, "the Great Little Whorehouse with the Heart of Gold". Then came Donny's Downloads, Vera's Virtual Vehicle Rides,

Pistol Pete's Shootin' Range, the Pocket Hilton Hotel (with its grand total of four bedrooms) and the Simply Peace chapel/temple/synagogue. (You could choose which religion when you went in). And then... well, then you were back at Clancy's Irish Bar again because, like I said, New Vegas is a torus station. The street goes round the inside of it.

Jacob tried out Clancy's, Mr Wu's, the casino and Mrs Morgan's. Inside these establishments, Jacob found various humorous, folksy and eccentric characters of both sexes, along with lots of pretty young girls and a few handsome young dudes. There were more of these folk out on the streets: Officer Murphy, for example, who stood outside Pete's with his hands on his hips, surveying the scene with his sharp and humorous eyes, or Ol' Pop Johnson on his rocking chair outside the Saloon, chewing his unlit pipe.

"Howdy Cap'n Stone. Long time no see, buddy," Ol' Pop called out.

"Howdy," grunted Jacob, half-pleased and half-irritated.

All of these Vegas people were rooted to the spot on which they stood or sat or, in the case of some in Mrs Morgan's, lay. All of them were controlled by the same single computer and all of them had spent the two-and-a-half months since the previous starship left motionless and in pitch darkness. In New Vegas, the music played and the lights twinkled and the faces came alive only when a spaceman docked and crossed over from his ship.

Jacob was paying a second visit to the restaurant, dining alone on a synthetic pap said to "have all the spice and excitement of Old Bangkok", when the game show playing on the TV over the bar was interrupted for some news.

"Hey folks," said the handsome anchorman, "this is a news flash brought to you by NVBC. We have a new visitor! Following the arrival a few hours ago of respected starways veteran Captain Jacob Stone we are now also hosting the *Exocon Enterprise V* and her up-and-coming head honcho Captain Doug Hempleman."

"Looks like you've got company, Mr Stone!" said Mr Wu from behind the bar. Mrs Wu and all three of the pretty animatronic waitresses looked over at Jacob and smiled.

They were decorative only, of course, those waitresses, since they were unable to walk. One of them also had a missing arm.

"Yeah I guess," said Jacob without enthusiasm, wiping his mouth.

"*Exocon Enterprise V*," said the newsman on the TV screen, "is one of the new Class-F multi-function ships that we've heard so much about lately, currently carrying cerium extraction equipment to Trixie Dixie colony from Proxima-3."

"You know Doug Hempleman, Captain Jake?" asked Mrs Wu.

"Never heard of him."

"He's quite a guy," Mr Wu said with a chuckle. "You should stay a few days, Captain, maybe check in to the Hilton, and hang out with Doug for a while. You two would get on like a house on fire."

"Check into the Hilton?" Jacob Stone gave a hollow laugh. "Check into that dump, when I can sleep for free in my own berth back on ship? That's not how I got to be a millionaire, buddy."

Mr Wu raised his animatronic hands creakily in humorous surrender.

"You're the boss, Captain Jake, you're the boss."

"Haven't got much time for young guys who get themselves given a fancy F-class ship and think they're it," growled Jacob. "Still, guess I'll check him out. It might fill up an hour. This guy play cards at all?"

"Spent an hour or two last time playing the guys down at the Saloon. There he is now, look."

From the TV screen looked down a still picture of a pleasant and surprisingly normal-looking man in his early thirties.

"Hmm," said Jacob sourly. "Barely more than a kid. Think they're it don't they? Think they're bloody it."

He shook his head.

"What kind of a card player is he, anyway?" he asked after a time.

"Pretty good, I heard," said Mr Wu.

"Pretty good? Just pretty good? Maybe I should teach him a lesson."

The two men met on Main Street, outside the Wild West Saloon. Inevitably, after months of solitude, they regarded each other at first with wariness and suspicion. But Hempleman quickly mastered this initial feeling and stepped forward with a pleasant smile and his hand extended in greeting.

"Hi! Doug Hempleman. You must be Jacob!"

His grip was firm and strong.

"Yup," said Jacob indifferently. "You a card player at all?"

He looked Hempleman up and down with unconcealed dislike. The other captain was twenty years younger than him, strikingly good-looking, and very trim. He was one of those, Jacob saw at once, who worked out every day in the little gym which every starship company, by law, provided for its crew. An hour a day was recommended by the doctors, but Jacob had no time for the damned things.

"Yes, sure," said Hempleman. "I like a game of cards. Maybe a drink first though? What do you say?"

Jacob shrugged, looked at his watch, and ungraciously assented, as if he was fitting Doug in reluctantly before a more rewarding engagement. They made their way to Clancy's and ordered beers.

"Nice to see you guys hooking up," said rosy-cheeked Mick Clancy from behind his bar, lifting the chemically synthesised drinks from the dispenser and placing them in front of the two space captains. Like several of the denizens of New Vegas, Mick was in need of repair. Part of his right ear was missing, and only his left eye blinked.

"Been at this game long?" Doug asked Jacob.

"Thirty-two standard years," Jacob said with grim pride. "Never more than three weeks planetside during that whole time."

"Jesus!" said Hempleman. "What kind of life is that? I've done this run three times – six years of my life – and this is the last. Then I'm buying my own little place by the sea in Prox-3 and giving up the starways for good. In eighteen months' time it'll be over, thank God. There's a lovely woman waiting for me back on Prox – I met her last time I was home – and we're going to get married as soon as I get back."

He fumbled in a pocket and handed a picture viewer to Jacob.

"This is her," he said, "this is my Helen. I can't tell you how much I miss her!"

Jacob let the viewer run through its sequence of images. Helen smiled, pulled a face, struck a mock-sexy pose, laughed. She *did* look lovely. She might not be quite as flawlessly pretty as some of the hundred thousand women whose images Jacob kept in his on-board entertainment system, but she *was* pretty all the same and she also looked funny and warm and kind. Unlike many of Jacob's hundred thousand, she looked liked a real human being. Jacob shrugged and handed the viewer back.

"Nothing but trouble, women, if you ask me," said Jacob. "F and F, that's my motto. Fuck 'em and forget 'em."

Doug looked at him appraisingly.

"Not much time even for that, eh, Jake, if you never stay planetside for more than a few weeks? No, I wouldn't be without my Helen, not for anything. Meeting her was like... like finding water in a desert... like I'd been hollow and empty up to that point and suddenly found I had a heart."

His voice became a little wobbly at this point and he paused in order to get his emotions under control. The life of a space captain can be a very lonely thing.

"Two more years," he said. "That's what we agreed. Two years apart. Build up the savings we need for a life we can really share together, and then no more wandering for me. Two years for *me* that is: it's four for her of course, which I do feel badly about, but then I tell myself that at least for her it's not time spent completely alone, so it'll pass a lot more quickly."

Again Jacob shrugged.

"Depends what you want, I suppose," he said coolly. "Me, I'm going for the *real* money."

"Sure."

Doug gazed into the middle distance. It was painfully obvious to Jacob that the other space captain had already grown bored of him.

"Anyway, Jake my friend," Doug said, bringing himself, with an effort, back to the present moment, "weren't the two of us about to have a game of cards?"

It wasn't much of a present moment to come back to, a plastic mock-up of an Irish bar surrounded by millions of miles of void, where the chemically synthesised drinks were served by a puppet with a broken blink mechanism. But Doug smiled kindly at Jacob, realising that, to him, this was virtually the whole world.

"Minimum stake of five dollars suit you, buddy?" he asked.

Jacob snorted derisively. He was determined to get one up on Prettyboy Hempleman with his pretty girlfriend and all.

"*Five?*" he guffawed as he sat himself down at the card table. "That's not real money. A hundred, and rising in steps of a hundred. Or there's no point in playing."

"Well... uh... okay," Doug agreed and touched the button to tell the machine to deal out the first hand. "I guess we can always stop if we want to."

An hour later and Jacob had lost nine thousand dollars. Things were not going according to plan.

"You had enough, Jake?" Hempleman asked him mildly. "You've been a very good sport. I must admit if it'd been me, I'd have dropped out when I was five hundred down."

Jacob made a contemptuous sound.

"Nine thousand is nothing. Not to a millionaire like me. Cards aren't coming up right, that's all. Bound to happen sometimes. Last time I played I won five million."

Again Doug regarded him gently but appraisingly, in a way that Jacob was rapidly growing to hate. He felt sure that Hempleman knew quite well that the five million win had been against a simulated player on the *Rio Quinto*'s on-board entertainment system, set to 'medium skill'.

"You *really* want to carry on then?" Doug said.

Jacob touched the button for more cards. Prettyboy Hempleman might be able to see right through him, but Jacob wasn't going to give him the satisfaction of proving his perceptions to be correct.

"Yeah, sure, may as well," Jacob said, "I guess it passes the time..."

Jacob lived for money – money was the only measure by which he could deem his own life to have been a success – so he hated the thought of losing any part of his precious stash. But one thing he hated more was the idea that this young whippersnapper, with his class-F ship and his pretty fiancée, might think he'd got one over on him.

How to end the game without looking like he was pulling out, though? He'd lost another five grand before a plan finally came to him.

"Got some passengers on board my ship," he informed the other captain archly.

"Passengers? Really?" Hempleman was very surprised. "I could have sworn your ship was a standard C-class mineral transporter."

"Correct. It's a standard C-class. No fancy F-class for me."

"I'm sorry Jake, I'm just not getting this. You have passengers in a mineral freight hold?"

Then Hempleman gave a strained laugh.

"I'm a fool," he said. "You're joking, aren't you, Jake? If you'd really had passengers they'd be here with us in Vegas. They wouldn't be waiting back on your ship."

"They *are* on my ship," said Jacob, "and they *are* in the mineral freight hold, and they're real passengers who paid their own fare. I bet you can't tell me how come."

"Not a clue, but I've an idea that you're about to tell me."

Jacob regarded Doug more archly than ever, savouring his own knowledge and the other's ignorance.

"They're tardies," he said at length, "that's why. Going to Little Earth for some sort of meeting or something, their agent said. Do you know what a tardy is?"

"Yeah. Sure. Hey, wow, that's really something. I've heard of them, of course, but I've never seen one."

"Like to see them?"

"Yeah. Yeah *sure*. I really would." Doug laughed. "Man, when you check into one of these dumps you really don't expect to see anything that's actually interesting or real. But tardies, wow!"

Jacob sighed, as if he were constantly being pestered about this, and it was starting to play on his nerves. But inwardly he smiled. He could see that Doug had completely forgotten the game.

"Yeah," he grunted, "everyone wants to see them."

"Of course they do. Little aliens from far away. The first truly intelligent alien species. Who wouldn't? Who wouldn't want to see them?"

"Yeah, well I've got a whole tribe of them I'm taking to Little Earth," said Jacob.

"A whole tribe, wow!" Doug exclaimed.

He considered this for a moment.

"Come to think of it," he said. "It'd have to be a whole tribe, wouldn't it? From what I've heard and read they'll travel as far as anyone wants them to go, but only if all their kin go with them. That's so isn't it? I've got that right? They're very family minded?"

"Can't say I know or care, to be honest. Want to come and check them out?"

"Sure! Let's go."

Doug Hempleman jumped up from the card table, Jacob noticed, without even glancing at the unfinished game.

"Bingo!" he said to himself.

They headed back to the station's hub and crossed from there over the bridge to the *Rio Quinto*. Doug screwed up his nose as they entered Jacob's squalid quarters and tried not to look at the mouldy plate and mug, the stained sheets, the squalid toilet with the door left open. They went to the hold airlock and put on pressure suits, then entered the airless hold itself.

Jacob turned on the lights. Huge containers packed with samarium stretched out in front of them in stacks four metres high. Stepping over a couple of small hive robots from the station that were scuttling from one maintenance task to the next, he led his guest along a gangway that ran down the centre of the hold.

"Their planet has an eccentric orbit, apparently," said Doug, speaking over the radio link between the two suits. "Half the year it never falls below 100 centigrade and there's no liquid water. The other half of the year it's warm and pleasant like Little Earth or Prox. Isn't that right?"

"If you say so," said Jacob.

They reached a container at floor level at the far end which differed from all the others in that it was painted white. Jacob opened a small door and turned on a light.

"Oh wow!" breathed Doug as they entered the chamber.

He was immediately entranced.

In the olive groves that ringed the crystal blue oceans of Prox-3, there were little creatures called cicadas that the early colonists had imported from Old Earth. Sometimes, walking in the hills, you'd find the discarded skin of one: hard, fragile, transparent and almost weightless, with eyes, wing cases and limbs just like the living creature, but completely hollow and dry. The tardies, about thirty of them, strapped in little seats down each side of the brightly lit container, looked very much like those empty skins. They were transparent too, and hard and fragile.

But these had hands and feet and little faces. They were unmistakably *people*, very small perhaps, less than half a metre tall, but people nevertheless. And they weren't really empty shells either, even if they looked that way. Their flesh was actually still there, shrivelled so much that it was just a dried-up smear inside the hard transparent surface. If the tardies were rehydrated these skins would fill out again with living tissues, and soften, and they would grow and move and come back to life.

"They're beautiful," said Doug. "Quite beautiful. You're lucky to have them, Jake. I wish I had some on my ship to look after."

He walked slowly between the two rows of seats, studying each individual in turn.

"Hello there, little fellow. I wonder what your name is… Oh and good day to *you* my dear lady, you look very much like you might be the one in charge."

Hempleman turned and beamed at Captain Stone.

"I bet you come down here all the time to check them out, don't you?" he said. "I know if it was me I wouldn't be able to keep away."

"Not really. Got better things to do."

Hempleman laughed.

"Better things? On a space freighter? You'll have to tell me your secret, buddy."

He turned back to the tardies.

"What happens when it's time, you know, to rehydrate them?"

Jacob shrugged.

"Not my job. I deliver the box. Someone at the other end sees to the rest."

"Sure," said Doug. "It's just that they are pretty unique creatures, you know. Their planet is *so* far away – they must have been travelling for many years before you took them on board – and they're pretty much unheard of in this sector. If I had on them on my ship, well, I would have wanted to find out as much as…"

But, realising it was rude to criticise Jacob's lack of curiosity, he broke off and answered his question himself.

"You just fill the chamber with moist air, is what I've read," he said matter-of-factly. "Fill it with moist air and they'll slowly come back to life. Or most of them will. Apparently one per cent or so rehydrate with the others, and show signs of life, but then immediately die. I guess it doesn't matter how well-adapted they are, you can't completely dry out a living organism without the risk of doing some damage to it."

He looked up and down the rows.

"Which means there's a distinct chance that one of these guys is not going to make it." He frowned, looking round him at the empty transparent shapes. "I wonder if that's the case, and if so which? It's weird that you can't tell."

"Not my problem."

Hempleman glanced at his fellow space captain with a slightly troubled frown.

"Uh, I guess not. Wow, will you just look at these little kids here! They're *tiny* aren't they? Imagine how cute they'll be when they come back to life."

The little dried up figures delighted him.

"They're so light, so... insubstantial. A breath of wind could blow them away."

"Yeah," Stone said, "and a fist could smash one of them to bits."

Hempleman winced but did not respond.

"Hey! Look at those two right at the end," he presently exclaimed, "sitting together on one seat. What's the story there? I don't suppose you know, do you?"

"Just got married, apparently, or whatever the heck tardies call it," grunted Jacob. "Guy who shipped them told me that she was from a different tribe or something. Scared to be alone, or some such."

Doug went to the diminutive pair and squatted down in front of them.

"She's holding his hand. Imagine that. Holding his hand and looking at him. And him looking at her."

With immense care he reached out his big, clumsy space-suited hand and touched their tiny joined fingers.

"Lucky devils," he said. "One minute they are getting drowsy in the dehydration chamber – that's how it feels to them, apparently, like going to sleep – the next they're waking up again together. Not like me and Helen. Another eighteen months we've still got to get through the slow way, day by day by bloody day, until we see each other again. Eighteen months for me, three years for her. No other way to reach her except through months and months of nothingness. The worst part is that for the whole of the next six months I'll still be travelling *away* from her."

He straightened up, stood looking at the little alien couple for few more seconds, then turned away. With contempt, Jacob noticed tears in the other space captain's eyes.

"Well," said Doug Hempleman, "better get back to the bloody old *Exocon* I guess. Get ready for the final haul out to Trixie Dixie, that godforsaken hole. I'm done with New Vegas."

Back in the malodorous captain's quarters he shook Jacob's hand.

"Nice to have met you, Jake, and all the best with the rest of your journey. Thanks *so* much for showing me those tardies. The highlight of my voyage they've been I can tell you, the highlight of *all* my voyages in fact."

"Well," said Jacob Stone ungraciously, "they say there's no accounting for taste."

"Oh and by the way," said Hempleman, "don't worry about the money for the cards, huh? It was just in fun really, wasn't it? And I'd have happily paid you twice that much just for a peek at those little tardy guys in there."

"Okay buddy," said Jacob, smirking to himself, as Doug returned over the bridge. "I'll try my best not to worry. I'll certainly try my best."

Jacob went back down to Vegas, with its colourful lights and its jolly music (honky-tonk outside the Saloon, the Can-Can outside the Gay Paree, 'Molly Malone' outside Clancy's). He bought a snack at Mr Wu's and made a couple of circuits of Main Street, accepting enthusiastic greetings from all the friendly animatronic characters: Mr Wu, Officer Murphy, big Momma Jackson, Ol' Pop Johnson in his rocking chair.

"Howdy there, Captain Stone. You on your way again soon, I guess?"

Their folksy cheeriness would turn to stillness and silence as soon as he'd rejoined his ship, and Main Street would plunge into a darkness that might be unbroken for weeks or even months, but now they behaved like they'd spent the whole four years since Jacob's last visit talking about him fondly, chuckling over his wry remarks, and looking forward to his return.

"I often smile to myself when I think about what you said to me last time," said Officer Murphy. "'How can a cop catch bad guys when his feet are fixed to the floor?' That's what you said, you sly dog. Good one Captain, good one. Still makes me smile."

But Jacob was bored with Main Street – the illusion of companionship was thin from the outset and it didn't last – and he settled for a bit of drinking instead. He had a 'whiskey' in Clancy's, a 'cognac' in the Gay Paree and a 'bourbon' in the Good Ol' Little Earth. All the drinks tasted vile and all pretty much the same, but they contained the prerequisite amount of ethanol. He followed them up with a chaser in Yoko's, a nightcap in the Wild West Saloon and one for the road at Mrs Morgan's gloomily watching an animatronic stripper gyrating round a pole. (She had one finger broken on her right hand. It dangled limply on a piece of wire.) Then he returned to the *Rio Quinto* to try and sleep.

He was not at ease though. He was agitated. The normal, sluggish, barely conscious flow of his life had been disrupted. There was something he needed to do to put it back in its regular channel but he couldn't think what it was. Only as he was lowering himself onto the crumpled sheets of his berth (as usual neglecting to remove his clothes or clean his teeth), did inspiration finally came to the drunken brain of Captain Jacob Stone.

He smiled grimly, sat back up again, and went to his toolbox to select a fine-pointed awl.

Jacob turned on the big hold lights and made his way slowly and unsteadily down the gangway between the containers of samarium, his breathing loud and laboured inside his helmet. He headed straight for the specially adapted container that held the thirty tardies, and then wobbled along between the rows of seats until he reached the two newlyweds on their single seat at the end.

"Hey there my beauties," said Jacob. "Hey there my pretty lovebirds. Old Daddy Stone has a little surprise for you when you get to Little Earth."

He leaned forward, peering into their delicate, empty, transparent faces, examining first the male, then the female and then the male again, patting the awl gently against his left hand all the while, as if he were an artist trying to decide the final brushstroke on some great masterpiece.

"Which one of you, eh? Which of you little lovebirds wants to be the one that wakes?"

Finally he made a choice.

He knelt, awkwardly and with much wheezing, in front of the dry shell of the young wife, reached behind the hollow bubble of her head, and pressed his little awl against the hard but fragile surface until it broke through into the small dried lump against the back of the skull that he surmised, correctly, to be her desiccated brain.

"Like the guy said, there's often one or two of you that wake up and then die. People expect that. There's often one or two."

He hauled himself, wheezing, back onto his feet, then stood for a moment, swaying, to admire his handiwork.

"A neat job though I say it myself," said Captain Stone.

He leaned forward into the empty transparent face, which was like a sculpture made out of blown glass.

"What do you think sweetheart?" he asked it. "Done you proud, wouldn't you say?"

He laughed wheezily.

"Certainly *done* you anyway."

He looked round and gave the husband a little avuncular pat on the head.

"Never mind, my dried-up buddy. Fuck 'em and forget 'em, that's old Daddy Stone's advice."

He laughed again at that, but when he turned and began to stagger back between the seats, he was trembling. And he shrank away from the gaze of the two rows of empty transparent eyes.

"*What?* What's your problem? Some of you die anyway. You heard the guy say it himself. You heard Mr Expert Tardy-lover. Some of you die every time. It might have been her anyway for all you know."

He reached the low door of the container.

"Think yourselves lucky I left your tribe alone, eh? That's what your buddy Hempleman said, isn't it? Your Mr Nice Guy. It's the tribe that counts for you people. At least I respected that."

Jacob slept for fourteen hours or more at a time. And when he wasn't sleeping he watched movies and played video games, and ate and drank, and looked at pictures of girls, and watched more movies, and thought about the money building up in his bank account. Just beyond the wall of his tiny quarters blazed the universe, but he paid it no heed.

"One million eight hundred and forty two thousand federation dollars. Lick that, Mr Nice Guy Hempleman, with your little house by the sea."

He never entered the white container again and tried not to look at it when he had to go into the hold, but he didn't give much thought to what he had done in there.

"It was only a pin-prick after all," he'd mutter, "and she might not have woken anyway, just like Hempleman said. And they're not really alive either, are they? It's not as if they were human or anything."

Then he'd let his mind drift to more pleasant things.

"One million eight hundred and forty two thousand dollars. How about that!"

And pretty soon it would be time to lie down again and sleep until the ship woke him to carry out his next round of daily checks.

This was his actual job, stipulated in his contract. The ship ran itself, but every standard day he was required to spend thirty minutes running through checks to establish whether any one of fifteen possible trigger events had occurred which might require human intervention to safeguard the ship and its cargo. None of them had ever occurred, not just on this voyage but on any of the voyages in all the thirty-two standard years that Jacob had spent riding spaceships back and forth across the void. Every single one of them would have passed off just as well if he hadn't been there at all. He was called captain but as it had turned out, he'd only ever been a passenger, or maybe a janitor at a pinch.

And after another six months the *Rio Quinto IX*, without its captain's help, duly put itself into orbit around the planet of Little Earth. Without his help, the ship negotiated with the planetary authorities. Without his help, robot shuttles docked at the *Rio Quinto*'s bow and drew out the one hundred containers from the hold, four at a time, the tardies' container being in the first batch.

Unloading took the better part of a day, with Jacob monitoring the whole process from a screen in his quarters (for it happened that no less than three of those fifteen prescribed triggers were events that could occur only during loading and unloading). He was in no hurry. He didn't enjoy the descent to a planet surface. It wasn't easy, after all this time, to emerge from his little den into the great gravity well of a habitable world, and see the ocean and clouds and continents, and to know that there was a whole complicated world of human relationships waiting down there, talking, arguing, laughing, doing deals, making love, and just generally getting along perfectly well without him.

When there were only eight containers of samarium left in the hold, and Jacob was waiting for a shuttle to come for the next batch, he was irritated to see instead a government launch docking alongside the external airlock. It was some sort of safety regulations check-up, he supposed. It happened from time to time in the more officious and metropolitan jurisdictions such as that of Little Earth. Safety people came on board with checklists and questions, and told him off for not keeping the gym in working condition, or not changing the air filter often enough. Jacob Stone sighed.

And was taken completely by surprise when five armed police officers came bursting in.

"I'm Lieutenant Gladheart Niyibizi," their leader told him, "and I am putting you under arrest.

"What for?"

He really was bewildered.

"For murder." She put handcuffs on him, indicating to the other officers that they should begin their search of the ship. "These are your rights, Mr Stone. You are not obliged to speak, but anything you say…"

"*Murder?* What? I've been in space these last two years for Chrissakes! Who could I murder in space?"

"One of your tardy charges, Captain Stone."

"Jesus," muttered Jacob.

For one brief moment it came to him just how much trouble he had managed to get himself into and just how wicked a thing he had done. Then he gave a characteristic snort of dismissal and contempt.

"That little tardy? What a lot of nonsense! It was only a pinprick, and anyway she wasn't really alive. So how could that be murder?"

"I'll show you something," said the lieutenant, linking her data pack to his system.

On his screen appeared the tardies, still sitting in their seats somewhere down on the planet surface, while their container was filled with moisture-saturated air.

"These particular tardies are converts to the Universal Church," said the Lieutenant. "I suppose you knew that? They've spent a total of nine years travelling across space to get here for the Church's General Synod, which only happens once every hundred standard years. It's a big occasion, a big fuss is going to be made of them, and they agreed to let their rehydration be filmed so that the whole gathering could see it."

Jacob shrugged.

Chris Beckettt

"The agent guy said they were religious or some such."

As the tardies' desiccated bodies absorbed the water, they trembled and quivered and jerked. They would have fallen to the floor if they hadn't been strapped to their seats. And Jacob could see the flesh rapidly expanding inside the apparently empty transparent skins. As they filled out, the tardies stopped being transparent and began to look solid. They were no longer empty shells but small silvery-coloured people. At one end of the chamber, presumably the end where the moisture was being introduced, some of them began to move.

One of them unbuckled her seat-belt. She stood up and stretched. Nearby an adult male was reaching out to one of the little children. The child had also woken and was tugging crossly at her belt. A couple of seats further down another, smaller female unbuckled and stood up. She looked back at the children too for a moment but then her attention was abruptly drawn away by something happening at the far end of the chamber.

The camera followed her gaze and at once the scene changed from one of calm, slow reawakening to one of crisis and desperation. The newly married husband was holding his wife's threshing body, his head turned away from her to shout for help. Not only was his wife's body twisted by violent convulsions, but something had gone terribly wrong with the rehydration process inside her head. Her newly reconstituted eyes were not looking out of the hollows that they were meant to see from, but were pressing up against the top of her transparent skull, staring out horribly in two different directions.

The young husband fumbled with her seat belt to release her, still yelling all the while. Other tardies came rushing forward. As they lifted and turned her, her convulsions were already subsiding into limpness. And then a gaping hole became visible in the back of her head. Lieutenant Niyibizi froze the picture as the camera closed in on the wound.

"Well that was nothing to do with me," grumbled Jacob Stone. "I just gave her a little pin-prick with a tiny little awl."

The lieutenant looked at him in disbelief.

"You've had all this time to think about it. Did it not occur to you for one moment, Mr Stone, that a pin-prick might get bigger when the flesh expanded?"

"Uh, I guess."

The lieutenant pushed a button on her wrist and instructed her officers to find the awl.

"And what was the purpose of that little pin-prick, Mr Stone? Do you deny you meant to kill her?"

Stone snorted.

"She wasn't alive anyway. No more than that mug over there, no more than that plastic fork."

In the trial Jacob Stone offered no defence at all other than repeating at every opportunity, and with increasing irritation, "It was only a pin-prick" and "She wasn't really alive". Nor did he show any remorse or provide any explanation except for boredom and being drunk.

Stone's face was indifferent as he was led off at the end to spend the remainder of his life in jail. It was as if he was saying, "You do what you like with me, I don't give a damn." But then, of course, he had already spent most of his adult life by choice in a tiny space not so very much bigger than a Little Earth prison cell. All that had really been taken away from him was the prospect of anything different at the end.

And truthfully he'd never been able to conceive of doing much more with his money than spending it in some sort of up-market version of New Vegas, with better and more realistic puppets, and whiskey that tasted real. His imagination didn't stretch much further than that. And nor did his shrivelled heart.

poppyfields

It had once consisted of a run-down industrial estate, an abandoned shooting range and a council landfill site. Now it was going to be a new housing project called Poppyfields. Contractors brought in bulldozers and diggers on the backs of trucks, put up high fences and uncoiled springs of razor wire along the top. Then the diggers began to dig and the bulldozers began to grub out bushes and knock down the remains of the firing range and the empty factory units, leaving only the concrete floors.

But when a digger started to excavate footings in the part of the site that had once been landfill, there was an unexpected development. There came a sort of malodorous fart from beneath the earth and the digger sunk into the ground to two metres' depth. The landfill site, it seemed, had not been properly impacted or biologically stabilised. Beneath the surface anaerobic bacteria were blooming in a rich marsh of old cereal packets and crushed chicken carcasses and leftover oven chips. It was in a state of ferment, seething with methane which bubbled up through the mush and collected in pockets as high-pressure, inflammable bubbles.

An argument broke out between the engineering contractors, the housing development agency and the city council, who were the former owners of the land, about who should bear the cost of sorting this out. Negotiations failed. Independent arbitration could not be agreed. The contractors took the housing development agency to court. The housing development agency issued a writ against the city council. The diggers and bulldozers came to a standstill. The Poppyfields site stood empty, seeds settled on the earth and red flowers bloomed over this legal battleground as they once bloomed over the trenches and shell-holes of the Somme. Poppyfields became a poppy field.

And presently larks made their nests on the ground. Rabbits burrowed under the fence. Field mice slipped through the chain link. Tussocks of wild barley appeared, and bindweed and vetch crawled up its stems. Tiny seedlings of hawthorn and brambles sprouted here and there that, given time, would have gradually turned the place from a field into a jungle, to be superseded in turn by oak forest. But Poppyfields did not care about the future.

Poppyfields lived its own life behind the razor wire. When it rained the water dripped from Poppyfields' leaves. When the wind blew, Poppyfields' grass and flowers bent back and forth like waves in the ocean. And when the August sun shone down at midday, Poppyfields' larks twittered, on and on, in the big blank blue of Poppyfields' sky, while mirages shimmered over the concrete slabs which had once been the floors of the industrial units but were now the home of lizards and wolf spiders, with buddleia sprouting in the cracks.

Poppyfields asked itself no questions. Poppyfields did not concern itself about its place in the world. Poppyfields did not wonder about the source of the energy beating down on it from the centre of the sky, powering its multifarious life. Poppyfields lost no sleep over the fact that, in due course, the County Court, or the High Court, or the Court of Appeal would make a decision, after which the houses and roads and recreation grounds would come and cover Poppyfields all over with tarmac and little boxes of brick. Poppyfields did not worry. But it lived, it lived anyway, secretly, on its own, behind the fence, feeding on the light that came to it from a nearby star.

Poppyfields lived and yet, at the same time, it was insubstantial. Not only Poppyfields but the entire universe that contained it, was really only a film, a membrane, thinner and more fragile than a child's soap bubble, stretched across a void. It was one of countless such membranes, countless millions of them, for universes are more numerous than Poppyfields' crickets and they are packed closer together than the grains of sand in Poppyfields' earth.

This was Poppyfields' secret, and yet it was an open secret. If anyone had looked through the fence at midday and seen Poppyfields there, shimmering like Armageddon in the atomic heat of the sun, they would surely have seen it. But hardly anyone did look through. Cars went past all day without anyone looking in.

Things might have been clearer to Angus Wendering if he had been able to overhear a conversation between his wife Judy and her best friend Anne, in the week after he and she had first met.

"I know Angus is nothing special," said Judy, setting down two glasses of chilled white wine on the table between them and returning to the conversation which they had broken off when she went to the bar, "but what I've decided is that there is no sense in waiting for Mr Right to come along. The thing to do is to find Mr Average and *turn him into* Mr Right."

This would have helped to explain why Angus sometimes felt like the caged rat in some behavioural experiment. He moved this way, he received an electric shock. He moved that way, he received another. He touched a lever and – aha! – no shock came but instead a pellet of food for him in the little tray. He touched the lever again and... Oh. No food. Only an extra-painful shock. So the answer wasn't just pushing the lever. Perhaps it was pushing the lever in a certain way, or at a certain time? Or perhaps it wasn't pushing the lever at all? Perhaps it was something else he happened coincidentally to have been doing the first time he pushed it?

When Judy arranged to spend the weekend with her mother, leaving on Friday directly after work, he had a heady feeling of freedom and release. An evening and two whole days to do as he liked! As soon as he got back from work he took a knapsack and packed into it a pork pie, an apple, a Kit Kat bar and a bottle of ginger beer, along with a notebook, the *Book of British Birds* and a pair of binoculars. When the cat was away the mouse went birdwatching.

And he went, of all places, to Poppyfields. Angus worked for the insurance company used by the building contractors at Poppyfields and he had once had occasion to visit the site in connection with the dispute over the underground marsh. During this visit he noticed how larks and linnets had taken advantage of the legal impasse and had colonised the disputed territory.

"Nature grabs every opportunity," he had enthused to Judy on his return. "It's just a mouldy old brown-field site but already the wildlife is taking over. I'd love to go down there one afternoon and see how many kinds of plants and animals I can find."

Judy administered a small electric shock.

"Whatever turns you on," she coolly remarked.

She wished to wean Angus off his interest in nature (a) because it wasted time which could be better spend on home improvements (b) because it did not strike Judy as very manly: *geeky* was the word that came to mind (c) because she was working on Angus to go on a management course to increase their earning power and make possible a move to a larger home than the two-bedroom box which they currently inhabited, and she wished to discourage any activity that diverted him from this goal.

He hadn't liked to raise the subject since and yet, when he heard that she would be going away, the first thing he had done was phone the contractors and arrange to pick up the key.

Poppyfields lay waiting. It was six o'clock and the air was still warm, though the mirages no longer shimmered over the concrete floors of the old industrial units. Pulling his car up on the grassy verge of the road that ran past Poppyfields' western perimeter, Angus walked to the gate and turned the key in the heavy padlock. The sound of the bolt drawing back sent up two quails that had been hiding in the grass nearby and Angus smiled. He *was* Mr Average in many ways. He would never be famous for his achievements. He would never be a leader. He had no ambition, no direction. Knowing this about himself, he had concluded that he must need Judy to supply what he was missing. That was why he put up with all those electric shocks. He was the floppy glove puppet, she was the firm hand. But he did have a certain capacity to *see* things, to become absorbed in the moment. The sudden bluster of the two quails rising went right through him, like a wave through still water. Perhaps the hand of the world itself can enter more easily into an empty puppet than into a glove that is stretched tightly already over an active, commanding hand?

He found linnets, he found skylarks, he found a mistle thrush, he found three different kinds of cricket, four kinds of spider and twenty-eight different species of flowering plant, and he wrote all the names down in his notebook, for no special purpose other than to mark the occasion. After about an hour he found a place to sit on the sun-warmed concrete of what had once been a plastic bag factory and unpacked his small picnic. He was munching his pork pie when he noticed a lark alighting not far off and put his binoculars to his eyes to try and see where it had gone.

He never found the lark, though. In searching for it, he noticed something else for which there seemed no explanation. A small patch of ground began to shudder like a mirage, revealing the ground of Poppyfields not to be the solid thing that it might appear, but to be a membrane like a child's soap bubble. Angus shuddered too and he felt as if he was on the brink of *remembering* something, some huge, obvious, world-transforming thing, something that was in fact obvious to him every night in dreams but which every morning he somehow forget in the process of waking up and adjusting himself the strange fact that of all people, of all beings in the universe, he had turned out to be Angus Wendering, a clerk in an insurance company in a provincial town in England.

And then, right in the middle of this patch of turbulence, there appeared a glimmering girl.

Universes divide like bacteria on the surface of a nutrient jelly: one becomes two, two becomes four, four becomes eight... moment by moment by moment.

Somewhere in this broth of universes, in one of the countless worlds, someone had invented a drug that could take a person from a particular point in space and time in one universe to the exact same point in another. It came in the form of small translucent spheres that glowed in their cores like distant nebulae and were known by those who used them as 'slip' or 'seeds'.

The girl had taken one of these seeds in a small recreation ground in a housing estate called Thurston Meadows which, in her own world, occupied the same space that Poppyfields did in Angus'. The seed had made a sort of bubble in space and time. The bubble, with the girl inside it, had separated from the membrane that was her world, and the membrane had sealed itself together again over the space where she had been. With nothing of her own except the clothes she was wearing, the things in her pockets and a bag containing twenty more pills clutched tightly in her right hand, the girl had emerged in Poppyfields. Her name was Tammy Pendant. Uncared for by her parents, claimed by no one else, she had grown up in the care of the state. Restless, resourceful, trusting no one, she lived like an acrobat, skilfully balancing herself over a bottomless abyss of longing, never staying in one place, always moving on before the ground had a chance to give way beneath her.

"Fucking hell," she muttered, looking round at the sea of red flowers – and then retched.

She got down on her knees and retched a second time, wiping the slime and the sweat from her face with the back of her hand. She had been a waif in her own world. Now she was doubly a waif. From a world where no one claimed her, she had come to a world where she did not even exist.

Then she spotted Angus.

At once, like a wild animal, she was on her feet, her eyes darting this way around as she weighed up the options for escape.

"Don't be scared!" called Angus. "I'm not going to hurt you!"

She began to run. But Angus was very fit. In a short distance he had got hold of her, pinning her arms to her sides.

"I'm not going to hurt you, all right?" he repeated. "Trust me. I won't hurt you at all. I just want to help. You can't get out of here without a key to the gate."

She looked up at him, narrowing her eyes. He was about twenty-five. He was a big man and very strong but his face with its blond lashes and thin blonde beard was almost painfully open, the sort of pink fair-skinned face that blushes at the smallest provocation. She had known a social worker once who was like that. Peter, the social worker was called. He worked in a children's home but had been completely incapable of maintaining any kind of order. He longed to be of help to the children, longed for them to like him, but they had all despised him, and mocked him whenever they got the chance.

"What is this place anyway?" Tammy asked.

This felt to Angus like more comfortable ground. He relaxed his grip, let go of her, began to walk towards the gate with Tammy following at a little distance.

"That's a long story," he said with a laugh. "It's supposed to be a building site. There's supposed to be a new housing estate here called Poppyfields..."

And off he went, off into all the details about the landfill and the underground marsh and the court case.

"...Of course I'm not working now," he concluded. "I just borrowed the key because I wanted to watch the birds. I'm a bit of a birdwatching fanatic, I'm afraid. Sad, I know. My other big thing is rugby. I..."

Tammy stopped again to heave and retch.

"Oh I am sorry!" exclaimed Angus. "Here's me prattling away and you..."

"Is this the gate?"

"Yes," he said. "Yes it is. But listen, what are you going to do when you get outside of it?"

She looked through the gate at the cars rushing by on the bleak new road that divided Poppyfields from a bleak park that had been laid out on the other side. The bright headlights and tail-lights of the cars were glimpses of the warm, lively places they were coming from or going to: homes, restaurants, cinemas, bars. But here inside the fence the daylight was rapidly fading and soon the only illumination would be the cold orange of the argon streetlights. By 2 a.m., even the passing cars would have stopped, except for the occasional solitary one rushing by through the motionless orange glow, the sound of its engine intruding for a moment to be swallowed up again by the silence.

A few tears rolled silently down Tammy's cheeks. Tomorrow she could go down town and look for the people like her, the outsiders, the fugitives, the druggies, the people who'd grown up in care: make contact with them, start to familiarise herself with the networks, start doing deals. But she was too exhausted for all that now and she had nowhere to go.

"Come on, Tammy," cried Angus, thrown him into a panic by her distress, "we'll sort out something! I'm not just going to leave you here!"

She reached out, took his hand, held it tight like a small child.

"I couldn't stay round yours, could I?" Tammy asked. "Not being funny or nothing. Just for one night?"

Angus cleared his throat. "Well, I…"

"Just for one night," she said. "I don't know where else to go to be honest."

"But there are hostels and things. I could phone up the social services or something. There are people who'd look after you…"

She grabbed his arm.

"No, *please!* They'd lock me up! Please don't phone no one."

Angus wished Judy were here. She'd have known what to do.

"Um, one thing," he said. "I'm just a bit worried about… Well would you mind telling me your age?"

"Nineteen," lied Tammy and she quickly added, "and don't you start off on how I don't look that old because that's what everyone says."

Angus opened the gate, then shut it behind them and closed the padlock. Poppyfields was alone again in the darkness, behind the fence, beyond the orange light. Poppyfield's owls with their infrared eyes were looking for shining mice. Poppyfields' hedgehogs were rooting for snails Poppyfields' bats were swooping and swerving after Poppyfields' beetles and moths. They didn't care what would happen next. Poppyfields didn't care.

"Well, perhaps for one night," said Angus unhappily.

As they drove across town, Angus considered with increasing dread the implications of what he was doing. It didn't look good, he realised, picking up a young girl and taking her home on the very night that his wife went away. It wouldn't look good even if she *hadn't* been a fugitive, owning nothing but the skimpy clothes she wore. It wouldn't look good even if he had *some* inkling about where she came from and what her history was. It wouldn't look good even she had been ten years older, or if she hadn't been one of the prettiest girls he had ever met, or if, when she took his hand, he had not felt desire, like a sharp cold electric shock, running straight from his fingers to his groin...

"Um... are you sure that it wouldn't be better if I phoned the social services or something. I'm not sure whether it's such a..."

Tears came to Tammy's eyes again.

"Please. I just can't deal with that shit now. You don't know what it's like. It'd do my fucking head in. Just tonight. Please, Angus!"

He swallowed. He was *just* like that social worker Peter, Tammy thought, the one who kids would sometimes come up to and poke with the tips of burning cigarettes. The kids would laugh, and he'd laugh too because he couldn't think how else to handle it.

"Okay," Angus said. "But, Tammy, it really has got to be just for one night."

They were getting quite near to where he lived.

"You'd better get your head down," he muttered.

"What? Are you ashamed of me?" asked Tammy, for the devilment of it, like when they had poked poor Peter with cigarettes.

"No, no!" he protested. "Why would I be ashamed? But you said yourself people might lock you up."

"Yeah but..."

"Just get your head down all right?" snapped Angus, fear finally overcoming his other feelings, and he turned into the housing estate where he and Judy lived.

He nearly didn't get round the corner. His hands were so slippery that he could hardly grip the wheel.

Tiny as Angus' and Judy's little box of a house might be, it still had en-suite off both its bedrooms and it still had an integral garage with remote controlled doors. Angus drove right in and made sure the door was fully shut behind them before he let Tammy out, safe from the gaze of neighbours in the enclosed space of his garage.

"Wait a minute," he snapped, as she made to follow him into the house. "I'll go and draw the front curtains first."

Tammy waited, lighting up a cigarette.

"Oh, um, we don't actually allow smoking in the house," said Angus, coming back from closing the curtains. "Perhaps you could just finish that out here before you..."

She crushed the half-smoked cigarette under her heel with a small cold shrug, so unlike the frightened tearful waif that he had seen beside the gate in Poppyfields that Angus found it hard to believe she was the same person.

"Do you want something to eat?" Angus said, avoiding her eyes. "Or the bathroom? I expect there's lots you want to know about...you know... this world. But perhaps that's for later, yes?"

"I could use a cup of tea. And a shower."

Tammy made herself at home. When she came down after her shower she had done up her hair, put on some of Judy's make-up and borrowed one of her tee-shirts to wear as a dress. She was, without doubt, the prettiest girl that Angus had ever been alone with, the prettiest and the youngest and the most obviously available.

"Um, listen," Angus said. "I've been thinking. I promised I wouldn't report you to the authorities Tammy, and I won't if you really don't want me to, but don't you think it might be the best thing? I mean I believe there are agencies now to help people like you, help you find a new life and all that. I mean you are welcome to stay here tonight but obviously I can't keep your existence a secret forever."

Tammy knew just how to deal with this.

"I thought you said you wanted to help me, Angus. But if you don't, well fine, I'll just walk right out of the door and you won't never see me again. Is that what you want?"

"No. No Tammy!" Angus cried out. "Don't get me wrong. I do want to help you. I really do."

"So where do you want me to sleep?"

"We've got a spare room. I'll show you. The bed's already made up."

"Are you sure you don't want me to sleep with you?"

Angus' face flamed. He tried to laugh in the loud cheerful way that he imagined a man of the world would laugh in such a situation, to show that he knew that she was only joking and that of course he didn't have the slightest interest in her in that way. But he was convincing on neither count.

"I'll… um… show you the spare room."

Just like that social worker Peter, thought Tammy. He'd go red too if anyone said anything that might be to do with sex. Why? Because sex was something he'd never mastered, any more than he'd mastered how to deal with children burning him with cigarettes.

Tammy couldn't sleep. The slip, the shifting drug, was in her veins. She was in this world, but only on the very edge of it, with the precipice right beside her. She kept feeling that she was falling and kept grabbing involuntarily for a handhold. Vivid images and sounds rushed through her mind, of the world she had come from, the world she had arrived in, the worlds she had glimpsed in between. She saw a thicket of thorn bushes, a brick wall appearing right in front of her face, a lorry rushing towards her, a child screaming. The scenes went round and round until her head felt it was bursting. And behind it all she felt emptiness pulling at her, nothingness, that void at the core of everything which she'd always had to struggle to keep from overwhelming her.

She got out of bed and crept across the landing to where Angus lay in the dark, also sleepless, in his marriage bed with its pink cushioned headboard, under the wedding photograph of himself and his gimlet-eyed wife, and beside the pink dressing table on which sat his wife's make-up and her mirror and her three teddy bears.

"Angus," she whispered.

Angus sat up like a jack-in-a-box, snapping on his light. Tammy was amazed to see that he was wearing blue and white striped pyjamas, like a character in some old film.

"Yes? Hello? What is it?"

"I can't sleep. I can't stop seeing things."

"Well, um, perhaps you could…"

"I'm scared of being alone. Could I just stay in here with you for a bit?"

"Um, listen, I don't think that's a very good idea."

"Please."

Tammy went over to his bed and took his hand.

"You wouldn't believe the shit that's in my head."

Once again tears began to roll down her cheeks.

Angus couldn't bear tears. He put an arm awkwardly round her shoulders.

"There there, Tammy," he murmured stiffly.

Tammy slithered up against him. This didn't look good, this wouldn't look good, this wouldn't look good at all.

"You're a kind man," Tammy said. "I don't know what I'd of done without you."

She snuggled up closer. She could tell that Angus was aroused.

Ten minutes later he was on top of her. Thirty minutes later he was telling her that he would give up everything for her: this magical glimmering girl who had materialised from another world before his eyes, and before his eyes alone.

"I love you Angus," she whispered, she murmured, she moaned, "I don't want you never to leave me." And all night she held him, and drew him to her, desperate to keep the emptiness at bay. Why had she abandoned her own world, after all, except in search of somewhere where she would feel less alone?

But at 6 o'clock in the morning, when Angus had finally sunk into a sated sleep, Tammy was still wide awake. She looked down at the mild, foolish, gentle man lying beside her and gave a small snort of loathing and contempt.

He stirred sleepily as she got out of bed.

"Where are you going Tammy?"

"I want a cup of tea."

"Bring me one too then. But don't be long. I want you here with me. I want you with me always. You make me feel my life has just begun."

She went into the other bedroom, put on clothes and went downstairs.

He would never see her again. Having already slipped back into sleep, he didn't hear the front door quietly opening and closing.

When he finally woke three hours later, he saw she wasn't beside him and flung on a dressing gown to follow her downstairs. He could hear the radio on in the kitchen.

"Tammy?" he called cheerily. "Sorry about that. I went right back to sleep."

His wife was coming home in less than eight hours' time but as yet he was untouched by that fact, or by all the other things that somehow had to be decided between now and then. He was just as contented and at peace with himself as he would have been if there were no obstacles at all to prevent his glimmering girl spending every night and every day with him between now and forever. It was as if he was inside a bubble which had separated itself from the rest of the universe.

"Sorry, Tammy," he said again with a laugh as he went into the kitchen. "I just went right out like a light again. It's..."

But the radio was chattering away in an empty room. There was no sign of Tammy other than the open back door, and the contents of several drawers and shelves which she had flung across the floor, looking for things which she could use or sell.

Then the bubble burst and Angus found himself standing instead in a ransacked home which had to be restored to normality in a matter of hours. He scoured the house for any possible trace of Tammy. He washed and dried the bedsheets, he swept and hoovered the ash from the garage floor. He gathered up the contents of the shelves and drawers. Of course he had no way of knowing whether Tammy might suddenly reappear, or write, or even phone and remind him of the love he had declared, the extravagant promises he had made. She had changed from his heart's desire to a dangerous stranger. And he was to live in fear of her, for days and weeks and months.

"Who is Tammy Pendant, Angus?" Judy demanded.

It was nearly a year later and Angus was in the spare bedroom painting the window frame.

Angus started, banging his head hard against the top of the window cavity.

"I don't know," he said. "Why do you ask?"

She held out a card. It was an ID card of some sort, with a photograph of Tammy looking out.

"Where… where did you find it?"

"In my magazine rack in the kitchen. Stuck in the middle of the magazines."

"Perhaps it fell out of one of them."

"It didn't."

"Perhaps we had a break in."

"A burglar who takes nothing but leaves a calling card?"

"Well it beats me then."

He turned hastily back to his painting.

"Don't you *dare* turn away, Angus! You know something about this. It's written all over you."

Angus was trembling.

"Okay," he said, "I'll tell you. I didn't tell you before because I knew you'd be angry. I went birdwatching down at Poppyfields that Friday you went to your mum's last August. She was there. She didn't have anywhere to go. She cried. She begged me to put her up for the night and I felt sorry for her and put her up for the night. In here of course. In the spare room."

"I should bloody well hope in here. She's only a kid!"

"She… she said she had nowhere to go."

"Good God, Angus, I've always known you were weak willed and easily manipulated. But can *anyone* pull your strings?"

The Mr Right project had hit one of its lowest points.

"I'm going out," he said.

Her anger was a like an icy gale blasting through every crevice of Angus' being. And he had no resistance to it, no way of warding it off.

"No you don't! You don't just run away when I'm talking to you."

"I'm going out," he repeated, pushing past her.

He picked up the car keys in the tiny hallway. Judy had followed him downstairs and now followed him into the garage.

"Don't be a *baby*, Angus."

And then: "Angus, you *are not to go!*"

He got into the car, backed it out onto the street. Judy came and stood in front of him so he roared off in reverse, lurching up and down the kerb, and then dived down a side road. He drove at random through the suburban streets until at last he found himself driving along that bleak road that passed between Poppyfields and that bleak little park. He stopped, got out and peered through the Poppyfields fence.

It was a building site now. The court dispute had been settled a month ago. The city council and the housing development agency were to go fifty-fifty on the costs of stabilising the underground marsh. The bulldozers had returned. Some of the footings for the new housing estate had gone in and even the skeletal frames of some of the little box houses, where one day people would do their gardens and watch TV and wash their cars, were starting to take shape. Poppyfields the wilderness had already almost gone, churned up by the tracks and wheels of the contractors' powerful vehicles.

As to the underground marsh, a specialist company had been brought in. They had identified the trouble spots and treated them, rather as a nurse might treat an infected wound, pumping down a powerful sterilising fluid into the fermenting patches and then pouring a special kind of liquid concrete in to hold everything in place. There would be no more sinking diggers, no more marsh gas bubbles, no embarrassing earthy farts.

But though they could stop the bubbles of methane and cover the skin of Poppyfields with brick houses, and drive out the larks and the poppies and the mistle thrushes, it came to Angus that there was one thing they couldn't change or stabilise. They couldn't alter the fact that Poppyfields itself was a kind of dream. No one could stop the bubbles that rose up not from buried marshes, but from other worlds.

"I will leave Judy," Angus decided. "I will go back and tell her now. It will be awful but in five minutes it will be over."

Terror and exhilaration are physically almost indistin-guishable. He couldn't tell where one ended and the other began. And he had no idea what would happen next. But he had made up his mind.

the peacock cloak

Grasshoppers creaked, bees hummed, a stream played peacefully as it meandered in its stony bed through the quiet mountain valley. And then Tawus was there in his famous cloak, its bright fabric still fizzing and sparking from the prodigious leap, its hundred eyes, black, green and gold, restlessly assaying the scene. Tawus had arrived, and, as always, everything else was dimmed and diminished by his presence.

"This world was well made," Tawus said to himself with his accustomed mixture of jealousy and pride.

He savoured the scents of lavender and thyme, the creakings and buzzings of insects, the gurgling of the stream.

"Every detail *works*," he said, noticing a fat bumble bee, spattered with yellow pollen, launching herself into flight from a pink cistus flower. Passing the object he carried in his left hand to his right, Tawus stooped to take the flower stem between his left forefinger and thumb. "Every molecule, every speck of dust."

Painfully and vividly, and in a way that had not happened for some time, he was reminded of the early days, the beginning, when, on the far side of this universe, he and the Six had awoken to find themselves in another garden wilderness like this one, ringed about by mountains.

Back then things had felt very different. Tawus had known what Fabbro knew, had felt what Fabbro felt. His purposes had been Fabbro's purposes, and all his memories were from Fabbro's world, a world within which the created universe of Esperine was like a child's plaything, a scene carved into an ivory ball (albeit carved so exquisitely that its trees could sway in the wind and lose their leaves in autumn, its creatures live and die). Of course he had known quite well he was a copy of Fabbro and not Fabbro himself, but he was an exact copy, down to the smallest particle, the smallest thought, identical in every way except that he had been rendered in the stuff of Esperine, so that he could inhabit Fabbro's creation on Fabbro's behalf. He was a creation as Esperine was, but he could remember creating himself, just as he could remember creating Esperine, inside the device that Fabbro called Constructive Thought. Back then, Tawus had thought of Fabbro not as 'he' and 'him' but as 'I' and 'me'.

And how beautiful this world had seemed then, how simple, how unsullied, how full of opportunities, how free of the ties and regrets and complications that had so hemmed in the life of Fabbro in the world outside.

Tawus released the pink flower, let it spring back among its hundred bright fellows, and stood up straight, returning the small object from his right hand to his dominant left. Then, with his quick grey eyes, he glanced back down the path and up at the rocky ridges on either side. The peacock eyes looked with him, sampling every part of the visible and invisible spectrum.

"No, Tawus, you are not observed," whispered the cloak, using the silent code with which it spoke to him through his skin.

"Not observed, perhaps," said Tawus, "but certainly expected."

Now he turned southwards, towards the head of the valley, and began to walk. His strides were quick and determined but his thoughts less so. The gentle scents and sounds of the mountain valley continued to stir up vivid and troubling memories from the other end of time. He recalled watching the Six wake up, his three brothers and three sisters. They were also made in the likeness of Fabbro but they were, so to speak, reflections of him in mirrors with curved surfaces or coloured glass, so that they were different from the original and from each other. Tawus remembered their eyes opening, his brother Balthazar first and then his sister Cassandra, and he remembered their spreading smiles as they looked around and simultaneously saw and remembered where they were, in this exquisite, benign and yet to be explored world, released for ever from the cares and complications of Fabbro's life and from the baleful history of the vast and vacant universe in which Fabbro had been born.

They had been strangely shy of each other at first, even though they shared the same memories, the same history and the same sole parent. The three sisters in particular, in spite of Fabbro's androgynous and protean nature, felt exposed and uneasy in their unfamiliar bodies. But even the men were uncomfortable in their new skins. All seven were trying to decide who they were. It had been a kind of adolescence. All had felt awkward, all had been absurdly optimistic about what they could achieve. They had even made a pact with each other that they would always work together and always take decisions as a group.

"*That* didn't last long," Tawus now wryly observed, and then he remembered, with a momentary excruciating pang, the fate of Cassandra, his proud and stubborn sister.

But they'd believed in their agreement at the time and, having made it, all Seven had stridden out, laughing and talking all at once, under a warm sun not unlike this one, and on a path not unlike the one he was walking now, dressed so splendidly in his Peacock Cloak. He had no such cloak back then. They had been naked gods. They had begun to wrap themselves up only as they moved apart from one another: Cassandra in her Mirror Mantle, Jabreel in his Armour of Light, Balthazar in his Coat of Dreams... But the Peacock Cloak had been finest of all.

"I hear music," the cloak now whispered to him.

Tawus stopped and listened. He could only hear the stream, the grasshoppers and the bees. He shrugged.

"Hospitable of him, to lay on music to greet us."

"Just a peasant flute. A flute and goat bells."

"Probably shepherds up in the hills somewhere," said Tawus, resuming his stride.

He remembered how the seven of them came to their first human village, a village whose hundred inhabitants imagined that they had always lived there, tending their cattle and their sheep, and had no inkling that, only a few hours before, they and their memories had been brought into being all at once by their creator Fabbro within the circuits of Constructive Thought, along with a thousand similar groups scattered over the planets of Esperine: the final touch, the final detail, in the world builder's ivory ball.

"The surprise on their faces!" Tawus murmured to himself, and smiled. "To see these seven tall naked figures striding down through their pastures."

"You are tense," observed his cloak. "You are distracting yourself with thoughts of things elsewhere and long ago."

"So I am," agreed Tawus, in the same silent code. "I am not keen to think about my destination."

He looked down at the object he carried in his hand, smooth and white and intricate, like a polished shell. It was a gun of sorts, a weapon of his own devising. It did not fire mere bullets. It destroyed its targets by unravelling, within a chosen area, the laws that defined Esperine itself, and so reducing form to pure chaos.

"Give me a pocket to put this in," Tawus said.

At once the cloak made an opening to receive the gun, sealing itself up again when Tawus had withdrawn his hand.

"The cloak can aim and shoot for me, if need be," Tawus muttered to himself.

And the cloak's eyes winked, green and gold and black.

The valley turned a corner. There was an outcrop of harder rock. As he came round it, Tawus heard the music that his cloak, with its finely tuned senses, had detected some way back: a fluted melody, inexpertly played, and an arrhythmic jangling of crudely made bells.

Up ahead of him three young children were minding a flock of sheep and goats, sheltering by a little patch of trees at a spot where a tributary brook cascaded into the main stream. A girl of nine or ten was playing panpipes. In front of her on a large stone, as if it were the two-seat auditorium of a miniature theatre, two smaller children sat side by side: a boy of five or so and a little girl of three, cradling a lamb that lay across both their laps. The jangling bells hung from the necks of the grazing beasts.

Seeing Tawus, the girl laid down her pipes and the two smaller children hastily set their lamb on the ground, stood up, and moved quickly to stand on either side of their sister with their hands in hers. All three stared at Tawus with wide unsmiling eyes. As he drew near, they ran forward and kissed his hand, first the older girl, then the boy, and finally the little three year old whose baby lips left a cool patch of moistness on his skin.

"Your face is familiar to them," the cloak silently observed. "They think they know you from before."

"As we might predict," said Tawus. "But *you* they have never seen."

The children were astounded by a fabric on which the patterns were in constant motion, and by the animated peacock eyes. The smallest child reached out a grubby finger to touch the magical cloth.

"No, Thomas!" her sister scolded, slapping the child's hand away. "Leave the gentleman's coat alone."

"No harm," Tawus said gruffly, patting the tiny girl on the head.

And the cloak shook off the fragments of snot and dust that the child's fingers had left behind.

Ten minutes later Tawus turned and looked back at them. They were little more than dots in the mountain landscape but they were still watching him, still holding hands. Around them, unheeded, the sheep grazed with the goats.

Suddenly, Tawus was vividly reminded of three other children he had once seen, of about the same ages. He had hardly given them a thought at the time, but now he clearly saw them in his mind: the younger two huddled against their sister, all three staring with white faces as Tawus and his army rolled through their burning village, their home in ruins behind them. It had been in a flat watery country called Meadow Lee. From his vantage point in the turret of a tank, Tawus could see its verdant water meadows stretching away for miles. Across the whole expanse buildings were burning and columns of dirty smoke were slowly staining the whole of the wide blue sky a glowering oily yellow.

When was that, Tawus wondered? On which of the several different occasions when fighting had come to Meadow Lee? He thought it had been during one of his early wars against his brother Balthazar. But then he wondered whether perhaps it had been at a later stage when he was in an alliance with Balthazar against Jibreel.

"Neither," said the Peacock Cloak. "It was in the war all six of you waged against Cassandra, that time she banned chrome extraction in her lands."

"Don't needlessly interfere. Offer guidance where necessary, head off obvious problems, but otherwise allow things to take their own course".
It would be wrong to say these were Fabbro's *instructions* to the Seven because he had never spoken to them. They were simply his intentions which they all knew because his memories were replicated in their own minds. When they encountered those first villagers, the Seven had greeted them, requested food and a place to rest that night, and asked if they were any matters they could assist with. They did not try and impose their views, or change the villagers' minds about how the world worked or how to live their lives. That had all come later, along with the wars and the empires.

"But did he really think we could go on like that forever?" Tawus now angrily asked. "What were we supposed to *do* all this time? Just wander around indefinitely, advising on a sore throat here, suggesting crop rotation there, but otherwise doing nothing with this world at all?"

The Seven had begun to be different from Fabbro from the moment they awoke. And paradoxically it was Tawus, the one made most completely in Fabbro's likeness, who had moved most quickly away from Fabbro's wishes.

"We can't just be gardeners of this world," he had told his brothers and sisters, after they had visited a dozen sleepy villages, "we can't just be shepherds of its people, watching them while they graze. We will go mad. We will turn into imbeciles. We need to be able to build things, play with technology, unlock the possibilities that we know exist within this particular frame. We will need metals and fuels, and a society complex enough to extract and refine them. We will need ways of storing and transmitting information. There will need to be cities. On at least one planet, in at least one continent, we will have to organise a state."

The Six had all had reservations at first, to different degrees, and for slightly different reasons.

"Just give me a small territory then," Tawus had said, "a patch of land with some people in, to experiment and develop my ideas."

In his own little fiefdom he had adopted a new approach, not simply advising, but tempting and cajoling. He had made little labour-saving devices for his people and then spoken to them of machines that would do all their work for them. He had helped them make boats and then described space ships that would make them masters of the stars. He had sown dissatisfaction in their minds and, within two years, he had achieved government, schools, metallurgy, sea-faring and a militia. Seeing what he had achieved, the Six had fallen over one another to catch up.

"How come they all followed me, if my path was so wrong?" Tawus now asked.

"They had no choice but to follow you," observed the Peacock Cloak, "if they didn't wish to be altogether eclipsed."

"Which is another way of saying that my way was in the end inevitable, because once it is chosen, all other ways become obsolete. To have obeyed Fabbro would simply have been to postpone what was sooner or later going to happen, if not led by me, then by one of the others, or even by some leader rising up from the Esperine people themselves."

He thought briefly again of the children in front of the ruined house, but then he turned another corner, and there was his destination ahead of him. It was a little island of domesticity amidst the benign wilderness of the valley, a small cottage with a garden and an orchard and a front gate, standing beside a lake.

"He is outside," said the Peacock Cloak, whose hundred eyes could see through many different kinds of obstacle. "He is down beside the water."

Tawus came to the cottage gate. It was very quiet. He could hear the bees going back and forth from the wild thyme flowers, the splash of a duck alighting on the lake, the clopping of a wooden wind chime in an almond tree.

He raised his hand to the latch, then lowered it again.

"What's the matter with me? Why hesitate?"

Clop clop went the wind chimes.

"It is always better to act," whispered the cloak through his skin, "that's what you asked me to remind you."

Tawus nodded. It *was* always better to act than to waste time agonising. It was by acting that he had built a civilisation, summoned great cities into being, driven through the technological changes that had taken this world from sleepy rural Arcadia to an age of interplanetary empires. It was by acting that he had prevailed over his six siblings, even when all six were ranged against him, for each one of them had been encumbered by Fabbro with gifts or traits of character more specialised than his own pure strength of will: mercy, imagination, doubt, ambivalence, detachment, humility.

True, he had caused much destruction and misery but, after all, to act at all it was necessary to be willing to destroy. If he ever had a moment of doubt, he simply reminded himself that you couldn't take a single step without running the risk of crushing some small creeping thing, too small to be seen, going about its blameless life. You couldn't even breathe without the possibility of sucking in some tiny innocent from the air.

"The city of X is refusing to accept our authority," his generals would say.

"Then raze it to the ground as we warned we would," he would answer without a moment's hesitation. And the hundred eyes would dart this way and that, like a scouting party sent out ahead of the battalions that were his own thoughts, looking for opportunities in the new situation that he had created, scoping out his next move and the move after that.

There had been times when his generals had stood there open-mouthed, astounded by his ruthlessness. But they did not question him. They knew it was the strength of his will that made him great, made him something more than they were.

"But now," he said to himself bitterly, "I seem to be having difficulty making up my mind about a garden gate."

"Just act," said the cloak, rippling against his skin in a way that was almost like laughter.

Tawus smiled. He would act on his own account and not on instructions from his clothes, but all the same he lifted his hand to the latch and this time opened it. He was moving forward again. And the eyes on his cloak shone in readiness.

Inside the gate the path branched three ways: right to the cottage, with the peaks of the valley's western ridge behind it, straight ahead to the little orchard and vegetable garden, left and eastward down to the small lake from which flowed the stream that he'd been following. On the far side of the lake was the ridge of peaks that formed the valley's eastern edge. Some sheep were grazing on their slopes.

Clop clop went the wind chimes, and a bee zipped by his ear like a tiny racing car on a track.

Tawus looked down towards the lake.

"*There* you are," he murmured, spotting the small figure at the water's edge that the peacock eyes had already located, sitting on a log on a little beach, looking through binoculars at the various ducks and water birds out on the lake.

"You know I'm here," Tawus muttered angrily. "You know quite well I'm here."

"Indeed he does," the cloak confirmed. "The tension in his shoulders is unmistakeable."

"He just wants to make me the one that speaks first," Tawus said.

So he did not speak. Instead, when there were only a few metres between them, he stooped, picked up a stone and lobbed it into the water over the seated figure's head.

The ripples spread out over the lake. Among some reeds at the far end of the little beach, a duck gave a low warning quack to its fellows. The man on the log turned round.

"Tawus," he exclaimed, laying down his field glasses and rising to his feet with a broad smile of welcome, "Tawus, my dear fellow. It's been a very long time."

The likeness between the two of them would have been instantly apparent to any observer, even from a distance. They had the same lithe bearing, the same high cheekbones and aquiline nose, the same thick mane of grey hair. But the man by the water was simply dressed in a white shirt and white breeches, while Tawus still wore his magnificent cloak with its shifting patterns and its restless eyes. And Tawus stood stiffly while the other man, still smiling, extended his arms, as if he expected Tawus to fall into his embrace.

Tawus did not move or bend.

"You've put it about that you're Fabbro himself," he said, "or so I've heard."

The other man nodded.

"Well, yes. Of course there's a sense in which I am a copy of Fabbro as you are, since this body is an analogue of the body that Fabbro was born with, rather than the body itself. But the original Fabbro ceased to exist when I came into being, so my history and his have never branched away from each another, as yours and his did, but are arranged sequentially in a single line, a single story. So yes, I'm Fabbro. All that is left of Fabbro is me, and I have finally entered my own creation. It seemed fitting, now that both Esperine and I are coming to a close."

Tawus considered this for a moment. He had an impulse to ask about the world beyond Esperine, that vast and ancient universe in which Fabbro had been born and grown up. For of course Fabbro's was the only childhood that Tawus could remember, Fabbro's the only youth. He was naturally curious to know how things had changed out there and to hear news of the people from Fabbro's past: friends, collaborators, male and female lovers, children (actual biological children: children of Fabbro's body and not just his mind).

"Aren't those memories a distraction?" the cloak asked him through his skin. "Isn't that stuff his worry and not yours?"

229

Tawus nodded.

"Yes," he silently agreed, "and to ask about it would muddy the water. It would confuse the issue of worlds and their ownership."

He looked Fabbro in the face.

"You had no business coming into Esperine," he told him. "We renounced your world and you in turn gave this world to us to be our own. You've no right to come barging back in here now, interfering, undermining my authority, undermining the authority of the Five."

(It was Five now, not Six, because of Cassandra's anni-hilation in the Chrome Wars.)

Fabbro smiled.

"Some might say you'd undermined each other's authority quite well without my help, with your constant warring, and your famines and your plagues and all of that."

"That's a matter for us, not you."

"Possibly so," said Fabbro. "Possibly so. But, in my defence, I have tried to keep out of the way since I arrived in this world."

"You let it be known you were here, though. That was enough."

Fabbro tipped his head from side to side, weighing this up.

"Enough? Do you really think so? Surely for my mere presence to have had an impact, there would have had to be something in Esperine that could be touched by it. There had to be a me-shaped hole. Otherwise wouldn't I just be some harmless old man up in the mountains?"

He sat down on the log again

"Come and sit with me, Tawus." He patted a space beside him. "This is my favourite spot, my grandstand seat. There's always something happening here. Day. Night. Evening. Morning. Sun. Rain. Always something new to see."

"If you're content with sheep and ducks," said Tawus, and did not sit.

Fabbro watched him. After a few seconds, he smiled.

"That's quite a coat you've got there," he observed.

Many of the peacock eyes turned towards him, questioningly. Others glanced with renewed vigour in every other direction, as if suspecting diversionary tactics.

"I've heard," Fabbro went on, "that it can protect you, make you invisible, change your appearance, allow you to leap from planet to planet without going through the space in between. I've been told that it can tell you of dangers, and draw your attention to things you might wish to know, and even give you counsel, as perhaps it's doing now. That is some coat!"

"He is seeking to rile you," the cloak silently whispered. "You asked me to warn you if he did this."

"Don't patronise me Fabbro," Tawus said, "I am your copy not your child. You know that to construct this cloak I simply needed to understand the algorithm on which Esperine is founded, and you know that I do understand it every bit as well as you do."

Fabbro nodded.

"Yes of course. I'm just struck by the different ways in which we've used that understanding. I used it to make a more benign world than my own, within which countless lives could for a limited time unfold and savour their existence. You used it to set yourself apart from the rest of this creation, insulate yourself, wrap yourself up in your own little world of one."

"I could easily have made another complete world as you did, as perfect as Esperine in every way. But any world that I made would necessarily exist within this frame, your frame, and therefore still be a part of Esperine, even if its equal or its superior in design. Do you really wonder that I chose instead to find a way of setting myself apart?"

Fabbro did not answer. He gave a half-shrug, then looked out at the lake.

"I've not come here to apologise," Tawus said. "I hope you know that. I have no regrets about my rebellion."

Fabbro turned towards him.

"Oh, don't worry, I know why you came. You came to destroy me. And of course it *is* possible to destroy me now that I'm here in Esperine, just as it was possible for you and the others to destroy your sister Cassandra when she tried to place a brake on your ambitions. In order to achieve her destruction you found a way of temporarily modifying that part of the original algorithm that protected the seven of you from physical harm. I assume you have a weapon with you now that works in the same way. I guess it's hidden somewhere in that cloak."

"But knowing it doesn't help him," whispered the cloak through

Tawus' skin.

Another duck had alighted on the water, smaller and differently coloured to the ones that were already there. (It had black wings and a russet head.) Fabbro picked up his binoculars and briefly observed it, before laying them down again, and turning once more to his recalcitrant creation.

"Be that as it may," he said, "I certainly wasn't led to expect an apology. They told me the six of you set out in this direction armed to the teeth and in a great fury. You had a formidable space fleet with you, they said, and huge armies at your back. They told me that cloak of yours was fairly fizzing and sparking with pent-up energy. They said that it turned all the air around you into a giant lens, so that you were greatly magnified and seemed to your followers to be a colossus blazing with fire, striding out in front of them as they poured through the interplanetary gates."

Tawus snatched a stone up from the beach and flung it out over the water.

"You are allowing yourself to be put on the defensive," warned the Peacock Cloak. "But remember that he has no more power than you. In fact he has far less. Thanks to your foresight in creating me, you are the one who is protected, not him. And, unlike him, you are armed."

Tawus turned to face Fabbro.

"You set us inside this world," he said, "then turned away and left us to it. And that was fine, that was the understanding from the beginning. That was your choice and ours. But now, when it suits you because you are growing old, you come wandering in to criticise what we have achieved. What right do you have to do that, Fabbro? You were absent when the hard decisions were being made. How can you know that you would have done anything different yourself?"

"When have I criticised you? When have I claimed I would have done something different?"

Fabbro gave a short laugh.

"Think, Tawus, think. Stop indulging your anger and think for a moment about the situation we are in. How *could* I say that I would have done something different? What meaning could such a claim possibly have when you and I were one and the same person at the beginning of all this?"

"We began as one person, but we are not one person now. Origins are not everything."

Fabbro looked down at his hands, large and long-fingered as Tawus' were.

"No," he said, "I agree. It must be so. Otherwise there would only ever be one thing."

"You made your choice," Tawus said. "You should have stuck to it and stayed outside."

"Hence the armies, hence the striding like a colossus at their head, hence the plan to seek me out and destroy me?"

Fabbro looked up at Tawus with an expression that was half a frown and half a smile.

"Yes," Tawus said. "Hence all those things."

Fabbro nodded.

"But where are the armies now?" he asked. "Where is the striding colossus? Where is this "we" you speak about? An awful lot of the energy has dissipated, has it not? The nearer you got to me, the faster it all fell away. They've all come back to me, you know, your armies, your brothers, your sisters. They have all come to me and asked to become part of me once again."

Some of the eyes on the cloak glanced inquiringly upwards at Tawus' face, others remained fixed on Fabbro, who had lifted his binoculars and was once again looking at bird life out on the lake.

"Fire the gun and you will *be* Fabbro," the Peacock Cloak told its master. "*You* will be the one to whom the armies and the Five have all returned. Your apparent isolation, your apparent diminishment, is simply an artefact of there being two of you here, two rival versions of the original Fabbro. But you are the one I shield and not him. You are the one with the weapon."

Fabbro laid down his field glasses and turned towards the man who still stood stiffly apart from him.

"Come Tawus," he coaxed gently, patting the surface of the log beside him. "Come and sit down. I won't bite, I promise. It's almost the end, after all. Surely we're both too old, and it's too late in the day, for us to be playing this game?"

Tawus picked up another stone and flung it out into the lake. The ripples spread over the smooth surface. *Quack quack* went the ducks near to where it fell, and one of them fluttered its wings and half-flew a few yards further off, scrabbling at the surface with its feet.

"The armies are irrelevant," Tawus said. "The Five are irrelevant. You know that. For these purposes they are simply fields of force twisting and turning between you and me. The important thing is not that they have come back to you. No. The important thing is that I have not."

Fabbro watched his face and did not speak

"I gave their lives purpose," Tawus went on, beginning to pace restlessly up and down. "I gave them progress. I gave them freedom. I gave them cities and nations. I gave them hope. I gave them something to believe in and somewhere to go. You just made a shell. You made a clockwork toy. It was me, through my rebellion, that turned it into a world. Why else did they all follow me?"

He looked around for another stone, found a particularly big one, and lobbed it out even further across the lake. It sent a whole flock of ducks squawking into the air.

"Please sit down, Tawus. I would really like you to sit with me."

Tawus did not respond. Fabbro shrugged and looked away.

"Why exactly *do* you think they followed you?" he asked after a short time.

"Because I was in your image but I wasn't you," Tawus answered at once. "I was like you, but at the same time I was one of them. Because I stood up for this world as a world in its own right, belonging to those who lived in it, and not simply as a plaything of yours."

Fabbro nodded.

"Which was what I wanted you to do," he said.

The day was moving into evening. The eastern ridge of peaks across the water glowed gold from the sun that was setting opposite them in the west.

"After the sun sets," Fabbro calmly said, "the world will end. Everyone has come back to me. It's time that you and I brought things to a close."

Tawus was caught off guard. So little time. It seemed he had miscalculated somewhat, not having the benefit of the Olympian view that Fabbro had enjoyed until recently, looking in from outside of Constructive Thought. He had not appreciated that the end was quite as close as that.

But he was not going to show his surprise.

"I suppose you are going to lecture me," he said, "about the suffering I caused with my wars."

As he spoke he was gathering up stones from the beach, hastily, almost urgently, as if they had some vital purpose.

"I suppose you're going to go on about all the children whose parents I took from them," he said.

He threw a stone. *Splash. Quack.*

"And the rapes that all sides perpetrated," he said, throwing a stone again, "and the tortures," throwing yet another stone, "and the massacres."

He had run out of stones. He turned angrily towards Fabbro.

"I suppose you want to castigate me for turning skilled farmers and hunters and fishermen into passive workers in dreary city streets, spending their days manufacturing things they didn't understand, and their evenings staring at images on screens manufactured for them by someone else."

He turned away, shaking his head, looking around vaguely for more stones.

"I used to think about you looking in from outside," he said. "When we had wars, when we were industrialising and getting people off the land, all of those difficult times. I used to imagine you judging me, clucking your tongue, shaking your head. But *you* try and bring progress to a world without any adverse consequences for anyone. You just try it."

"Come on Tawus," Fabbro begged him. "Sit with me. You know you're not really going to destroy me. You know you can't really reverse the course that this world, like any world, must take. It isn't only your armies that have fallen away from you, Tawus, it is your own steely will. It has no purpose any more."

But the cloak offered another point of view.

"Destroy Fabbro and you will become him," it silently whispered. "Then you can put back the clock itself."

Tawus knew it was true. Without Fabbro to stop him, he could indeed postpone the end, not forever, but for several more generations. And he could rule Esperine during that time as he had never ruled before, with no Fabbro outside, no one to look in and judge him. The cloak was right. He would *become* Fabbro, he would become Fabbro and Tawus both at once. It was possible, and what was more, it had been his reason for coming here in the first place.

He glanced down at Fabbro. He looked quickly away again across the lake. Ten whole seconds passed.

Then Tawus reached slowly for the clasp of the Peacock Cloak. He hesitated. He lowered his hand. He reached for the clasp again. His fingers were trembling because of the contradictory signals they were receiving from his brain, but finally he unfastened the cloak, removing it slowly and deliberately at first, and then suddenly flinging it away from him, as if he feared it might grab hold and refuse to let him go. It snagged on a branch of a small oak tree and hung there, one corner touching the stony ground. Still its clever eyes darted about, green and gold and black. It was watching Tawus, watching Fabbro. As ever, it was observing everything, analysing everything, evaluating options and possibilities. But yet, as is surely proper in a garment hanging from a tree, it had no direction of its own, it had no separate purpose.

Across the lake, the eastern hills shone. There were sheep up there grazing, bathed in golden light that picked them out against the mountainside. But the hills on the western side were also making their presence felt, for their shadows were reaching out like long fingers over the two small figures by the lake, one standing, one seated on the log, neither one speaking. Without his cloak, in a simple white shirt and white breeches, Tawus looked even more like Fabbro. A stranger could not have told them apart.

A flock of geese came flying in from a day of grazing lower down the valley. They honked peaceably to one another as they splashed down on the softly luminous water.

"When I was walking up here," Tawus said at last, "I met three children, and they reminded me of some other children I saw once, or glimpsed anyway, when I was riding past in a tank. It was in the middle of a war and I didn't pay much heed to them at the time. I was too busy listening to reports and giving orders. But for some reason they stuck in my mind."

He picked up a stone, tossed it half-heartedly out into the lake.

"Their ruined home lay behind them," he went on, "and in the ruins, most probably, lay the burnt corpses of their parents. Not that their parents would have been combatants or anything. It was just that their country, their sleepy land of Meadow Lee, had temporarily become the square on the chessboard that the great game was focussed on, the place where the force fields happened to intersect. Pretty soon the focal point would be somewhere else and the armies would move on from Meadow Lee and forget all about it until the next time. But those children wouldn't forget, would they? Not while they still lived. That day would stain and darken their entire lives, like the smoke stained and darkened their pretty blue sky. What could be worse, when you think about it, than filling up a small mind with such horrors? That, in a way, is also creating a world. It is creating a small but perfect hell."

He snatched up yet another stone, but, with a swift graceful movement, Fabbro had jumped up and grasped Tawus' wrist to stop him throwing it.

"Enough, Tawus, enough. The rebellion is over. The divisions you brought about have all been healed. The killed and the killers. The tortured and the torturers. The enslaved and the enslavers. All are reconciled. All have finally come back."

"Everyone but me."

Tawus let the stone fall to the ground. His creator released his hand, sat down again on the log and once again patted the space beside him.

Tawus looked at Fabbro, and at the log, and back at Fabbro again. And, finally, he sat down.

The two of them were completely in shadow now, had become shadows themselves. The smooth surface of the lake still glowed with soft pinks and blues, but the birds on its surface had become shadows too, warm living shadows, softly murmuring to one another in their various watery tongues, suspended between the glowing lake and the glowing sky. And more shadow was spreading up the hillside opposite, engulfing the sheep one after another, taking them from golden prominence to peaceful obscurity. Soon only the peaks still dipped into the stream of sunlight that was pouring horizontally far above the heads of the two men.

"Everyone but you," Fabbro mildly agreed, reaching down for his binoculars once more so he could look at some unusual duck or other that he'd noticed out on the water.

Tawus glanced across at his Peacock Cloak, dangling from its tree. That tawdry thing, he suddenly thought. Why did I choose to hide myself in that? The cloak was shimmering and glittering, giving off its own light in the shadow, and its eyes were still brightly shining, as if it was attempting to be a rival to those last brilliant rays of sunlight, or to outglow the softly glowing lake. It was all that was left of Tawus' empire, his will, his power.

He turned to Fabbro.

"Don't get the wrong idea," he began. "I don't in any way regret what…"

Then he broke off. He passed his still trembling hand over his face.

"I'm sorry, Fabbro," he said in a completely different voice. "I've messed it all up haven't I? I've been a fool. I've spoiled everything."

Fabbro lowered his binoculars and patted Tawus on the hand.

"Well maybe you have. I'm not sure. But you're quite right, you know, that I *did* just create a shell, and it *was* your rebellion that made it a world. Deep down I always knew that rebellion was necessary. I must have done, mustn't I, since whatever you did came from somewhere inside me? Rebellion was necessary. I'd just hoped that in Esperine it would somehow take a different path."

Only the highest tips of the peaks were still shining gold. They were like bright orange light bulbs. And then, one by one, they went out.

About the Author

Chris Beckett was born in Oxford, England, in 1955. His first published story, "A Matter of Survival", appeared in the British science fiction magazine *Interzone* in 1990, and he's since been publishing short stories regularly in magazines and anthologies on both sides of the Atlantic, as well as three novels: *The Holy Machine* (first published in the US by Wildside in 2004 and since published in a new edition by Corvus in 2010), *Marcher*, published in 2009 by Cosmos, and, most recently, *Dark Eden*, published by Corvus in 2012, to widespread critical acclaim.

This is his second short story collection. His previous collection, *The Turing Test*, published by Elastic Press, was the winner of the Edge Hill Short Fiction Award in 2009 from a short list that included a Booker prize-winner, a Whitebread prize-winner and a Booker-shortlisted author.

Having originally studied psychology at Bristol University, Chris Beckett trained as a social worker and has worked in that field for most of his adult life. He is now a part-time lecturer in social work at the University of East Anglia in Norwich.

He lives in Cambridge with his wife Maggie and sundry animals, and is visited there from time to time by his three grown-up children, Poppy, Dominic and Nancy.

For more information on Chris Beckett's writing, please visit www.chris-beckett.com

Lightning Source UK Ltd.
Milton Keynes UK
UKOW05f1326250813

215930UK00002B/21/P